THE VINE III

FROM HEAVEN AS A DOVE

Arlene Adamo

*Dedicated to the memory of
Anne Stumpf*

*Then John gave this testimony: "I saw the
Spirit come down from heaven as a dove and
remain on him. I would not have known him,
except that the one who sent me to baptize
with water told me, 'The man on whom you
see the Spirit come down and remain is he who will
baptize with the Holy Spirit.' I have seen and I testify
that this is the Son of God."*

John 1:32

1

Mona pulled open the frosted glass door and walked out into the large bustling reception area. Several people immediately recognized her and tried to catch her eye. A couple of the bolder ones even attempted to discreetly maneuver over her way. No one dared approach her directly, for fear of overstepping the mark and putting an end to their career before it even began. All they could do was silently hope that the woman closest to *the man* himself would take notice.

Of course, Mona could have avoided all of this attention and simply had an assistant come out to escort in her next appointment, but then she would miss out on experiencing the raw buzz of this room. The Einhorn Records reception area was a place filled with passionate emotions and dreams of music. Coming out here helped to reassure her that the recording business was still just as fresh and as full of hope as ever.

Silently scanning the crowd, it did not take her long to find the one she was looking for. Even though he was turned away from her, in discussion with the young man next to him, his cheaply cut mop of graying hair was easily recognizable. "Danny!" she called, as she walked over.

Upon hearing her voice, Danny instantly turned around. Years of living under the stress of the entertainment industry had made his face look ten years older. "Mona!" he exclaimed, jumping to his feet. "How are you, beautiful?"

Mona secretly cringed. *Why on earth does he think he has a way with women—if he only knew?* "I'm doing great Danny, just great. Now, I assume this would be Sexton Spin," she said, nodding at the fashionably scruffy young man who remained sitting.

"You know it! A born star!" declared Danny.

The young man looked up sleepily at Mona and muttered, "Hey."

Danny kicked the man's boot, "Sexton, stand up in the presence of a lady."

Sexton slowly got up from his chair. Danny apologetically looked at Mona. "Sorry, but you know how these artists are, Mona dear—all talent, no social skills."

Mona smiled politely. "Well, shall we go see *the man*?"

"Yeah, time to meet *the man*," said Sexton with a grin.

As Mona turned towards the door, Danny nudged Sexton in the side. The last thing he needed was for this idiot to kill the deal. Like so many others in the business, he had lost money in the recession. If he was going to keep his head above water, he needed to land this contract. *Should have listened to my mother and become a podiatrist. People will always spend money on their feet.*

Mona led them through the frosted door and down the long hallway.

"Is he in a good mood today?" asked Danny.

"Oh Danny, he's always in a good mood when you're bringing him talent," answered Mona cheerfully.

They came to the large wooden double doors. Each one was engraved with a magnificent reared up unicorn, the symbol of Einhorn Records. Mona pulled open one of the doors and let Danny and Sexton enter the office first. The circular two-storey room glowed with the beautiful sunlight that streamed in through a great wall of windows. Outside was a breathtaking view of New York. The city glistened like an endless fantastical sea of glass and steel. A large round oak desk nestled in the alcove of windows dominated the room. Scattered about the office were tables and shelves all covered with unicorn figurines. The varying sizes and shapes of the unicorns seemed to mimic the various sizes and shapes of the buildings outside.

"Please have a seat," said Mona, gesturing towards the comfortable looking sitting area to their left.

"Thank you," replied Danny, who waited until Mona sat down before sitting down himself.

Sexton did not sit, but instead began to wander around the room, examining everything he could see. "Wow, man. This dude is crazy into unicorns."

"Yes," said Mona, "Einhorn is German for unicorn."

"Cool," replied Sexton, who picked up one of the more delicate looking pieces.

"Put it down, Sexton," said Danny, who was beginning to feel nervous. He hated being made to wait, and it was now made worse by the worry he felt about Sexton. He wasn't sure what this idiot kid might say or do next.

Sexton walked over to look at the two framed photographs on the desk. One was of a handsome young man, and the other was of an old woman. "Who are these people?" he asked.

"The woman was his mother. The other is just an old friend," said Mona.

"Friend, eh?" said Sexton. "So, the dude is queer like they say." He then looked directly at Danny and asked, "Should I, you know, make him an offer? 'Cause, like I told you before, if the price is right…"

"No Sexton!" cried Danny a little too loudly. He looked at Mona. "I apologize. What can I say? He's an artist—a free spirit."

He's a goddamned moron, thought Mona. "No problem," she said, then turning to Sexton added, "Sexton, it would be best if you let Danny do all of the talking."

"Precisely what I told him," said Danny.

Sexton said nothing, but from the look on his face it was clear that he was now sulking. He went back to examining the various unicorns on a nearby table.

Suddenly, the door opened and in walked a pleasantly plump older man. Although he did look his sixty-nine years, his youthful way of dressing and the spring in his step made him seem much younger. "Jack!" exclaimed Danny, quickly rising to his feet to shake hands.

"How are you, Danny?"

"I'm wonderful! Just wonderful!" he answered, shaking Jack's hand a little too vigorously.

Jack nodded to Mona, who smiled back at him. He then looked over in the direction of Sexton and pushed his glasses higher up his nose.

"And this is, of course, our rapidly rising star, Sexton Spin!" exclaimed Danny, with all the enthusiasm of a proud father.

Sexton made a move towards Jack, but as he did his elbow hit one of the unicorns, knocking it off the table. It fell to the floor smashing into a myriad of pieces.

You dumb shit, thought Danny. *If you cost me this deal…*

Jack looked at Sexton, who guiltily looked back. "Never mind," Jack sighed. "Come and sit down."

Sexton walked over to Jack and held out his hand, "I'm sorry about the unicorn sir, but it's very nice to meet you," he said sweetly.

Danny was relieved. Perhaps there was nothing to worry about after all. Perhaps Sexton was more mature than he had given him credit for. But just as he was thinking that Sexton blurted out, "You're much shorter in person."

Jack did not respond but simply gestured for everyone to sit. He then sat in the largest armchair.

"I don't want to take up too much of your valuable time Jack, so I will cut to the chase," said Danny, hoping that the meeting would be short and he could get Sexton out of there sooner rather than later. "You realize of course that we have here the world's newest and soon to be greatest pop idol!" Danny was already to launch into the rest of his well-rehearsed spiel when Jack interrupted him.

"Thank you, Danny. I know everything there is to know. We have prepared a contract—and a very generous contract at that. Take it with you today. Have your lawyers look it over, but I'm certain that it will be to your liking."

At first, Danny was silent as it began to sink in. *The contract was already prepared? Could it really be this easy?* His face lit up with a huge smile. "Jack, what can I say? This is great news! And you know you are getting a real producer. Believe me when I say that this boy will come through with flying colors."

Jack was feeling like he just wanted to be rid of the pair of them as quickly as possible. He had already attended too many meetings for one day and wanted only to go home and relax. "Speak with Jewel on the tenth floor. You've dealt with her before, Danny.

She'll provide you with the necessary documents, and then we can get Sexton officially signed on."

"They said you'd know a good thing when you saw it," said Sexton, whose sense of entitlement precluded any bit of gratitude.

Oh God, he's talking again, thought Danny, *I've got to get him out of here.* "Well Jack, this is going to be one of those magical moments in music history. I just know it." Danny quickly stood up. "Sexton, my boy, let's go get some papers signed."

The two men shook hands with Jack and Mona and then headed out the door. As soon as it closed, Mona burst out laughing. "Oh, I'm sorry Jack. I don't mean to laugh, but that was just too much."

Jack smiled at his long-time friend. "It's alright. It's either laugh or cry, so go ahead and laugh."

"Oh Jack, that fool broke your unicorn."

"It's just an object, Mona—nothing but an object."

"I still feel bad about it. Should I call someone to clean up the pieces?"

"Leave it for now. There is plenty of time to sweep it up. Just sit with me a while. I need some pleasant company."

"Alright," Mona settled back in her chair. "Are you feeling well today?" she asked in concern.

Jack smiled, "Not to worry. This old man is not about to die on you yet. I'm just tired. That's all."

"You know that I could have handled those two clowns myself. You needn't have met with them at all."

"No Mona," said Jack. "It's important to look a man in the eye when you make a deal with him. Otherwise, you can easily forget that it is not just about some piece of paper. It's about people. When your life is full of compromise, you have to stay true to some principles, no matter how small."

"You didn't want to sign him, did you Jack?"

"Of course not—you could see he was ridiculous. And you know that there are far more talented singers out there—singers who are also able to write their own songs. But he's of the Bloodline, and you know that no one will give me sufficient airtime for someone who is not of the Bloodline. That's just how it's set up."

"Oh, yes—the Bloodline," replied Mona. "Everything's all about that."

"He'll make us richer so that we can continue with the work of the Underground, but there are times when I wonder about the cost. Is filling the world with less than inspiring music and fool-idols a sin for which I will never be forgiven?"

"Well, at least we will be going to hell together," joked Mona.

"We try so hard. Don't we? We try to do what is best, but when your hands are tied... Is it enough, Mona? Are we doing enough? And how is she ever going to awaken if the most we can offer is Sexton Spin?"

"You really believe that she is still out there—that she is still coming?"

"I have to, Mona—for Stuart's sake I have to." Jack looked towards the picture of Stuart on the desk. *Look at us now, my love— you, eternally young and me a flabby old man.*

"Sometimes I doubt," said Mona, "but I still keep the faith too. When I see that endless parade of Sexton-like characters, I have to believe to keep myself from going completely insane."

"I know what you mean. It's just so difficult some days. I used to hear Stuart's voice almost as clearly as if I were awake and in the room with him, but now I'm not sure where he is. I always relied on him. He always told me which way to go and which ones to sign. Now, I sometimes feel like maybe he's left me."

Mona wasn't sure if she had ever seen Jack looking so low. It seemed as if he were about to cry. "No Jack!" she exclaimed. "Don't think like that. He'd never leave you. He told you he wouldn't—don't you remember. In the dreams, he said he'd stay. Look how far he's brought you. Keep believing. He'll show you the way. You're just a little tired. That's all it is. Get some rest and you'll hear him again. You just need a little rest."

* * *

As they came to a stop in front of the opulent over-sized black walnut doors, the butler turned and began to carefully explain the protocol to Mr. Todd.

"Sir, it is most important that you always refer to him only as *Your Majesty*," he said.

Todd chuckled. "*Your Majesty*? Really? Isn't that a little over the top?"

The butler's face did not hide his annoyance. *Americans are so naturally uncouth*, he thought to himself. "Mr. Todd, I would advise you to take this very seriously. If you wish to do business, then you must refer to him only as *Your Majesty*. It is his preference."

"I won't have to bow or curtsy or anything, will I? Because I think I forgot my curtsying dress at home." Todd hadn't liked dealing with the snooty fussiness of the English during his time in the Middle East, and he liked it even less now. *How dare any Englishman look down his nose at a red-blooded American.*

"Please take this seriously, Mr. Todd. I am trying to help you," replied the butler, who wanted to ensure this meeting went smoothly. If it didn't, he would be the one who would have to live with the emotional fallout from his master.

Despite wanting to put this miserable little slave in his place, Todd knew the man was right. There would be a lot of money at stake, so there was no room for an old soldier's pride to get in the way. "Okay. Fair enough. I'll call him anything he wants."

"Furthermore, do not under any circumstances turn your back on him."

Todd smiled, "In my business Jamezy, I never turn my back on anyone."

The butler then ceremoniously opened the two doors, stepped back, and gestured for Todd to enter. Todd slowly walked in. When he felt the doors close behind him, a chill ran through his body. The room was typical of old English manors with its high ceilings and tall windows covered by heavy dull draperies. It had a dingy atmosphere, and a hopelessly dank smell. *All this place needs now is for Dracula to come swooping down from the ceiling.*

"Come in, Mr. Todd," said a well-dressed man, who appeared to be in his late fifties. He was casually leaning against the mantle of a large black marble fireplace.

Todd came closer but kept a respectable distance. His well-honed instincts told him that this was not the kind of man to mess with. "Your Majesty," he said politely with a small bow of the head.

"Please sit." The man pointed to a firmly stuffed settee.

Todd sat down, but the man continued to stand.

"I believe I have an assignment for you, Mr. Todd," said the man, as he toyed with a small jade statue on the mantle. "They say that you are the best there is when it comes to this sort of thing."

"You heard right. My company has a one hundred percent success rate, Your Majesty," replied Todd.

"So, I understand. And that is precisely why I contacted you. I want only the best there is for this…this assignment. Now, before we get down to details, what you must know is that this is very personal for me. It strikes at my very heart and soul. There can be absolutely no errors."

"I understand," responded Todd. "Most of what we do has a personal element, and we take very seriously the needs of our clients. You have no worries there. Satisfaction is one hundred per cent guaranteed."

The man took in a deep breath. "I am very glad to hear you confirm this. There is only one thing I want in this world, Mr. Todd, and I believe that you are the man who can deliver. I want you to kill the man who killed my dear father."

Todd was confused by what he had just heard. "But your father wasn't murdered. He died from a blood-clot in the brain." It was then that he noticed a vein pulse with anger in the man's head and thought it best to add, "I apologize for being so blunt, Your Majesty, but I always do thorough research on a client before considering any job."

"My father *was* murdered!" the man shouted, slamming his right fist into his left hand. "I realize that a blood-clot was the official cause of death, however, that was not the whole story. The clot was the result of an altercation with a low-bred man days prior—a man who has never been brought to justice and who has enjoyed freedom for far too long. Now, I want that man dead! I want revenge!"

"I understand, Your Majesty," said Todd, who was happy to see so much anger. The more passion a client had for the assignment, the more that client was willing to pay. "Is the man here in England?"

"No. He left England some years ago. Currently, he resides in The United States of America."

Todd was relieved to hear the target was in the U.S. This would make the job so much easier. "That's perfect. America is very conducive to the type of thing we do."

"And what exactly do you do, Mr. Todd? I need to understand what I will be getting for my money."

Todd had explained how it worked many times before, but he never tired of explaining it again. He was proud of the system. "Basically, this is how we proceed. First, we locate what would be best described as a messed-up loser—an appropriate patsy who will carry out the job." Todd smirked. "I have to say that the internet has made that part so much easier than it used to be."

"I see," said the man, eagerly. He had a weakness for murder mystery novels and was now feeling very excited about being part of such a real-life plot.

Todd was encouraged by the man's enthusiasm. "So, once we locate our loser who is already brimming with hate and anger over stupid things, we then covertly play him. We fill his head full of more crazy ideas and provide him with drugs that will assist the process. With systematic precision, we turn his increasing hatred towards the target we want removed. As he becomes more and more obsessed with the target, we just keep it going until he is, basically, ready to blow. This process can take anywhere between three months to a year, depending on the individual and the job. When all signs point to our unwitting killing machine being ready, we then set the rat loose."

"What a brilliant strategy!" exclaimed the man. "Truly inspiring!"

Todd smiled at the compliment. "Guns are of course the choice weapon, because of their effectiveness, so I'm glad to hear the job is in the U.S. The absence of any real gun laws gives us access to the most lethal weapons. It's best if the idiot has a gun that can't miss, so we never have to clean up after him. Of course, you realize that these guys always get either shot down by police or arrested. In the end, the public gets their blood by prosecuting this crazy fool and no one is the wiser about how it's really done. It's the perfect assassination."

"Oh Mr. Todd, I am impressed!" grinned the man.

"All in a day's work, Your Majesty," said Todd proudly. "So, who is it that you want terminated."

The smile dropped from the man's face and his lips curled in anger. "He is the owner of Einhorn Records. The world just calls him *Jack*."

"Jack!" Todd was surprised. He had never been asked to take out anyone of that magnitude. "They love Jack in America. That's a big fish to fry, Your Majesty. You need to know up front that the bigger the fish, the higher the price."

The man slammed his fist down into his hand again. "I want that man dead! Each and every time I see his smiling Philistine face on the telly, I cringe at the thought that he is still living. My dearest father has been lying cold in his grave all these years while that dog continues to walk this earth. Kill him, Mr. Todd! Money is no concern as there is nothing I will not pay to see him die!"

"Well then," said Todd, eagerly rubbing his hands together, "it seems that we are in business." Todd looked into the man's cold ice-blue eyes and a shiver ran down his spine. That was when he decided it was best to add the words, *"Your Majesty."*

2

Jack sat at his desk trying to read through an important financial report. He had fallen behind in his work lately and didn't know how it happened. Somehow, he just seemed to be losing focus.

The rain pelted against the windows, and he wished it would stop. When he first moved to this office, it was always a good thing whenever it rained. It was like watching a cleansing baptism of the city. Now, it seemed as if the rain only made mud in the roads and sooty streaks on the windows.

Jack looked at Stuart smiling in the photo. Even this was not bringing him comfort today. *Have I lost my way, old friend? If I have, can you help me find it again?*

Just then the phone rang. Jack didn't feel like picking it up. He didn't want to talk to anyone today. He just wanted to shut himself up somewhere quiet and not think about anything. The phone kept on ringing, and he just stared at it. Another person wanting something from him. He was tired of people always wanting something. Couldn't they leave him alone for a few minutes? The phone continued to ring, and Jack realized that it was not going to stop unless he did something about it, so he picked up the receiver. "Yes." he said.

"Danny Green is on the line, Jack. Would you like to speak with him, sir?"

Jack sighed. He wanted to say, 'No, tell him to get lost and stay lost. This day is gloomy enough without Danny making it any darker.' But Jack knew that Danny would just keep calling back if he did not take the call now, and maybe there was already some trouble with Sexton Spin. If it was trouble, it was important to know about it sooner rather than later. "Alright Susan, put him through," he said.

A few seconds of silence and then he heard Danny's voice, but it didn't have the usual I-have-a-deal-for-you gusto. There was strangeness in it Jack had never heard before. "Hi Jack. It's so good of you to take my call. I realize how busy you are, and so I appreciate you giving me this time."

He still wants something, thought Jack. "Hello Danny, what can I do for you?"

"I just wanted to touch base with you on Sexton. Everything, as you know, is going very well. You've seen the numbers yourself. What did I tell you? That boy would deliver and he sure as hell is. I know my stuff, Jack. I know how to pick the winners."

"Yes Danny, he is doing very well."

"You pick the winners just like me, Jack. That's why we do such great business together. You know them and I know them. We both have instinct Jack—real instinct."

Oh, he's building up to something. Jack glanced over at Stuart. *For certain, he wants something big.*

"Well, because we share that sort of sixth sense, you'll understand what's coming next. I have a winner for you, Jack—a big winner! But he's being selective on who he wants to sign with. It has to be a unique record company—a company that understands real talent. Believe me when I tell you that this guy will take us places— places even you have never been before."

Jack was getting tired of listening to the sales pitch. "What's his name Danny?"

"Well, he's been around a long time. He's made big money in the past. But now he wants to move on to even bigger things." Danny took a big breath. *Come on, don't be a coward just say it.* "It's Elijah—one of the greatest performers of the last century."

"Elijah!" said Jack. "Elijah the Techno-pop King from the '80's! Are you having me on Danny?"

Ah damn, he's not going for it. "Listen Jack, he's ready to make a comeback. This is what the world has been waiting for. He still has thousands of devoted fans out there—and he's completely clean now. No drugs, no alcohol, no anything—he's clean."

Jack was confused. This was not like Danny at all. He always picked the sure things and wasn't an out-on-a-limb sort of guy. "Why Danny?" Jack asked. "Just be honest for a moment and explain to me why you are pitching Elijah of all people?"

Danny knew Jack well enough to know that there was no point in trying to hide the truth. He'd have to risk being at least partially truthful. "I owe him, Jack. I don't want to talk about why I owe him, but I do. I owe him big. Call me superstitious, but when you owe a man, you have to pay him back. Otherwise, it's going to come back on you. That's my secret belief, and I don't share it with anyone, Jack. But I can trust you. You're different."

Jack was surprised by what Danny said. This was not like him at all. He was usually a take-whatever-you-can-get-and-run sort of guy. That Danny would actually have some sort of principles—principles strong enough to even try and pitch Elijah was a little shocking.

"Anyway, Elijah came to me," Danny continued. "And he asked me to find him a deal. He wants to make a comeback, and he says he's ready. It's not for me to judge whether he's ready or not. But just so you know Jack, this isn't business as usual. I wouldn't be part of the package. He'd be all Einhorn's. You'd have full control. Will you at least take a look at him, Jack? He's available to meet with you anytime."

Jack was still having a hard time trying to reconcile this Danny with the Danny he had known for so many years. It was like he was talking to a different man. It was disarming.

"Jack, are you still there?" asked Danny, who was waiting for an answer."

"I'm sorry Danny," said Jack. "I would like to help you, but this is business. I can't sign a man like Elijah. It would not just be a risk—it would be a certain catastrophe."

"I understand Jack," replied Danny. "But don't say *no* right away. Think about it. Think about it for at least a few days and I'll check back with you then. Now, I know that you're a very busy man, so I won't take up any more of your time. But just think about it. That's all I ask."

Jack knew there would be no point in dragging it out. He would have to be firm and tell him like it is. "No Danny," he said. "I can tell you right now that the answer is absolutely *no*."

For a moment there was only silence, then Danny sighed and meekly said, "Well thanks for hearing me out, Jack. I appreciate it."

"Goodbye Danny," Jack said, as he hung up the phone. He leaned back in his chair and thought about the strange conversation. *Sign Elijah? That man must be going mad.*

Just then there was a knock on the door and in walked Mona. Jack had told her many times not to bother knocking, but she often did it anyway as a courtesy to him. "Good morning!" she chirped.

Jack was relieved to see her smiling face. "Hello Mona. What perfect timing. I need your help to get through some of this backlog," he said, picking up some papers and then letting them flutter back down to the desk again.

Mona pushed a chair beside Jack's and began to leaf through some of the papers. "You shouldn't always try to do so much yourself," she said.

"Are you trying to tell me that I am getting too old?" asked Jack.

"Yes Gramps, you are way too old. By the way, your white shoes and matching belt will be delivered this afternoon."

Jack laughed. "One day if you come in here and I am wearing just that, it won't be so funny anymore. Oh, and by the way, you will not believe the phone call I just received," said Jack, leaning back in his chair.

"They haven't asked you to do a reality show have they? I think you'd be great on Lawn Bowling with Celebrities." Mona laughed as she imagined Jack in a bowling shirt.

Jack smiled. "No. It was even stranger than that. It was from Danny Green."

"Well, Danny is more than a little strange, Jack. I've been telling you that for years," laughed Mona.

"He wanted me to sign on a new singer—well actually an old singer. He wanted me to sign Elijah." Jack looked at Mona and waited for the reaction he was expecting.

Mona looked at Jack in surprise. *Was he joking?* But the look on Jack's face told her this was no joke. "Elijah!" she exclaimed. "The Techno-pop King! Has Danny lost his mind? Comics worldwide still make jokes about him and his leather pants. And for goodness' sake, the man must be close to fifty by now!"

"He said that he owed Elijah," said Jack. "I never had Danny down for the superstitious type, but he seems to believe that he owes some kind of metaphysical debt. He wants to set things right and practically begged me to take on this man."

"I'm surprised," said Mona. "That doesn't sound like the Danny we know. Do you think he may be on drugs or maybe it's just that he's off them?"

"It's a possibility. You know how it is in this business."

"So, what did you say?" asked Mona, wanting more details.

"Of course, I said *no*. It's not just the fact that Elijah would cost more than he would ever make, but as you know, he was deliberately *set loose*."

Mona shook her head. "You mean he was a human sacrifice." She did not like to mince words with Jack when talking about the Bloodline and their strange practices. She preferred telling it like it was.

Jack sighed and adjusted his glasses. "Yes, he was a sacrifice. The recording company saw him sinking and decided to let him go. I'm sure they even did things to help quicken the descent. They believe that the occasional sacrifice can give them more power and strength. It's madness, but who am I to try and tell them it's wrong."

"And what would they do if you signed him?"

Jack picked up his pen and tapped it on the desk. "They would see it as a hostile act and likely shun both me and the company. Over time, they would rally their allies and eventually destroy Einhorn. Their superstitions run deep and they take them very seriously."

"Some days I am just so disgusted with this Bloodline garbage," said Mona, looking past Jack and outside at the gray clouds above the city. "I'd just like to scream at them to *grow up and get real*! Maybe one day I'll do just that."

Jack laughed. "Tell me when that day is approaching because I don't want to miss it."

Mona laughed too. "Anyway, I originally came in to ask you if you wouldn't mind if I left a couple of hours earlier today."

"Do you have a hot Friday night date?" asked Jack playfully.

"A hot date? Oh Jack! A woman of my age has one of three choices: either a very old man who sees me as a potential nurse; a man my own age, who is probably married, and sees me as a desperate and easy one-nighter; or a silly young man who doesn't see me at all, but who is madly and hopelessly in love with my credit card limit. Pretty sad options I'd say."

Jack smiled at Mona's joke, but he knew her well enough to know that she was lonely. He really wished he could help her. "Don't give up completely," he said. "You never know what's around the corner. Even an ordinary guy from Liverpool like me, found love once."

* * *

The office was in a small dark basement rented from a convenience store owner who lived and worked in the upper areas of the old redbrick building. It had a separate entrance in the back alley, which made it easy to come and go with little notice. The dank room had actually been offered for rent a very long time, but prior to this, the landlord had never been able to attract a tenant who found value in his poorly renovated property. His advertised "modern office" still looked like a damp cellar to prospective renters. When two well-spoken businessmen showed up, said it was "perfect" and were willing to pay six months in advance and in cash, it was like winning the lottery.

The office, which had come fully furnished with two old metal desks, a large steel filing cabinet and some newly upholstered office chairs, was lit by a single fluorescent fixture that made a continuous humming noise. The concrete floor was covered with new gray industrial carpeting that gave off a mild toxic odor.

At one of the desks sat Mr. Todd, hunched over his laptop. His face had that permanent serious weathered look one often sees on old soldiers—a look between life and death but leaning more towards death.

At the other desk sat a much younger man with a fresh New England face and wispy blonde hair. He wore the underwhelming overpriced clothes typical of an affluent college student and was busily working away on a brand-new PC. As he read through the text on his machine, his face suddenly lit up. "Mr. Todd, I think I have our weevil!"

Todd looked up from his desk and smiled. Minton was the best troller he had ever found. "That didn't take long," he said.

"It never does," grinned Minton. "And the good news is that this guy is already tailor-made for the job. He has a blog where he keeps updates on socialist space aliens attempting to take over America. He hates gays and Hollywood. And—get this—he's even already written an article about how Jack is corrupting the minds of the people with alien directed music. This is a gift from above—or maybe below."

"Have you worked out the angle already? Because the sooner we get this job done, the better." Todd was eager to get it finished in record time. He had lost money in the economic collapse and needed to collect the full payment before they repossessed one of his four homes.

Minton swiveled his chair around to face Todd. "From what I gather, this guy is completely alone. He talks a lot about *feminazis* so he definitely has some sort of sexual issues. A vixen should easily do the trick. That's the angle I'll take. She'll of course have to be virginal and innocent, but a good vixen always is. That's important to hook him in. It shouldn't be a problem to quickly work my way into his sad lonely heart. These guys are pretty much all the same."

Nothing is more useful than an Ivy League education in psychology, thought Todd. "How long do you estimate?" he asked.

"This should be a piece of cake. From the things he says, I'm certain he already has a pick of guns stock-piled under his bed. I'd say as little as three months—six months tops."

"Good!" said Todd. "This is a high priority client, and I'd like to give him some sort of rough timeline. We can't take the risk of him becoming impatient. This is major money and we have to keep him sweet."

"So, any suggestions for a name?" asked Minton. Todd just looked at him in confusion.

"For the vixen, I mean. Anything that invokes youthful innocence—after all she's a fair maiden who needs protection from dangerous socialist monsters from outer space."

Todd laughed. "How about Britney? I once knew a whore named Britney, but I don't think that was her real name."

"I like it! Britney it is," grinned Minton. He turned back to his computer and clicked the contact button on the site. "Today, my unlucky little weevil, you are about to meet the girl of your dreams. Okay Britney, let's give him a time to remember!"

3

The long black limousine slowly made its way to the grand columned entrance where a uniformed valet was waiting. As the valet pulled open the shiny black door, Jack confidently stepped out onto the red carpet. Dressed in his finest tuxedo, he was feeling quite youthful and handsome as he climbed the stairs to the party. It was just like the old days when he had first found success in New York.

Once inside, he looked around at the crowd but didn't see anyone he recognized. This was odd because Jack knew a lot of people. He could never attend a party without knowing nearly everyone there. Perhaps if he found the bar, he would be able to find some old friends. He began to scour the area hoping that they would, at the very least, have proper English beer on tap.

Not seeing any sign of the bar, Jack moved further into the room. The crowd around him was now becoming thicker. A fear started creeping over him, as he began to feel people pushing in on every side. What if it didn't stop? What if more and more people pushed into the already full room? What if he were crushed to death by this mob?

Desperately wanting to find the exit, Jack couldn't remember from which direction he had come. Nothing looked familiar, and it began to feel as if all the air was now being sucked from the room. He needed to get outside—to get back into an open space where he could breathe again.

Just as the feeling of panic was rising to a point where he thought he would start to scream, there was a whisper in his ear. "A man asked for your help Jack, and you refused. Do you still love me?"

Jack knew that voice. He knew that voice better than he knew his own. *It's Stuart! He is here at the party!* "Stuart!" he called, as he quickly turned around.

From a distance, he could see only Stuart's back as he walked through a doorway and disappeared into another room. "Stuart!" Jack shouted as he struggled to push through the crowd. It seemed to take forever before he reached the doorway, at which point, he became fearful that he might have lost him. Once inside the room, however, he could see Stuart standing with his back still towards him and staring out a window. "Stuart!" Jack shouted again as he rushed forward and grabbed him by the shoulder, "Oh Stuart!" he cried. But when the man turned around, it wasn't Stuart at all. It was Sexton Spin.

Sexton grinned at Jack and said, "Great party man. Like some?" At first Jack didn't know what he was talking about but then realized that Sexton was referring to something he had in his hand. When he looked down, he saw that he was holding a raw bloody heart that was still beating. Jack could even hear it thumping.

Lifting the heart to his face, Sexton opened his mouth wide and took a large bite making a horrible squishing noise. The thumping sound instantly stopped and blood squirted out in all directions. Jack felt sick when it splattered disgustingly hot against his cheek. *Oh no! Oh horror! God save me!*

Jack's eyes suddenly flew open. For a moment, he did not even recognize his own bedroom ceiling. His heart was pounding in his chest, and his breathing was rapid. Putting his hand to his forehead, he wiped away the damp sweat. *It was all just a nightmare—just a terrible horrible nightmare!* The image of Sexton biting into that living heart was still fresh in his brain, as he tried to calm his nerves. *Don't have a heart attack old man*, he thought, as he concentrated on slowing his breathing and relaxing his body. It was then that he remembered Stuart.

Stuart was in the dream! And he spoke in the dream! Despite the nightmare part, there was Stuart! It had been such a long time, but the waiting was now over. Finally, he had heard Stuart's voice again. And even though he had not seen his face, there was no doubt in his mind. That was Stuart!

Jack could feel warm tears falling down the sides of his face and into his hair. He thought about Stuart's words and how they had been so clear—clearer than they had ever been before. Then he thought about what Stuart had said. "Why would you ask if I still love you? Of course, I still love you," he called out to the empty room. "You know I can't help but love you."

* * *

Another boring weekend finished and another boring Monday just beginning. Could it get any worse? thought Mona as she walked down the hall towards Jack's office. Today she would talk to him about taking some time off. It had been a while since she had a vacation, and Paris would be just the thing to break this wicked spell of monotony. Jack surely wouldn't have a problem with it, given how hard she had been working these past few months.

When Mona opened the door and stepped into the office, she could see only the back of Jack's desk chair as it was turned facing the window. "Don't you ever get tired of looking at that city?" she asked, closing the door behind her.

Jack quickly spun around. "Mona!" he exclaimed. "I heard him! Last night, I heard his voice!" He could feel his eyes filling up with tears. *Don't start crying, you silly old man.*

"Oh Jack!" cried Mona, rushing over, and hugging him. "That's great! I told you he wouldn't leave you."

"Yes," said Jack. "Yes, I've waited a long time—praying every day that I would hear that voice again. And now the day has come, and so here I am almost wishing that I hadn't heard him at all. Can you believe that, Mona? So intensely I wanted to hear him, and when it happened, it was so marvelous—so wonderful, but what he said is so troubling."

Mona stepped back and looked Jack in the eye. "Why?" she asked. "What did he say?"

Jack sighed. "He said, *a man asked for your help, and you refused.*"

Mona was puzzled. "What man? What does he mean?"

Jack looked down at his desk and picked up a pen. At first, he said nothing as he nervously twirled it around in his fingers, but then he looked back up at Mona and replied, "I've thought about it and there is only one man he could mean. It's Danny. I refused to help Danny when he begged me to sign Elijah. That's who he was talking about."

Mona shook her head. "Oh no! That can't be it. You must have it wrong, Jack. That would make no sense at all. You know what would happen if you signed Elijah."

Jack got up from his chair and went over to the enclosed glass display case where he kept the unicorns he had brought with him from England. These were the most precious ones in his collection—the ones that Stuart had once touched. He stared at them. The white one was a birthday. The speckled one was a Christmas present. The extremely silly pink one with the gold painted crown was just a Friday night whimsy. Each one represented a special memory—but Stuart was far more than just a memory. He was as much about the present and the future as he was about the past.

Turning back towards Mona, Jack knew he had to make her understand. "I've thought long and hard about what he told me. I've run it through my head a million times, and I'm not wrong, Mona. Stuart wants me to sign Elijah. And if I do such a thing, we both know what this will mean. They will not like it. Not one bit. And they will come after us for certain. But I have to listen to what Stuart tells me. I have to be true to him. It's the only way."

Mona couldn't believe what she was hearing. *Why would Stuart ask him to do something so crazy? He had to have his wires crossed somewhere.* "Jack, how can you be so sure? This is serious."

"Of course, I know it's serious. I'm not making this decision lightly, but what must be done, must be done."

Mona was afraid—afraid for Einhorn Records, afraid for herself but, most of all, afraid for Jack. "Oh Jack, consider what will happen. Will the Underground be able to protect you?"

"The Underground?" laughed Jack. "Sometimes I'm not sure if there is such a thing anymore. Once we did fight for something, but now? There are days when the Underground and the Bloodline just seem to be one and the same. Is there any difference in their goals? Both want money. Both want power. Both advance almost exclusively their own. And both, it seems, will sacrifice anything to get what they want. No Mona, Stuart's right. I have to do this. I have to sign Elijah. Come what may, I have to follow my heart."

* * *

Britney:
Glad u came back to talk with me again. Still live with my parents but they don't understand me. They r stupid bleeding-heart liberals. U understand, don't u?

AlienKiller666:
Yes I understand.

Britney:
It's nice to know someone does. What color is ur hair?

AlienKiller666:
Brown.

Britney:
Nice. I like brown hair.

AlienKiller666:
What color is yours?

Britney:
Blonde. Like golden blonde. It's straight and past my shoulders. I mostly keep it in a ponytail.

AlienKiller666:
Sounds nice too!

Britney:
Do u like music?

AlienKiller666:
Only good music.

Britney:
Me too. Don't like Sexton Spin. He's gay.

AlienKiller666:
He's really gay.

Britney:
Yah, like that other guy from Einhorn records. You know the one? Mr. Ugly. Seen him on TV the other day.

AlienKiller666:
You mean Jack?

Britney:
Yup.

AlienKiller666:
You know that he works for the aliens.

Britney:
Really! No wonder I didn't like him.

AlienKiller666:
I think maybe you have a sense for spotting aliens and their people.

Britney:
Wow! U think so?

AlienKiller666:
You figured out Jack didn't you?

Britney:
Yah, guess I did.

AlienKiller666:
I think we have a lot in common.

Britney:
I'm glad I found u.

AlienKiller666:
Me too.

Britney:
Parents just came home. Gotta go. They r nosey.

4

"How are you feeling today?" asked Mona, carrying a box of Jack's favorite tea. She set it down on the desk in front of him.

"I would be lying if I didn't say that I was feeling a little nervous about the entire thing. I have to keep reminding myself that this is the right thing to do. I have to keep my faith."

Mona moved over behind Jack and began to rub his shoulders. She hated to see him this distressed. "If this is what you feel you have to do, you know that I will stand with you. You can count on me."

"Thank you, Mona. And I'm so glad to hear that you are completely behind this project because...well, because I'm going to be assigning Elijah to you."

Mona abruptly took her hands from Jack's shoulders. "Umm Jack...yes, I will support you, but I can't do this! It's just too...too crazy. How am I supposed to orchestrate a come-back for this man? His career is not just in the toilet. It's been flushed way out to sea. This is a task I don't think I could handle even if I was feeling at the top of my game. The truth is I was planning to ask you for some vacation time. I haven't been feeling well lately and what I need is to get away—far away. The last thing I need right now is to be asked to spin hay into gold."

Jack turned to face Mona and took her hand in his. "For so long I've waited to hear Stuart's voice again, and now I have. I heard it louder and stronger than ever before. This is important, Mona—so important that I cannot just trust anyone with this work. I need you. You are the only one who can help me with this. You are the only one I trust with this important job."

Before Mona could protest again, there was a knock on the door.

"Come in," said Jack, letting go of Mona's hand.

Danny Green poked his head inside. "They told me to just go right on through."

"That's fine Danny," said Jack, getting up from his desk. "Come in and sit down." He gestured towards the sitting area.

Danny came through the door followed by a tall unassuming man. Both Mona and Jack were surprised that they barely recognized him. He'd been out of the public eye for a very long time.

"Well, here he is," said Danny, pointing at Elijah. "Elijah, this is Jack."

"It's a pleasure to meet you," said Elijah, smiling as he shook Jack's hand.

Yes, that's the smile I remember, thought Jack, finally seeing something that still looked like the star Elijah once was. "It's good to meet you, Elijah."

Danny was happy to see Jack warming up to Elijah. All the way over, he was nervous that it would somehow fall apart. He looked over to see Mona walking towards them. She did not look pleased.

"And this is the beautiful Mona," said Danny.

Elijah looked over at Mona. "It's nice to meet you," he said smiling. Mona was shocked when she felt herself blush. *Oh my God, I can't believe I just did that! Did anyone notice? Sure, I was a fan once. What girl my age wasn't. But that was a long time ago. He can't do that to me now—not at my age. I know better.* "Hello," she said in her most serious business voice.

"So," said Jack, clapping his hands, "shall we sit down and discuss what's next?"

"Whatever you say," said Danny, trying to be as obliging as possible. If all went right, he may finally get a good night's sleep. It seemed like this Elijah thing had been hanging over his head forever.

Everyone sat down except for Jack. "Would anyone like a tea or coffee before we begin?" he asked.

At first, no one answered, but then Elijah spoke. "English tea would be just fine, if you have it. Do you by any chance have decaf?"

"Yes," said Jack. "I do. Anyone else? Danny? Mona? I also have coffee?"

"No thanks," replied Danny who, even though his doctor had warned him about caffeine and heart attacks, was still jittery from the extra-large latte he drank earlier.

Mona didn't really want anything. All she wanted was to get out of that room and on a plane to Paris, but what could she say? "Sure Jack, tea sounds good to me too."

Jack went over to a nearby wall and slid open a pocket door to reveal a small tidy kitchenette. Elijah was surprised to see him begin to prepare the teas himself. It reassured him that this was the right decision.

"So, Elijah," said Jack, as he filled the kettle, "what made you decide that you wanted to return to the music business. It's been a long time."

Before Elijah could speak, Danny quickly interjected. "He's still got it, Jack. The fever never leaves 'em. You know rockers. They never get old. They just glow brighter like any star."

Mona held back from laughing. *Danny boy is really laying it on thick today.*

"It's okay Danny. I can speak for myself," said Elijah. He then looked at Jack. "To be perfectly honest, I didn't want to ever sing again. In fact, I made a vow to myself years ago that I would never try to make a comeback. It took me a long time to get over what this business did to me, and I wanted no part of it. I had reached a point where I had a reasonably comfortable and quiet existence, and I wanted to keep it that way."

Jack was surprised that this was the same person whose erratic behavior in the 80's had caused so much controversy. But then again, how much of it was truth and how much of it was rumor.

"I spent a lot of time reading and trying to forget the past. But then I began studying the work of Lao Tzu, and it all became clearer to me. When I read these words:

It is better to do one's own duty, however defective it may be, than to follow the duty of another, however well one may perform it. He who does his duty as his own nature reveals it, never sins.

…it somehow seemed to sum up all I had been through. It made me realize how the music I was making back in the 80's was not my own. I did it very well, but it was not of my nature. It was the duty of another. Now I just want a chance to do what I should have done in the beginning. I want to do nothing more than my duty according to my nature."

For a moment, everyone was silent. Danny clenched his hands in worry. *Why would Elijah talk all airy-fairy like that? It's going to put Jack off for sure. We were so close and now he's gone and blown it. Jesus Christ! Jack was my only hope.*

The boiling kettle clicked off and Jack began to pour the water over the tea bags in the three cups. After he was done, he turned towards Elijah and said, "For me, that is as good a reason as any to want to return. Let's see if we can make it happen for you."

Danny breathed a sigh of relief.

Mona had been surprised by Elijah's answer. She expected him to be just another self-absorbed rock star looking to placate his ego. *Don't be fooled,* she told herself, *they all learn to talk like that. It means nothing.*

Jack brought over the tray with the tea and placed it on the table. "Milk? Sugar?" he asked.

"No thanks," said Mona and Elijah simultaneously. They then looked at each other briefly.

Jack handed them their cups, sat back, and took a sip from his own. "I believe that you've already signed the contract, so it's only a matter of getting you to work. We will have to do a little bit of a— uh—well, a makeover. No offence, but right now, you look more like a grocer than a star."

Elijah laughed. "No offence taken. Anything you want, I'm willing to do, as long as it doesn't involve knives or needles."

"Now Elijah, don't be hasty," said Danny, who was worried about making any sort of conditions. *Beggars can't be choosers.*

"No, it's alright Danny," said Jack. "That's a fair enough request. No knifes or needles, but maybe a little hair color?"

Elijah laughed. "That's fine, as long as it's not electric yellow. I gave that up years ago."

"Yes, we all remember that very well," said Jack with a smile. "Mona will be working closely with you. She's not only an exceptional producer, but she'll also help you with the bookings, PR, and all that. You need to take very seriously whatever she has to say. Mona is the best in the business."

Elijah looked over at Mona and smiled at her once again. This time she was ready for him. She was not going to be blind-sided by the remnants of some star-struck-silly-girl crush. "Yes," she said in a matter-of-fact tone, "I will be expecting you to follow my instructions to the letter. There will be absolutely no drinking or drugs, and you must check with me before accepting any social invitations or attending any function. It's not going to be easy to get you back to even singing in small clubs. You will need to co-operate fully and if you do not, I guarantee that I will be all over you."

"That sounds good to me," said Elijah, still smiling.

Mona blushed for a second time. *Damn! Why would I choose those words?* She looked over at Jack, who seemed to be a little amused at her embarrassment.

Jack set his cup on the table and said to Elijah, "Mona is correct that you must follow her instructions carefully. She has done similar projects and knows what she is doing. It is imperative that you stay in touch with her every day and that you do not hide anything from her. Remember, she's here to help you."

"I understand," said Elijah. "And I'd just like to say that I am very grateful for this opportunity. I fully realize this is a significant risk for Einhorn records and I promise I will not let you down."

"Good," said Jack, glancing over at the picture of Stuart. "I have a strange feeling that this could be one of the most important things any of us will ever do."

Danny Green looked anxiously at his watch. He'd just make it to his next appointment if he left now.

"Do you have somewhere to be, Danny?" asked Jack. "Because if you do, I think we are done here."

"As a matter of fact, I am running behind schedule. But what's new about that?" Danny quickly jumped up from his chair. "Thank you again, Jack," he said as he shook Jack's hand. "And you Mona," he said turning to smile at her. "And Elijah—take care and all the best," he said as he headed for the door.

"Danny!" called Elijah.

Danny stopped at the door and looked back.

"The journey of a thousand miles begins with one step," said Elijah. "That's Lao-Tzu. Thanks for helping me with that one step, Danny. It will never be forgotten."

Danny warmly smiled, waved, and walked out the door.

* * *

Jack removed his jacket and threw it down on a chair. He then sat down on the sofa and took off his shoes. It had been a very long day, and he was looking forward to having a nice long hot shower and then watching a little television before going to sleep. After signing Elijah that morning, he couldn't help but feel uneasy all day and he was still unable to shake the feeling. *Faith does not always come easy,* he thought to himself.

He looked over at the painting hanging on his living room wall—the last gift from Stuart. The years had not faded it one bit, and the great white unicorn still had its horn firmly through the throat of the dead ape. It was a forever gift and reassured Jack about everything.

Just then the phone rang. Jack didn't recognize the number displayed, and anyway it was a little late for a friend to be calling him. He immediately suspected that it must be someone who had heard about him signing Elijah. Being a community rife with gossip, the music business had few real secrets. *They will certainly not be phoning to congratulate me.*

At first, he thought he'd leave it to the message machine but then decided that this shouldn't be avoided. It had to be handled quickly and firmly. "Hello," he said, picking up the phone.

"Jack, this is Dick—Dick Hinken."

"Good evening Mr. Hinken. How are you?" Jack said, knowing what was to come next. Hinken represented Elijah's old recording label.

"Not too good, actually. I understand that you have signed Elijah. Is this true?"

You know it's true so why ask? "Why yes Mr. Hinken. This morning Elijah joined our team at Einhorn. Is there a problem?"

"Of course there's a problem!" Hinken had begun to yell. "You know how it works! You know the rules! You don't bring guys like Elijah back from the dead! It upsets the balance!"

"That was not my intention, Mr. Hinken," said Jack calmly. "The man asked for a second chance, and I said that I would give it to him. Everyone deserves a second chance."

"Most people don't even deserve a first chance! How dare you do this!" From his voice, Jack could tell that Hinken was getting angrier. "A man like you is lucky to be where he is. You have no family, Jack—no family!" Jack knew that he was referring to Jack not being part of the Bloodline. "Who will protect you when it all goes downhill? And it will, Jack—mark my words, it will!"

"Look Mr. Hinken, I know how to read the signs, and the signs told me that this was the right course of action. I'm very sorry, but I have to go with the ultimate authority."

"*I'm* the ultimate authority in this matter! Read signs? You think you can read signs better than a direct descendant of Jesus Christ? Has the power we've given to you gone to your stupid head?"

Jack wanted to say that any power he had he earned through hard work, but he knew better than to argue.

"I am very sorry that you feel that way," replied Jack. "But really there is nothing more you can say that will change my mind. Elijah is signed, and I will do everything I can to ensure his success. That is my job."

For a moment, there was only silence on the other end as Jack waited for Hinken's response. Just when he began to wonder if the man was even still there, Hinken suddenly hissed, "You'll be sorry all right, Jack—damned sorry! You'll be sorry you were ever born!" With that he hung up.

Jack sighed and set the phone down. He looked up again at the painting. "Oh Stuart, everything is now on the line. Hinken won't stop until he destroys both me and Elijah. I hope I understood what you were telling me. If I have it wrong, then please let me know while I still have the chance to turn around." Jack waited, but except for the dull hum of the traffic outside, the room remained completely silent.

5

Mona sat at her computer, busily finalizing the press release that was to go out the next day. She was having a difficult time deciding on the exact wording. Such things were usually delegated to her staff, but this was a very delicate matter, and she wanted to be sure that it was handled in the best possible way. She felt certain that the media would pick it up, but what they would do with it was another matter. They would definitely make some jokes. And after what Jack told her about his conversation with Hinken, she knew that he would stop at nothing to put a bad spin on everything he could. Hinken was a very powerful man in the entertainment industry.

As she contemplated whether it was better to use the word 'renewed' or 'refreshed,' there was a knock at the door. "Yes, come in," she called out, a little annoyed by the interruption.

The door opened. It was Elijah. "Good morning, Mona," he said, closing the door behind him.

Mona could see that the Einhorn image people had given him a thorough makeover. He looked ten years younger with his black hair and new wardrobe. She decided it was best if she didn't compliment him on his new look. It was important not to let him feel too confident about the entire situation. Too much confidence could lead to too much ego.

"So, do you like the new me?" asked Elijah, spinning around.

Mona was determined not to get lured into a personal response. She had to keep this on a strictly professional level. "You are definitely much more marketable now," she said matter of fact.

Elijah laughed and sat down in the chair opposite her desk. "What's next," he asked with a big smile.

Mona tried to keep her eyes on her computer screen. "We need to decide on a single to be released ahead of the album. I understand that you have a considerable amount of material already to go, and that you have started working with our music producer

Joanne. She's suggesting that your song *Love Rising* would make the best single. I'd like to work with you on the final production of that song. Joanne is very good, but I am better."

"Yes, I have hundreds of songs," said Elijah. "After my career ended, I spent a lot of time writing. I didn't really ever think it would go anywhere. It was mostly written for personal reasons, but it's very good material. I think you'll be impressed."

"Just keep your ego under check and listen to the advice of your producers," said Mona. "I do know that Joanne thinks *Love Rising* would be a perfect launching pad. Although I haven't heard it yet, I trust her judgment. Do you have any objections to starting there?"

"No," Elijah simply replied. "I think *Love Rising* is a perfect place to start."

"Good." Mona picked up a pen and tapped it against her desk. "She thinks that we can release it as early as the end of next week. We want an early jump on that summer song market. The introductory press release will go out this week. Once your comeback becomes common knowledge, under no circumstances are you to talk to anyone about anything. All communication comes through me and me alone. Also, try not to go out too much. We don't want you seen until we are ready for them to see you. Do you have any questions?"

"Yes, I have a question." Elijah looked directly into her eyes. "You didn't really want to take this job, did you?"

Mona looked back at him in silence, and then down at her desk pretending to be checking the information on the paper beside her keyboard. "It's a job like any other. I'm a businesswoman and I take my work very seriously. This is not easy work at the best of times, and your circumstances have made it even more demanding. What you assume is resentment, is merely focus—pure focus."

"Alright then, if you say so."

"Anyway," said Mona clearing her throat, "I want to see how it goes once the single is released. If it catches on—great. If it doesn't then we will have to do some more intensive PR work. Be prepared for that."

"I'm prepared for anything," replied Elijah.

"Good," said Mona, standing up to signal that the meeting was now over. "You seem committed. As I said before, keep a low profile for now and just wait for my instructions. If you have any questions or concerns, you have my cell number. Don't bother me after hours if it's not important. But if you think it merits emergency status, then feel free to call."

"Thank you. I'll do that," he said, rising from his chair. He held out his hand to Mona. She hesitated for a moment, but then briefly shook his hand.

Elijah walked over to the door and opened it, but just before he stepped outside, he looked back at Mona and said, "I'm looking forward to working with you. I realize it won't be easy and that there's a lot of hard work ahead of us, but you make me feel reassured about everything. I just wanted you to know that." He then left, closing the door behind him.

Mona sat down in her chair and stared at the door. "Damn!" she said aloud to herself. "Damn, damn, damn it! Damn, that man smelled good!"

* * *

Britney:
Did u sleep well last night?

AlienKiller666:
Like a baby. Those sleeping pills you sent me did the trick.

Britney:
Knew they would. Nothing like a raid on Mommy's medicine cabinet. She's got a whole pharmacy. If u need some anxiety meds let me know.

AlienKiller666:
Thanks. Good for now.

Britney:
One day u should come visit me in New York.

AlienKiller666:
That would be great!

Britney:
Saw that fag the other day. You know the one. Jack.

AlienKiller666:
Where?

Britney:
In a restaurant. Mommy and me were having lunch and he came in. He's uglier in person.

AlienKiller666:
Yeah, the aliens like the ugly ones to do the dirty work.

Britney:
I was sitting there thinking how easy it would be to just shoot him. He's a big target. Ha Ha!

AlienKiller666:
The world would be better off.

Britney:
We don't have a gun. My parents hate guns.

AlienKiller666:
Anti-American to hate guns. Traitors!

Britney:
Do u have a gun?

AlienKiller666:
I have thirteen right now.

Britney:
Thirteen! Wow! What's ur biggest one?

AlienKiller666:
I have four different types of fully automatic weapons. They're my most deadly ones.

Britney:
Cool! Wish I knew how to shoot.

AlienKiller666:
I'll teach you someday.

Britney:
Promise?

AlienKiller666:
I promise.

Britney:
Ur not like the boys at my college. Most of them are anti-gun.

AlienKiller666:
Fags!

Britney:
Yah, fags!

AlienKiller666:
When will you come and see me?

Britney:
It's not easy to get away from my parents. They r so protective.

AlienKiller666:
I'd really like to see you. Your picture is beautiful!!!!!!

Britney:
O that was a bad hair day.

AlienKiller666:
I think your hair is terrific!

Britney:
U say the nicest things. I want to see u too. One day u can come here
to New York. Maybe even bring a gun. That would be cool!

AlienKiller666:
Yeah! Sounds good!

Britney:
Just looked at the clock. I'll be late for class if I don't leave now. Talk to u later. XOXO

41

6

"Jack, it's not working."

"Where are you, Mona?"

"At the gym. I needed to work out after the day I've had. I've tried everything to get that single played, and absolutely no one picked up the press release. I thought maybe some TV host would at the very least do a joke, but nothing."

"We are being very seriously blackballed."

"And it's a great song, Jack. It really is. If I could just get it out there, I know people would love it."

"Wait a few days and let me think about what we should do next."

"No Jack. I'm not waiting anymore. I'm mad—real mad! Who do they think they are doing this—messing with people's lives! This song is a hit, and come hell or high water, Elijah is going back on stage again."

"You're surprising me, Mona."

"I've just had enough, and now I'm taking it to the trenches."

"The trenches?"

"Paparazzi, Jack. I have a friend who is an agent for a number of supermodels, and he owes me a favor. I'm going to get Elijah a date he can take to dinner at Le Chien d'Or in LA. The paparazzi are there every weekend just waiting outside the front doors. It's a long shot, but I'm going to take my chances and hope that one of them takes a few photos. Even something on a tabloid back page is better than nothing."

"Mona, do whatever you need to do. I'm behind you a hundred percent. It's good to see you this fired up. I can't remember the last time you were so passionate about your work."

"I've never had a job as challenging as this, but I'm not going to let it get me down. Elijah is going back to the top, and I am going to take him there. I just need to make him visible again. Bloodline or no

Bloodline, no one can control the hearts of the people. They can sway them this way or that temporarily, but in the end the people will decide. And I know the people not only want, but they *need* Elijah."

* * *

Elijah slipped his arms into the black leather blazer, completing his new ensemble. He then examined himself in the full-length mirror. *Not bad. Not bad at all.* Since making the decision to come back to the music business, he had worried about looking like just another sad middle-aged man trying to be young again. It was a relief to see a distinguished yet youthfully vibrant person looking back at him. He had not lost his dignity.

Initially, he had tried to talk Mona out of setting up this date. Although he had done this type of publicity stunt before, he was never very good at it. It always took a great deal of effort and left him feeling exhausted afterward. However, he decided to go along with it for Mona's sake. She was working so hard for him and was completely convinced that this was the right course of action. Refusing to go would be letting her down, and Elijah did not want to let her down.

As he adjusted his lapels and shirt collar in the mirror, the hotel phone rang. He picked it up.

"Good evening, Sir. This is the front desk calling just to let you know that your limousine is waiting."

"Yes, thank you. I'll be right down."

Elijah looked one last time in the mirror to make sure everything was okay. *Well old man, time for a show. Let's see if you've still got it.* He went to the door and opened it, only to see Mona standing there with her fist raised, ready to knock.

"Oh! Hi," she said, a little startled.

Elijah wondered why she would show up like this. "Hello Mona. I was just leaving. The limo is waiting downstairs."

Mona had a worried look on her face. "We're going to have to cancel it. Let me in and I'll explain," she said, as she pushed by him.

"Why? What's happened?" Elijah asked, closing the door.

"He cancelled on us—the idiot!" Mona was fuming. It surprised Elijah who had never seen her like this before. "That guy owed me a big favor, but at the last minute he decides that he can't take that sort of risk for his client. Bull! He chickened out. He didn't

43

want to take the risk for himself. Sniveling, miserable little coward! Oh Elijah! I'm so sorry I didn't come through for you," Mona said, realizing that she had pinned far too much hope on this publicity stunt.

"It's not your fault, Mona. It was out of your hands. We'll just have to come up with something else," said Elijah, trying his best to reassure her.

"I should never have trusted that weasel! In this business, you don't make friends only unstable alliances. I'll phone down and cancel the limo." Mona reached for the hotel phone.

"Wait!" said Elijah. "Why cancel? The restaurant and meal have already been paid for—right? So why don't we just go anyway."

"The whole point of this evening was to get you some exposure," replied Mona. "To show the world that Elijah is the desire of young famous beautiful women. I don't think dinner with me will have the same effect and could even make things worse."

"So, it's not a date with a trendy supermodel. It's a date with sophisticated lady with excellent taste in restaurants and in men."

Now Mona laughed. "You can't be serious. Look at me. I'm not even dressed for it."

"You look fine. Just like a businesswoman should. Come on. I've heard that the food at

Le Chien d'Or is an experience not to be missed. Why throw away Jack's good money? Let's go!"

Mona thought about it. It was crazy, and there were risks involved. But then again, it's not like they were serious risks. Probably the paparazzi would not even bother with them. Without a well-known supermodel on his arm, Elijah would not be considered of interest. And besides, the food was supposed to be amazing. "Alright then," she said, finally giving in. "We wouldn't want to waste Jack's good money."

"Wonderful!" exclaimed Elijah, opening the door and holding it for her. He bowed and waved his arm. "My Lady, your limo awaits!"

* * *

Jack sat in front of the television, trying to focus on the documentary he was watching.

44

The butterfly is now emerging from her chrysalis-stage. Her wings are not yet fully unfolded and must be inflated with her blood and dried in the warm air before she can fly into the safety of the sky.

Unfortunately, this was not enough of a distraction to keep him from thinking about the Elijah situation. Hinken was definitely planning to take this as far as he could, and Jack couldn't help worrying about what else might be in store. Even Sexton Spin was not getting the media attention he should be getting. Hinken was beginning to put the screws on all of Einhorn.

Hoping to find a more fast-paced show to help take his mind off of things, Jack began to channel surf. Finding nothing of interest, he switched over to a cable news network. It seemed to be a slow night with not much happening, but just as he was about to go back to the documentary, the anchorman announced breaking news.

And this just in—apparently once famed singer Elijah has viciously attacked a photographer outside of an upscale restaurant in Los Angeles. Elijah, best known as the Techno-pop King, dropped out of the music scene in 1989 after problems with alcohol and drugs devastated his career. Police have not yet confirmed whether drugs or alcohol were factors in this attack. We should have more on this breaking story in a few moments.

They briefly showed an unflattering photo of Elijah taken in 1989 before cutting to a commercial. *Do you suffer from erectile dysfunction…*

Jack quickly switched off the television. He just couldn't look anymore. *How could this have happened? Did Mona know about it?* He grabbed his phone and hit the speed dial. It rang through but was immediately picked up by voice mail.

"Mona, what's going on? What's this about Elijah attacking someone? Call me as soon as you get the chance."

He set down the phone and looked at the blank screen in front of him. There was no point in turning it back on. This was a slow news day so these people would milk it for everything they could. It would probably not be long before they would assemble a panel of pundits to do an analysis about God-knows-what. And then there was Hinken. He would surely get involved behind the scenes and try to stick the knife in further.

Jack needed to get a hold of Mona. He needed to know what really happened before he listened to any more media babble.

Reaching over and picking up the picture of Stuart that sat on the end table, he stared at it and pleaded, "Please reassure me! Remind me that this was the right course to take. Tell me that we will get through this!" Stuart just remained silently smiling.

* * *

"Mmmm…this is so good!" said Mona, nourishing every bite. "It just melts in your mouth. I don't usually eat dessert especially after such a rich meal, but this is just too amazing to pass up." Mona had eaten at some of the finest restaurants in New York, but she still couldn't believe how delicious the food was at Le Chien d'Or.

"Here try this," said Elijah, offering her a taste of his *clafoutis aux cerises.*

Mona took a small amount on her fork and placed it in her mouth. "Dreamy." She then laughed. "Oh, I can't believe I used such a stupid word, but this food is so incredible! I'm glad you convinced me to do this."

"You see…I'm not just a beautiful face. I have brains too," he said smiling.

Mona smiled back, as she tried not to worry about having such a good time. A little voice inside her head kept telling her that she would eventually pay for all of this pleasure. *Damned Midwestern guilt!*

"So, Mona, where are you from originally?" asked Elijah, taking the last bite of his dessert. "Your accent says you're not from New York."

"I was hoping that my accent was completely lost," replied Mona. "Whenever I go back home, they always tell me that I sound like a New Yorker."

"So, where's home?"

"Well, it's not my home anymore, but I was born there—small town Indiana."

"We have something in common—sort of," said Elijah. "In some ways Indiana is similar to where I came from."

"Kansas. Isn't it?"

"Yes Kansas. We're both from God's country."

"God's country?" laughed Mona. "I could hardly wait to get away—all those small-town people with their small town minds. God's prison is more like it."

"It's not so bad," said Elijah. "Over the years, I've learned that big city people also have small town minds. It's just hidden behind a facade of being current. There's no escape from the small town."

"You're probably right," she laughed. "I suppose no matter where you go people have the same mentality. But what I really liked about the city, when I first arrived, was the anonymity of it all. In New York, I could walk down the street and not feel like I was being watched by a hundred judgmental eyes. I was just a part of the crowd, which was something refreshing. In my town, I always stuck out like a sore thumb, and people don't like looking at sore thumbs. They get angry at you for just being there. What I do miss though are the beautiful open spaces. That's the only reason I ever bother to go back at all."

"And how long have you been at Einhorn?"

"Forever. When I first came to New York it was the early '80's and the recession was hitting hard. The only job I could find was in a greasy spoon. It was miserable work and my boss was a complete jerk—one of those guys who, because they are paying an hourly wage, think you should be working every single minute. One day Jack happened to walk in when my boss was giving me a really hard time. I suppose he took pity on me and offered me a job. I've been with him ever since."

"You are close to him, aren't you?"

"Jack's like a father to me. The way my real father never was."

"Oh, I'm sorry."

"Don't be sorry. How many people in this world can claim to have a real father? Not many."

"Certainly not me—I never knew mine."

Mona moved her fork around her empty plate. "One thing I could never figure out was how you were connected to the Bloodline. Because you are—right?"

"I'm what some of those people refer to as a half-blood. I was the consequence of an indiscretion by a senator on the campaign trail. He rode into town in his big black car and swept a small-town waitress off her feet—for a few minutes anyway. So, here I am!"

"Really! What was his name?"

Elijah laughed. "It's best for you if you didn't know. All I can say is that you would easily recognize it if I told you."

"Okay, I won't push it."

"Actually, the numbers of those like me are likely staggering. I should start a website called The Bloodline Bastards Club. It could be very popular before the powers that be close me down."

"You know that they are trying to close you down already."

"I know," sighed Elijah. "I knew that they would try. Although I don't understand completely what their thinking is, I get the gist of it."

"I'm glad you understand."

Elijah sipped the last drop of tea from his cup. "Anyway, we're having too good a time to talk about business tonight."

"I agree," said Mona cheerfully.

"In fact, why don't we get into that big fancy limo and just drive around town a bit. See the sights like a couple of excited tourists. It's been a long time since I've been in LA."

Mona laughed. Riding around town in a limo, going nowhere in particular was something she hadn't done in years. "The company has already taken care of all the bills," she said. "So, we can leave anytime."

Elijah stood up and offered her his arm. "Shall we go then, my lady?"

Mona smiled. It seemed so natural when she locked arms with him and then headed for the door.

As they stepped out into the warm California night, they both took in a deep breath. Mona looked around for the limo, but it was nowhere to be seen. "He may have been asked to move it," she said, taking her phone from her handbag. "I'll just give the driver a call and see where he is."

Nearby there were a few photographers leaning against walls and lampposts. They were looking extremely bored, as they waited for their celebrity targets to appear. It was a very slow night. "Hey!" a small wiry fellow suddenly exclaimed, "isn't that the dude from the '80's? You know…leather pants guy…what's his name…Isaiah."

"It's Elijah, not Isaiah, moron," replied one of the others, who wasn't going to waste any of his time trying to photograph some old has-been.

"Elijah, Isaiah—who cares? It could be a story if I make it one." The small wiry man walked over to Mona and Elijah and began to snap their pictures.

"The Techno-pop King is alive!" he chided. "And who you havin' dinner with tonight, Elijah—your mom?"

Elijah was ready to say something to this nasty little gremlin, but Mona put her hand on his arm and warned him, "Don't say or do anything. Our limo will be here shortly."

"Yeah Techno, listen to your old whore," said the photographer, hoping to get a shot of Elijah looking angry. Angry shots of faded celebrities could usually bring in a few extra bucks.

It was clear from Elijah's face that he was beginning to lose patience. He was just about to open his mouth and say something when Mona suddenly moved in between him and the little man. The little man, intent on getting a close-up of a furious ex-star, tried to push his camera in closer. The lens suddenly hit Mona hard in the face, making her wince in pain.

Without thinking about it, Elijah grabbed the small man by the shirt and smashed him up against a nearby brick wall. Suddenly there were cameras all around, flashing photos of Elijah holding this man, half his size, up against the wall.

"No Elijah!" screamed Mona, pulling him off of the photographer. "Let's go! The limo's here! Hurry!"

Once inside the car Mona began to shout, "What did you do? You know his kind! Why did you fall for it?"

"I'm sorry, but are you alright? He hurt you."

"Do you think I need a man to defend me? I'm a big girl and can take care of myself! Now look what you've done? You've ruined everything!"

For the rest of the trip back, they both remained silent. When the limo stopped in front of the hotel, Mona did not wait for the driver to open the door. "Mona I…" said Elijah, who wanted to say anything that might possibly make things right.

"Never mind," she said, now standing outside the car. "I just don't want to talk about it." She then hurried past the doorman and inside the hotel.

7

AlienKiller666:
I haven't heard from you for three days. I was worried.

Britney:
Sorry. Parents took me on a trip to Maine. They didn't let me take my phone or computer because they said it would be an "organic" vacation. They r such hippies.

AlienKiller666:
I hate hippies.

Britney:
Yah! Hippies suck!

AlienKiller666:
Glad you're back.

Britney:
Me too. I missed talking to u.

AlienKiller666:
I missed you too.

Britney:
I think the parents were trying to set me up with this guy. The son of their stupid friends.

AlienKiller666:
There was a guy?

Britney:
Yep. One of those liberal elite snob types. His mommy and daddy bought him his own boat.

AlienKiller666:
Hate that kind. Did you think he was good looking?

Britney:
Really hot! All the girls were looking at him but I don't like that type.

AlienKiller666:
What's your type?

Britney:
More like u.

AlienKiller666:
You have good taste. We both do.

Britney:
Did u get the new pills I sent?

AlienKiller666:
Good stuff! They keep me going.

Britney:
Remember to up the dosage if u can't feel it anymore. But don't overdo it.

AlienKiller666:
I won't.

Britney:
I still want to meet u.

Alien Slayer666:
Me too.

Britney:
My parents r planning a European vacation soon. They will be gone for weeks. Maybe u could come then.

AlienKiller666:
Sounds real good. When?

Britney:
Not sure yet. I'll have to check the dates. I want to see u.

AlienKiller666:
Me too.

Britney:
Saw that fat queer again.

AlienKiller666:
You mean Jack?

Britney:
Yah, in the restaurant. I think he saw me looking at him. It gave me the creeps.

AlienKiller666:
Don't go near him! He's dangerous!

Britney:
I know. I could feel it. It's like u and me are the only ones who know what's really going on. Everybody else is so stupid. So blind.

AlienKiller666:
I try to warn people in my blog.

Britney:
Yah. Ur a real hero! I only wish more people listened to u.

AlienKiller666:
It's amazing how stupid sheeple can be.

Britney:
It's so pathetic. They r all slaves to the aliens.

AlienKiller666:
Not me and not you! We'll never be slaves.

Britney:
Yah! We'll always be fighting the good fight. I really wish u were here right now.

AlienKiller666:
Me too.

Britney:
One day soon.

AlienKiller666:
Yeah, one day soon.

Britney:
Gotta go. Someone's at the door.

* * *

Jack opened the door. It was Mona. He was surprised that she had not just let herself in. Usually, she would simply ring the bell and then use her own key. This had been their arrangement for years. She must be extremely upset not to feel comfortable enough to walk in freely.

"Come in and tell me what happened," he said.

"I'm so sorry," she cried, stepping into the foyer.

"Let's go sit down and talk. We might as well be comfortable." Jack followed after Mona down the hall and into the grand living area.

"Would you like anything to drink?" he asked, as Mona settled into a large stuffed chair.

"No...no thanks. I'm sorry, Jack. It's all my fault! It shouldn't have happened," Mona looked down and stared at the diamond pattern in the Persian rug.

"Tell me what happened and I will decide whether or not it is your fault."

Mona looked back up at Jack with pleading eyes. "I shouldn't have gone with him! I know better. My contact cancelled the deal with the supermodel so Elijah didn't have a date. He said that it would be a waste not to go and enjoy the meal anyway, and suggested we go together. I knew I should say 'no' but I didn't. I'm so sorry, Jack. I guess I just had heard so much about that restaurant, and I was really hungry at the time. I know that's a ridiculous excuse. It was so unprofessional of me."

Jack leaned back in his chair. He could see that Mona was becoming increasingly upset. "Please slow down and explain exactly what happened," he said.

Mona sat back and folded her arms across her stomach. She didn't expect to feel so emotional while trying to relay the events to Jack. There had been other set-backs with other singers, and she always dealt with them as they came. So why was she now feeling such panic? This wasn't like her at all. Taking in a deep breath, she said, "When we were leaving the restaurant, the photographers were waiting outside. At first, they simply ignored us and then this little squirrelly guy comes over and starts in. You know the way they do. He did the old *attack-the-female-to-get-at-the-guy* trick and Elijah fell for it."

"He insulted you?"

"Yes. He said some things. At first, it seemed to be under control and then Squirelly got a little aggressive and hit me in the face with the camera."

"Was it an accident?"

"Maybe yes, maybe no. Who knows?"

Jack folded his hands on his lap. "So that is when Elijah lost it—after it became physical?"

"Yes. I'm sorry, Jack. I've really messed up this time." Mona shifted in the chair. "I haven't even looked at a newspaper or turned on the TV yet. I'm afraid to ask, but how bad is it?"

"It's bad," replied Jack. "Plenty of front-page coverage, and I'm sure the comedians will have material for weeks. How is Elijah doing?"

"To be honest, I haven't even spoken with him since it happened. And I took the next flight home, so I left before him. At the time, I was just so mad and I suppose I blamed him for everything. I just couldn't face him."

Jack looked very concerned. "Mona, what are you doing?" he exclaimed. "You know better than to leave him alone at a time like this! Definitely it's a mess, but you've gone and left him completely alone. That's not right. Here's a man who took a risk to stand up for you and now you treat him like this? It's still your job to ensure his career is recharged, and there is no way that you are going to run away now. I won't let you. Certainly, you were a little embarrassed and angry, but so what? Personally, I don't care what happened outside that restaurant, or what the world wants to make of it. You have work to do. Everything rides on making sure that Elijah is successful."

Mona was both surprised and a little annoyed at Jack scolding her like that. She was not some silly little girl to be reprimanded by her elders. Fully prepared to defend herself, she began to explain, "But Jack you were not there. I was there so I know. I know that…" Mona stopped. She didn't know what to say next. What exactly was her excuse? She looked at Jack who had that expression on his face. The one that said, *let's keep it real Mona.* She heaved a sigh and sunk back into the chair. This wasn't really about Elijah or what had happened. This was about her looking for an excuse—looking for a way out of something that was becoming too complicated—something she could feel was taking her out of her comfort zone. Jack was right. She was acting like a silly girl. Elijah was her responsibility and she couldn't simply walk away from him. This one slip shouldn't stop her now. Before the whole thing fell apart, she had been so full of determination. She had to find that determination again.

"I'm sorry. You're right, Jack. I need to buck up. I have a job to do."

Jack stood up and walked over to her chair. He put his hand on her cheek, bent over, and kissed the top of her head. "That's the Mona I know," he said. "Now get a hold of him, and get this thing sorted. We need to start remedying the situation as soon as possible. Don't worry about the rest for now, we'll figure a way to fix it."

* * *

Mona pushed the buzzer for the seventh time. She knew he was up there and just not answering. Certainly, his front step must have been bombarded by journalists earlier in the day, and he likely thought it was just another reporter come to harass him. "Come on, check the video surveillance," she said, as if he could hear her. "Open up Elijah, it's me." She was just about to push the buzzer again when she heard the click of the automatic lock. Quickly she grabbed hold of the door handle and entered.

When Mona reached the apartment door, it was slightly ajar. She pushed it open, but there was no sign of Elijah. "Hello!" she called out. There was still no reply so she closed the door behind her and began to walk down the short hallway towards what she could see was the living room. "Elijah!" she called out a little worried.

"Please come in. Come in and sit."

When she entered the darkened room, she could see he was sitting alone on the sofa with the shades drawn. She clicked on the lights, and Elijah covered his eyes with his hand.

"Are you alright," she asked, coming closer. He was dressed in old sweats, and didn't look as though he had showered or shaved that morning. It was obvious that he was more than a little distraught.

"I'm not sure," he replied, taking his hand from his eyes and looking straight at her.

Mona felt sick to see him like this. She shouldn't have left him alone. Why had she been so selfish and insensitive?

"I've been trying to phone you all day, but you don't answer. So, I thought I'd come over. I came to apologize," she said, as she sat down on an opposite sofa. "I shouldn't have gotten angry at you, and I shouldn't have left you alone in LA. What happened with the photographer wasn't your fault. I should be thanking you for trying to help me. Elijah, I'm really sorry."

Elijah sighed. "No, you were right the first time. It was my fault. I should have known better. I know what those guys are. I know the score. Because of my zealousness, it's now all fallen apart."

Mona could see how deeply Elijah was feeling this setback. If only she had stayed with him, maybe she could have prevented this. She had to get him thinking positive again. "It's no one's fault," she said. "It's just one of those things that happen. In this business things change in an instant, but we can't let that stop us. Together, we need to make a plan and move on."

"There's nowhere to go from here!" cried Elijah. "We have to face it. I blew it—for you, for Jack and for me! This whole thing was a mistake—just a huge mistake! I never should have imagined that a comeback was possible. I should have stayed right where I was—comfortably out of the limelight."

Mona could no longer stand to see Elijah like this. "So, you pinned a little weasel against the wall!" she exclaimed. "You know he deserved it. We both know what really happened. What does it matter what other people think?"

Elijah shook his head and replied, "In this business, what other people think always matters. Right now, I'm an even bigger joke then I was before, and there's even talk of criminal charges. It's a mess."

Mona surprised herself when she reached across the coffee table and grabbed his hand. "Einhorn will support you completely with any legal matters. And so, what if everyone is talking about you? Isn't that what we want? It's true that right now it's not exactly positive, but we can turn that around. Finally, they are mentioning the release of your single and we are getting all kinds of hits on the website. You can meet this crisis head-on. I know you can."

Elijah looked over at her and sighed. "I lied," he said.

Mona was taken aback by what he just said and let go of his hand. "What do you mean, you lied?"

Elijah looked over at a bookshelf in the corner. "I lied when I told Jack about why I wanted back to the business. Well, it was not entirely a lie, but I did leave out something. It's something important. You see, I didn't want to come back at all. I was through with the music business and all of its disappointments. I'd had enough, but something happened that kept pushing me in that direction. It sounds ridiculous to say it out loud, but it had to do with dreams. Dreams made me want to try again."

"Dreams? What are you talking about?"

"This is going to sound strange," he said, "but for many years I've had this reoccurring dream. Lately it's become more frequent and more intense." Elijah looked at Mona and waited for her response before telling her more.

"Go on then," she said. "You can't leave it there. You have to tell me about the dream."

Elijah seemed a little embarrassed as he began to explain, "This dream is just so vivid and emotionally powerful," he said, now staring into the palm of his hand. "It's unusual—always filled with bright and amazing colors, and yet when I wake up, I can't even begin to picture what those colors looked like. The sounds in the dream are clear and perfect in a way I cannot explain. And each time it happens, it's always the same. It begins with me on stage, but not as a young man from the past. It's different this time. I'm older. I know things. I feel the stage differently. I relate to the audience in a better way.

"As I stand there on the stage and look out over the hordes of people, somewhere behind me the band is playing. I'm preparing to sing, and there's a very real and passionate anticipation from the audience. That's when I suddenly realize, I've forgotten the words to the song. A crazy panic just washes over me and I'm horrified. The people are all staring at me—wanting desperately to hear the song, and all I can think is that the band will soon reach the part where I have to sing, but I don't know even the first word. All I want to do is run, but there's no way out. There are no doors or stairs leading away from the stage. I'm trapped.

"Then I begin, in my mind, to recite Psalm 23. You know how it goes, *The Lord is my Shepherd, I shall not want....* I don't know why I do this, but I do. That's when I suddenly see her. At the end of the stage, I see a woman climbing out of the crowd. I can see she's dressed all in white, but I can't see her face. It's obscured by the bright stage lights.

"At first, she just stands there for a moment and then I hear her voice. It's remarkable! The pitch is the most beautiful thing I have ever heard—like a flawless chorus of tiny bells. And this woman is saying just one thing over and over again. *Sing for the world, Elijah!*

"In an instant, all my fear—all my pain simply disappears and the words I had forgotten now flood in and fill me. But I know they are not the words of the original song—these ones are better—perfect! I open my mouth and they flow out like refreshing water upon the crowd. That's when I realize the words are somehow transforming them. And it's not just them, it's me too. I can feel it in myself. The words are also transforming me!

"And all the time I am singing, this woman—this *angel* stands there glowing brighter and brighter, as we all watch in wonder. Finally, her light just—just—her light just wraps up me, the band and everyone else in the room. It's the most amazing feeling and everyone is feeling it at the same time. It's a shared experience. The words keep flowing out of my mouth and somewhere deep within my mind I think, *I'm home.*

"That's when I wake up. I wake up and I cry because I'm back alone in my room. She's gone and all I want is for her to come back—come back and make me feel that way again. Each time I have this dream I'm left with the feeling that I need to get on stage once more. I need to try and make this happen for real. That's why I wanted to come back—because of this dream." Elijah nervously wrung his hands. "I know—I know it sounds crazy. Can you see now why I couldn't tell you and Jack the whole truth?"

At that moment, Mona wanted to tell him everything. She wanted to grab his hands and tell him about Jack, about Stuart, about the girl, but she knew it was not her secret to divulge. Instead, she smiled and said, "What's so crazy about that? So, you want to make a lovely dream come true. You want to make people feel wonderful. How can that be a bad thing?"

Elijah looked up and into her eyes. "I can't believe that you don't find it all just insanity. I haven't told anyone about this before because I'd be an even a bigger joke than I already am."

Mona could see how alone and confused he was feeling. "Elijah, you are no joke!" she exclaimed. "You're an incredible artist! If there are some who just want to hold you down, that's not your doing. Get back to yourself and who you are! Don't let a few people try to define you and make you into what they want you to be. Don't let them stomp on your dreams. You're an amazing singer and an amazing man!"

Elijah continued to look into Mona's eyes. *You're telling me the truth, aren't you? You're telling me what you are really thinking. You do think I'm amazing.* A tiny smile gently stole across his lips.

When Mona saw what she had done, she felt a sudden heat run from her toes to the top of her head. Worried that she may be visibly blushing, she quickly looked away and tried her best to regain composure. "We just need to get back on track," she said. "We need to stay focused and decide on the next step. I've brought you this far and I'm sure as heck not going to throw in the towel now."

Elijah couldn't help but laugh. It had been a very long time since he heard the expression *sure as heck*. His laughter made Mona smile.

"You've made me feel so much better," he said. "Thank you. I appreciate it. And you're right. It's time to get it together and move forward. There is no point wallowing in self-pity and that's just what I've been doing. Life goes on. The world keeps turning. So, tell me, what's next on the agenda? What's your plan B?"

"That, I don't know."

Elijah laughed again. "So, we are just free falling?"

"For the moment."

"And do we at least have parachutes?"

Mona was enjoying the new playfulness between them. "Elijah," she said, "incredible people like us always have parachutes. We just sometimes aren't always sure where to find the ripcords."

"And is there a way to find these elusive ripcords?"

"We will do the same thing people like us always do in these cases," she said with a big smile. "Get ourselves centered, maybe say a little prayer and wait for a magic green light to shine on the right spot. As soon as that happens then we pull those cords and fly to earth like a couple of magnificent birds!"

"I think you may be even crazier than I am," Elijah laughed.

To hear him joke around like that was like music to Mona's ears. She knew then that she had said all the right things. Elijah was back on track. "Maybe you're right," she happily replied. "But sometimes a little crazy is just what the doctor ordered."

8

Jack sat at his desk, trying to keep his concentration on the computer screen in front of him. With the Elijah fiasco continually haunting his thoughts, he kept losing focus. Taking off his glasses, he rubbed his tired eyes. *Mona will handle it,* he kept telling himself. *No need to worry.*

Just then the phone rang. He answered it on speaker, "Yes?"

"Mr. Hinken is calling, sir. Should I put him through?"

Jack didn't shy away this time. This time without hesitation he said, "Yes Susan. Put him through."

"Mr. Hinken is now on the line, sir."

"Hello Dick," Jack said, with friendly confidence. He had never before called Hinken by his first name, but it seemed that this was a good day to start.

"I'm surprised you are in such a good mood," said Hinken, "considering your man is down and he's not getting back up. What you've done is unthinkable, as well as way beyond your station. However, because it's you, I'm willing to give you a second chance. Finish him off, Jack. Finish him off for good. You do this and we will forget that this whole Elijah thing ever happened. Everything will go back to the way it was before. But if you don't do this, I'll do it for you, and then *you'll* be next."

Jack knew this was no bluff. Hinken meant every word. But Jack did not have to think twice about his answer. He knew what he had to do. "No Dick," he said. "That is not going to happen. No one is going to finish off Elijah."

"Excuse me?" shouted Hinken. Even people high up in the Bloodline did not dare tell him *no*.

"No," repeated Jack, "I am not going to destroy a man to appease your foolish superstitions. Yes, I'm not part of the Bloodline and thank God for that. My loyalty is to my own human values—values that do not include treating other people as though they were

61

nothing more than mere pawns in a chess game. I'm better than that—better than you."

"You idiot!" Hinken yelled. "You've lost your mind!"

Jack could feel his own temperature rising. He had all he could take of this man and his threats, and he wasn't going to take any more. "Then be warned, Dick—*there's method in madness,*" he shouted back, "a method so foreign to you and to other small men like yourself that you cannot even begin to conceive of its power!" Jack had surprised himself—and he had even quoted Shakespeare! He had not quoted Shakespeare since Stuart had been murdered. It felt good that it should just flow from his tongue once again.

As Jack waited for a response, there was only silence. It took him a moment to realize that Hinken was no longer on the line. The man had not even bothered to reply, just simply hung up. But this was not the end. He knew Hinken would stop at nothing to try and destroy him now. But it no longer mattered. Jack was full of a conviction he hadn't felt in years. There was no way Elijah was going to be destroyed—not this time. He would make sure of it—but how?

He looked over at the picture of Stuart. Picking it up, he gently touched the glass. "Like so many years ago, I am once again at the edge. Help me, my darling. I need a little of your magic. Please help."

* * *

Britney:
I had a dream about u last night.

AlienKiller666:
Really?

Britney:
Yah. About u and me.

AlienKiller666:
What happened?

Britney:
Nothing much but we were living together in a cabin in the middle of nowhere. Just u and me. There's more but I can't say.

AlienKiller666:
Why not?

Britney:
It's personal.

AlienKiller666:
Please tell!

Britney:
No. U will think I'm not a nice girl.

AlienKiller666:
No I won't.

Britney:
No! I can't tell.

AlienKiller666:
Please!

Britney:
Ok but don't think I'm a bad girl. Promise?

AlienKiller666:
I'd never think that.

Britney:
Oh I'm too embarrassed so I'll just say that we were in bed together.
Do u think that's bad of me?

AlienKiller666:
No. I think that's good.

Britney:
Really?

AlienKiller666:
Yes, because I luv you.

Britney:
I've waited a long time for u to say that. I luv u too.

AlienKiller666:
We need to meet soon.

Britney:
Not yet. When my parents go away. Then we can have the whole
house to ourselves.

AlienKiller666:
When do they go?

Britney:
They r still working on their plans.

AlienKiller666:
They'd better hurry. I need to see you.

Britney:
Guess what happened yesterday? It was a little scary for me.

AlienKiller666:
What was it?

Britney:
Mommy took me to that restaurant again. The one where Jack goes.
He was there and I sort of accidentally bumped his table. Then he did
something weird.

AlienKiller666:
What did he do?

Britney:
It kinda sounded like he hissed at me.

AlienKiller666:
Aliens do that when they are angry! Are you ok? Did he do anything
else?

Britney:
No, only that. But it was real scary. It wasn't like a human or animal sound. It was weird.

AlienKiller666:
I'll kill him!

Britney:
No! I don't want u to do anything that puts u in danger.

AlienKiller666:
But aliens hold on to vendettas for the smallest things. I know. I've studied them for years.

Britney:
If I ever see him again, he won't remember me. I was afraid to tell u because I knew how u would get. That's what I luv about u. U always make me feel protected.

AlienKiller666:
If anything ever happened to you, I'd go postal on every alien I could find.

Britney:
Oh Mommy's calling. I think she wants to discuss the Europe trip. She's been trying to get me to go too, but I want to stay here so I can see u. It may only be weeks away.

AlienKiller666:
A week is like an eternity without you.

Britney:
Awww! Ur so romantic. Talk to u tomorrow. Luv u!

AlienKiller666:
Luv you too!

* * *

The door to his office suddenly burst open, making Jack jump in his chair. He was surprised to see Mona rushing towards him. She threw her arms around his neck and kissed his temple. "There's a video!" she exclaimed. "A wonderful, marvelous, fabulous video!"

Jack had never seen Mona so excited before, and he couldn't help laughing a little. She was like a child at Christmas. "Slow down," he said, "and tell me what exactly you are talking about."

Mona sat on the desk and tried to regain her composure. She couldn't stop smiling. "A German tourist, Jack—a tourist was there the whole time and took a video of the entire thing! I didn't even see him. It all happened so fast. But he was there and now it's all over the internet—the real deal with Elijah and the photographer. The entire encounter is there and it vindicates Elijah. In fact, it makes him look more like a hero than anything else." Mona looked out the window behind Jack and exclaimed, "Thank you Mr. Heinz Schmidt wherever you are!"

"And have the mainstream media begun to pick this up?" asked Jack, pushing his glasses up his nose. He glanced over at Stuart's smiling photo.

"Oh, they will. It's everywhere and people are talking. Thank God people are talking!"

"This is good, Mona," said Jack, relieved that there was now at least a glimmer of hope. "But the next step will be crucial. I'm not sure which door will open because Hinken will certainly be making sure to keep as many shut as possible. Whatever door it is, care must be taken. We have to be leery of pitfalls and traps."

Mona leaned over and patted his shoulder. "Don't worry Jack. I care more about this right now then I have about any job before. A lot of it has to do with a conversation I had with Elijah. He told me why he really came back to music—the whole truth and nothing but the truth."

"So, what is the whole truth?"

Mona sighed. "He's had dreams, Jack—well actually—one dream—a reoccurring dream about a woman who, because of his songs, turns into a shining light—a light that changes people. This dream is what brought him back to the business. He returned to make this dream come true. You know what that dream means. It can only mean one thing."

Jack closed his eyes and felt the warmth of emotion wash over him. "A woman who is a light," he breathed. When he again opened them, he found himself staring at the photo of Stuart. *You were right again, my love.*

"It all fits together—doesn't it?" said Mona. "It all makes sense."

Jack took her hand in his. "Yes, it makes more sense every day—a new piece to the puzzle."

"We can do this, Jack! I know we can."

Jack could feel Mona's hope and determination. He looked at her and said, "You need to stay focused. Go and keep an eye on how things are moving on the internet. See who is picking up the story and who isn't. Be ready to take advantage of the first opportunity."

"Aye aye Captain," said Mona, jumping down from the desk and then heading towards the door.

"Mona!" called Jack.

When Mona turned around, she was surprised by what she saw. Sitting there in the light of the sun, Jack seemed so much younger and alive than she had seen him look in a very long time. Although she never confessed it to him, she had been worrying about his health lately. It warmed her heart to see him looking like he could take on the world again. "Remember, my friend," he said, with the biggest smile she had ever seen him smile, *"music is the food of love, so play on!"*

9

Mona hurried down the hall, towards Jack's office. She had set up a morning meeting with Elijah and Jack. There were some very important things to discuss.

As she walked through the door, she was instantly immersed in the beauty that filled the room. The steadily rising sun glistened off the unicorn menagerie in such a way that it turned the office into a sort of magical fairyland. She always preferred morning meetings with Jack just because that was the time when this miracle happened. As long as the weather forecast called for sun, she was guaranteed an inspirational show.

"Come and sit. Would you like a tea?" asked Jack, who was in his usual chair.

Mona was surprised to see that Elijah was already there and sipping tea on the sofa.

"Good morning," he said, with a smile.

"Good morning," replied Mona. She then turned to Jack and said, "No tea for me thanks. I'm fine." She sat down in a chair next to Jack's. "I'm not late, am I?"

"No," replied Elijah, "I was early."

Mona glanced at Elijah who was still smiling at her. His smile caught her off guard, just like it had the first time. She quickly put her head down, took her phone from her pocket, and pretended to scroll through her emails.

"What updates can you give us, Mona?" asked Jack.

"I was really hoping for more," she replied. "But so far it's mostly requests for interviews with small radio stations."

"Don't underestimate the power of starting out small." said Jack. "These interviews can be done over the telephone which means Elijah can easily do a lot of them over a short period of time. We can reach a considerable number of people that way, and perhaps even get some playtime for *Love Rising*. What do you think, Elijah?"

"It sounds good to me, and I promise that I will be prepared for the questions. You don't have to worry."

"I'm not at all worried," said Jack smiling. He then turned to Mona and asked, "Are there any television offers?"

"Well…" she said, "I wanted to talk about that. There is one show that has made a request. It's the Hailee and Haley Hour."

"That's great!" exclaimed Elijah. "They have a huge audience."

Mona shifted in her chair a little. "No, that's not so great. Is it Jack?"

Jack looked over at Elijah who looked back in confusion. "You see Elijah," he began to explain, "The Hailee and Haley Hour has connections to your old friend Dick Hinken. If they invited you to appear, it is meant only as bait to lead you into a trap. They'll rip you apart."

Elijah considered for a moment what he had been told. He knew Jack was right about it likely being a trap, but he didn't feel afraid. He felt sure that he could jump anything they might put in his way. "But this show is watched by millions," he said. "There couldn't be a more perfect opportunity to announce my album release. A platform like this could provide us with a major breakthrough. And who says they have the ability to rip me apart. I'm more than willing to take that risk."

The last thing Mona wanted was another public catastrophe. "Absolutely not!" she asserted. "It would be a suicide mission."

Jack leaned back in his chair and looked at Elijah. "Have you seen the show?" he asked. "Those women have been well trained. They know how to tear a person down in just a few minutes. You won't even realize it's happening until it's over. I don't know if we'd be able to pick up the pieces after that."

"I've seen the show," replied Elijah. "And I know what those women are. I realize the danger. But I also know that I can do it. Yes, I had a setback. And yes, you have every right to wonder if I will have the fortitude to handle myself. But I assure you that I know what I'm doing. You have to have faith in me." He looked over at Mona, who then looked questioningly over at Jack.

For a moment, Jack wondered if sending Elijah into that lion's den could be the most foolish choice he could ever make, but he'd already made the biggest wager of his life by confronting Hinken. What was one more risk? Elijah seemed to have full confidence that this would work out. And didn't every great moment in history begin with a leap of faith? "Alright," he said, "I'll trust that you know what you are doing. Mona, contact the show and arrange for the booking."

Mona was still doubtful. After seeing Elijah fall to pieces over the paparazzi mess, she wondered how he could possibly handle those two well trained she-foxes. Surely, they would go for the jugular and he would be completely helpless. She didn't like the thought of him at their mercy. It was almost painful.

Elijah looked at Mona and could see the doubt in her eyes. He smiled and said, "Don't worry, I'll do fine. Please try and have some faith in me—even a little would be nice."

Mona knew that it wasn't about faith. Faith was not the issue. It was about an intense urge to protect him. The idea of him going on the chopping block frightened her. But what could she say without revealing her feelings—feelings she did not want to admit even to herself. "Yes Elijah, I have faith in you," she answered. "I'll go back to my office now and make the call."

* * *

Mr. Todd was sitting in the dingy basement office, sorting through various pieces of news and information on the internet. In this work, seemingly insignificant bits of data could prove to be essential to a successful operation.

All of a sudden, Minton, who was busy at a second computer, burst out laughing. He had the harsh cruel laugh of a drunken frat boy—the same kind of undisciplined guttural laugh that Todd found intensely aggravating. Minton moved his fingers rapidly over the keyboard. Click, click, click, and then followed by his grating laugh again.

Todd wanted to scream, SHUT THE HELL UP, but he knew it was important not to let Minton know what he was thinking. The time may eventually come when he could finally look the man dead in the eyes and tell him what was really on his mind. But for now, Minton was still extremely useful. "What's so funny?" Todd asked.

Minton glanced over at Todd and giggled with excitement. "This is my favorite part," he said. "I've just confessed that I'm a virgin and asked him to go easy on me the first time. The weevil has promised to be *oooh* so gentle." Minton burst out laughing. His face

70

was beginning to redden and there were balls of sweat forming on his brow.

Todd did not want to hear about the sordid details. He found Minton completely repulsive when he became like this, but what could he do? He had to keep his feelings hidden. For now, Minton was still the best he had ever found. He knew exactly how to work and manipulate these guys. Much of the company's success rate was down to his talents, but it would be a problem if he ever realized it. He had to be kept on a short leash. Minton was just a stupid rat-catching dog, and a particularly disgusting one at that.

"How soon do you estimate?" Todd asked.

"He's close," replied Minton, "real close. I'd say only about a month away."

Todd was surprised that things were progressing so quickly. "That's well ahead of schedule. I'll begin making preparations for a new location."

"Can you tell me what town this time?" asked Minton.

"No. You'll know when we get there."

"As long as you provide me with all the regular perks, take me wherever you want, baby I'm yours." Minton once more began to click away, snickering to himself while he typed.

Todd felt even more disgusted. Why couldn't he find someone who would do the job with some degree of emotional discipline? He had to deal with this kind of thing all too often in the army. *Glee apes*, he called them, because of the way they killed with such idiotic enthusiasm. When he needed the ugliest jobs done, *glee apes* were the ones he called in. They were swift, brutal, and never remorseful. But they were also unpredictable. Todd hated them as a lower form of life. Even though it was he who gave the orders, he knew he was not like them. He could never do what they did. He was of nobler stock.

Todd decided he needed some fresh air and stood up to leave. Just then, Minton let loose a wild uncontrolled laugh with such intensity it began to choke him. This caused him to then snort like a pig and thick pale snot flew out of his nose, landing on the computer screen. Todd couldn't take anymore. Without a word, he quickly turned away and headed for the stairs.

* * *

Mona opened the door and walked into the restaurant. Immediately, she was struck by the elegant and tasteful décor. *Whoever designed this place did an incredible job. It looks like something out of a classic movie.*

"Good afternoon, Madame," declared the impeccably dressed Maitre d' with a slight bow.

"Hello. I'm meeting someone. It's Elijah," she said, hoping the name alone would illicit some type of a response. In their business, every interaction was a chance to gage public opinion.

The man's face lit up. He was obviously pleased to have such a celebrity in his restaurant. "Oh yes Madame. Right this way please."

Mona followed him to a far and private corner, away from the kitchen and other patrons. They had given Elijah an excellent table. This was another good sign. People were really beginning to respond positively to him.

"Hello Mona," said Elijah, standing up and holding out a chair for her. Mona felt a little uncomfortable and wished he had just let the Maitre d' do it. She wanted this meeting to be as business-like as possible.

"Hi. You picked a nice restaurant."

"I always do," said Elijah. "If there is one thing I learned on the road those many years ago, it was how to appreciate a good restaurant."

"I want to talk with you about the Hailee and Haley Hour tomorrow. I received some news that may be a problem."

Before Mona could tell Elijah what the news was, the waiter approached them with menus in hand. "May I get you something to drink?" he asked, as he placed the menus in front of them.

"Yes please. I'll have a glass of your house red and Elijah will have a bottle of sparkling water," said Mona, without even thinking about first checking with Elijah. Suddenly realizing that she may have overstepped the mark, she quickly looked over at him to gage his reaction, but Elijah was obviously not offended. Instead, he appeared rather amused.

"Very good, Madame," said the waiter, who then left.

"So, what's the bad news?" Elijah asked.

"They've changed things around and now you only have a five-minute slot. Two and a half minutes to talk to the hosts, and two and a half minutes to perform."

Elijah was obviously upset. "They can't do this! How can I do *Love Rising* or any of my songs in two and a half minutes?"

"Look Elijah," she said with a sigh, "there was always the possibility that they would try something like this or even cancel completely. We discussed that before. The good news is that they didn't cancel. You will still be on the show, and isn't that what you want? We have to look on the bright side of things. Let's stay positive."

Elijah looked at her and thought for a moment. He then slapped his hand on the table and said, "You're right. I have to stay positive. After all, I wasn't cancelled. I'll just have to work with what they are willing to give me. It can be done. It may take a little extra effort and more creativity, but it can be done."

The waiter appeared with their drinks. "May I take your orders now?" he asked, as he placed the drinks in front of them.

"Give us a moment," said Mona, sending him away again. She took a sip of wine and then looked at Elijah. "I've already considered our next step and will have people working all through the night on a plan for you. Perhaps a part of your single would work if we can arrange it right. It's not the best scenario, but we can deal with it. It's better than nothing at all."

"No," said Elijah.

Mona looked at him in disbelief. "What do you mean *no*?"

"No, I can't do it like that. This time around things have to be different," he answered. "I need to come up with something that is all mine—something from my heart alone. It can't be anyone else's arrangement. This time, I want to own my songs completely. Mona, I know this is not the way you usually do things, but please believe me when I say that this is the only way to go."

"Elijah, we have experts for that sort of thing. Just leave it to them. They know what they're doing. Doing it on your own would be far too risky, and there is too much riding on this appearance."

"No, not this time," insisted Elijah. *This time I cannot let anyone else tell me who I am. Even people I trust.*

Before Mona could voice her objections, the waiter returned. "Are you ready to order now or would you prefer more time?" he asked.

Elijah looked over at Mona. "I might recommend what I'm having, the poulet de sainte-hélène. It's an amazing dish."

Mona just wanted to be rid of the waiter as quickly as possible so they could get back to their conversation. "Yes, it sounds fine," she said.

"An excellent choice, Madame," chimed the waiter as he picked up the menus from the table and then walked away.

Elijah looked intently at Mona. To her surprise, he then reached across the table and grabbed her hand. She immediately wanted to pull away, but how could she without seeming extremely rude? There was no escape. She was now both touching him and looking into his eyes. *This is a business meeting*, she kept telling herself. *Nothing more than a business meeting.*

"Mona," he said, "those experts are only experts in repeating a tired old pattern—a pattern guaranteed to be easily recognizable and palatable. But I want to give them something different. Throughout my career I did what others told me to do and provided whatever was palatable, ordinary, and too often sub-standard. This time I want to give them a feast that they will never forget. And this can come only from me. I'm the artist. I work the magic of this craft. You must trust me."

All the time he held her hand and spoke, Mona could feel her body temperature rising. She wanted to run away—to make it stop. What good could come out of this kind of complication? Looking down at the table, she tried to concentrate only on the blank white cloth in front of her. She tried as best she could to fix her gaze but couldn't stop her eyes from wandering over to where his hand was covering hers. "Alright, you do what your instincts tell you to do, and I'll trust you," she said, without looking at him.

"Thank you," said Elijah softly, as he patted her hand. He pulled his arm back and sat up straight.

Mona glanced up to see him smiling warmly. *This is getting worse*, she thought, as she felt the heat rise up in her even more. *Get control woman! It's only a silly mid-life crisis thing*, she told herself as she quickly looked past Elijah and stared at a woman in a rose covered dress sitting at the next table. She tried hard to imagine where the woman might have purchased such a lovely dress—anything that might take her mind off of the burning feeling that remained in her hand.

10

Mona sat anxiously in the front row of the mostly female audience. She could feel the intense excitement of the chattering women around her. They had just been professionally warmed up and given friendly instructions on how to respond during the show. Today they would be a part of something bigger than their own routine lives, and the prospect was almost overwhelming for some of them.

"And now…" A man's voice suddenly boomed through the studio. "America's most popular and, might I add, beautiful daytime hosts Hailee and Haley!"

The crowd grew even louder with most of them jumping to their feet and applauding wildly as the perky blonde co-hosts waddled out in their tight dresses and five-inch stilettos. The ladies continued across the stage, warmly waving to their adoring fans. When they reached the infamous red couch, they carefully took their seats. Mona could feel her heart beating.

"Good morning to y'all!" declared Hailee. This was her trademark signature that opened every show and the audience loved it.

"And what a good-looking audience we have today!" added Haley. The crowd again went wild.

Mona nervously tapped her foot on the floor. Had she made a mistake letting Elijah prepare his performance alone? She didn't have a clue what he had planned and was worried. This was not how she did things. Her life and especially her work-life were all about planning and being prepared. She had made enough mistakes in the past to know the disastrous consequences of not having things carefully plotted out beforehand. Now, the thought of not knowing what was going to happen next was almost too much to bear.

Hailee smiled at the camera and read from the teleprompter. "Today we have an amazing line-up for y'all. First, we have the delightfully funny Mr. Bob Clive, as well as TV's quirkiest chef, Jean Moreau, singer Elijah and a very special guest making his first appearance right here on our show. A big star I know y'all have been just dyin' to see."

There was a long suspenseful pause and then Haley announced triumphantly, "Well, let me tell them. It's none other than Magee the canine superhero of the new number one hit at the box office, *Aussiedoodle to The Rescue!*"

The crowd burst out in shouts and applause. Mona cringed. This was definitely going to be an attempt to take Elijah down. She took in a deep breath and said a silent prayer.

* * *

Jack sat in his office leafing through the latest copy of Rolling Stone Magazine. He looked up at the television hanging on his office wall, and then at his watch. The Hailee and Haley Hour was almost over. Elijah's interview should be coming up soon. Jack un-muted the television.

"And how is Magee adjusting to his newfound fame?" Hailee asked with a big smile, her hand gently stroking the head of the well-trained dog.

The woman in the seat beside her replied, "Well, he hasn't let it go to his head yet, but a funny thing happened last week when he got loose then came back wearing a brand-new diamond studded collar."

When the audience burst out in laughter and applause, the dog nervously twitched and its eyes bugged out with fear. The creature's instincts were telling it to run, but years of strict training kept it locked in one place.

"Oh, doggy bling!" exclaimed Haley. "I love it!"

The audience laughed again.

Jack looked again at his watch. He was beginning to worry that they would go overtime with Magee. Was this their plan all along? To let Elijah be bumped by a dog?

"Now sadly we need to say goodbye to Magee. Such a beautiful baby, isn't he? Yes, he is," said Haley, scratching the animal behind the ears.

The audience burst out in enthusiastic applause as Magee and his trainer made their way off of the stage.

The camera closed in on Hailee's smiling face. "And now, our final guest of the day has been out of the spotlight for some time but

76

has recently decided to try to make a comeback. Y'all may remember him as the Techno-pop King back in the 1980's before his career was tragically cut short by *personal problems*. Now he is here today with a new single, and a new album that will be released tomorrow. So won't y'all please welcome the once Techno-pop King, Elijah."

The audience applauded politely.

Jack watched as Elijah strolled towards the red couch. Dressed all in black, he was looking larger than life. Just before he reached the step up to the couch, he turned and gave the audience a friendly wave and a sweet handsome smile. Then, like a pro, he greeted the co-hosts by taking their hands and kissing each one on the cheek. They both seemed a little surprised and Jack knew from the look on their faces that Elijah must have been instructed beforehand not to do this. Lesser guests were always instructed not to get too familiar when greeting the nobility of daytime TV. Only the stars ever touched Hailee and Haley.

Elijah sat down between the two women. He was looking not only good, but extremely confident also. Jack could tell it was beginning to unnerve the ladies. Hinken would have spelled out their roles in this interview. They were supposed to turn the tide against him. They were not supposed to find themselves falling for his charms.

Haley glanced for a moment at the camera and mischievously grinned. "So, Elijah, no leather pants today?" she asked.

The audience, who for years had heard every joke imaginable about the infamous leather pants, laughed. Some of them had never even seen one of Elijah's early performances, but the joke had become a cultural legend.

Elijah's smile deepened and he leaned back, putting his arm ever so slightly behind Haley. "No, sorry to disappoint you," he replied with confidence and ease, "but I'm afraid I retired those some time ago." So far it was like water off of a duck's back.

"Aww come on!" piped in Hailee. "Won't you put them on again? What do y'all think audience? Wouldn't you like to see Elijah move in those pants once more?"

The audience responded with loud applause, laughter, and the odd wolf whistle.

Elijah didn't flinch. Instead, he answered, "I'll make you a deal. When you ladies come out here wearing your most colorful outfit from the '80's, and I remember some of them very well, then I will too."

The audience laughed and clapped even louder. Elijah was winning them over.

Hailee was slightly taken aback, not only because the laughter was now directed at her, but also because Elijah was giving away her age. Trying to keep her cool, she smiled sweetly and said, "I understand that you will do a song for us today, Elijah. Is this your new single?"

You know it's not, thought Jack, *you people made sure that he would not sing even one of his songs.*

"No," replied Elijah. "Instead of singing something from my new album, *Love Rising,* which also happens to be the title of my hit single, I've prepared a special treat for the Hailee and Haley Hour—a little surprise just for you."

"Sounds interesting," said Haley. She then looked out at the audience and announced, "So here to perform something, that we don't know what it is yet, is the once Techno-pop King, *Elijah*."

The audience applauded as Elijah masterfully walked over to stage left.

* * *

During the interview, Mona fumed as she watched those women try to belittle Elijah. *Those bitches couldn't measure up to him if they tried.* She was proud of the way he was handling himself under such pressure. So far no one had gotten the better of him. He had deflected every cheap shot fired his way.

Even though Mona could feel the audience responding positively to him, as he walked across the stage to the microphone, she was now more worried than ever. He had not even arranged for a proper band. Instead, he had only a single woman with a harp to accompany him. This could easily turn into a disaster. Tomorrow, the leather pants jokes could be replaced by harp jokes.

As soon as Elijah reached the microphone, he signaled the harpist. Her fingers began to glide gracefully across the strings, and the first sweet notes brought the audience to complete silence. He then opened his mouth and began to sing. From the beginning, it was pure perfection! The air filled with the warm rich sound of his voice as he sang the most beautiful rendition of *Ave Maria* Mona had ever heard.

Mona forgot about Hailee and Haley. She forgot about the doubts she had before. She forgot about everything as she found herself surrendering completely to Elijah's song. Being so mesmerized by the magic of his music, Mona did not even notice when tears began to gently roll down her face.

After he had finished and the harpist softly faded out the last remaining notes, there was a brief moment of stunned silence. Then suddenly, the audience jumped to their feet in wild applause. Mona did the same. She looked over at Hailee and Haley and saw that they too were standing and applauding. They were also wiping away their own tears.

He's done it! Mona applauded even louder, raising her hands high over her head.

On the stage, Elijah made a small humble bow. That trademark smile never left his face as he looked affectionately out at the fans in front of him.

You're so beautiful, thought Mona still applauding along with the rest of them. *Just so beautiful!*

11

Jack was sitting back in the armchair, looking through the many emails Mona had forwarded to his laptop. They were all requests for an appearance by Elijah. And these were just the ones that had come in that morning. Since his amazing performance on television only a week earlier, it seemed everyone was now interested. Most of the top talk shows and magazines were eager for an interview. Not only that, but Elijah's album was selling remarkably well, and the song *Love Rising* was now the top download. Everything was taking off in a way Jack had never imagined. He looked over at the glass case with Stuart's unicorns. *What's next? Where do I take it from here?*

Suddenly, Mona came bursting into the room. She sat down on the sofa and for a moment didn't say a word. Jack could see she seemed upset about something. He was just about to ask her what was wrong when she exclaimed, "Jack, I need to talk with you. I think it's time that I moved on to something else. Elijah is now right on top, and there are plenty of others in the company who are quite capable of handling it from here. I need a new challenge."

Jack was very surprised. "I—I don't understand. Wouldn't you want to see it through to the next level? There is still so much to be done."

"No," said Mona a little too quickly. "I found this so interesting that I would like to do the same thing again. There are plenty of has-beens out there. Let me at them," she nervously laughed.

Jack got up, set his laptop on the table, and moved over to the sofa to sit close beside her. "What's going on?" he asked in concern.

Mona would not look at him. "What do you mean? Nothing's going on. I just feel like my part of the job is finished and I need to move on. Elijah is a big success. I did it. It's done. Time to move on to the next waif in waiting."

From the tone of her voice, Jack knew that she was being less than truthful. She could pretend very well with agents, press and producers, but she could not fool him.

"Tell me the truth," he said. "I'm your friend—your best friend, I might add. You know that you can share anything with me."

He knows I'm hiding something. He always knows when I'm hiding something. Mona drew a heavy sigh. What could she do? She'd have to tell him the truth if she wanted to find a solution to this problem. "Oh Jack, there's something wrong with me." She hadn't meant to say it like that, and immediately regretted starting out on such an emotional note.

Jack was now very concerned. "What do you mean? Are you sick? What's wrong Mona?" he asked, reaching over, and touching her arm.

"Am I sick? I suppose you could call it that. Oh, I don't know—I'm a middle-aged woman not a sixteen-year-old girl. Why should this old rock star have such an effect on me? What's wrong with me, Jack?"

For a while, Jack had suspected Mona might have an attraction to Elijah but held off saying anything. Now he could see it was more serious than he first thought. *"Love is a familiar; Love is a devil: there is no evil angel but Love,"* he said.

"What?" Mona was a little offended that he seemed to be making light of her situation.

Jack could see she was getting more upset. Putting his arm gently around her shoulders, he answered, "It's Shakespeare. From Love's Labour's Lost to be precise."

"And we all know how his plays ended," said Mona.

"So, do you love him?" Jack thought he might as well just ask it straight out.

"I...I don't know," replied Mona. "At first, I thought it was only the residuals of a silly star-crush from my youth. Back then I was a fan—like so many young women. I wasn't unique in thinking he was the hottest rock star on the stage. But you grow up and out of these things, and I was sure I did. Then, when I first met him in your office and felt that twinge, I told myself it was nothing—that it would just go away. At least, I hoped it would. But it's just become worse. Oh Jack, the other night, I really embarrassed myself!"

"What happened?"

Mona looked at the floor. She didn't really want to share this with anyone. It was too personal. But if there was any hope of Jack taking her request seriously, she must make him understand what it was like for her. This was not simply a silly whim. It was now altering her life.

"I was at Elijah's place," she explained, "and we were going over a few things regarding his itinerary for the next few days. We were sitting side by side—kind of close—anyway I find myself getting more and more..." Mona hesitated to continue. She and Jack had shared a lot of things over the years, many of them very personal, but now she was finding it very difficult to go on.

"Mona, you know you can tell me anything. I would never think badly of you," said Jack.

Mona took in a deep breath and continued. "Well, I was feeling increasingly—oh, I suppose there's no easy way to say it—increasingly aroused."

Jack suppressed a small laugh. He had never seen the ever-in-control Mona at such a loss. It was a bit of a refreshing moment for him.

Mona kept her head down and continued, "So when I feel this way...and so intensely like it was...I well...sometimes I kind of...without even knowing I'm doing it...I kind of...well...pant."

Jack couldn't hold in the laughter this time. He threw his hand over his mouth as he began to chuckle uncontrollably.

"Oh, Jack don't laugh," she said, a little annoyed at Jack's outburst, but at the same time beginning to laugh too. "It's not funny!"

Jack was glad to see any offence she took was tempered by the humor in the situation. "So, you pant?" he laughed. "Do you mean like a dog?"

"No!" exclaimed Mona. "Of course not like a dog. It's...it's more like a cat."

Jack started laughing more. "Do cats pant?" he asked.

"Sort of...well maybe. Perhaps, I shouldn't describe it as panting. That makes me sound too crazy. I'll just say that my breathing became a little funny—different. Anyway, like I said, I don't really notice it, being so caught up in the experience. So, I'm sitting there, trying to concentrate on his schedule for the next week and that's when he noticed."

Jack smiled and asked, "Are you certain? How do you know he noticed?"

"Oh, it was so embarrassing, Jack!" Mona ran both hands through her hair. "He said something about my breathing not sounding right and asked if I was feeling okay."

A small chuckle escaped Jack's lips. "How did you answer him?"

Mona put her hand to her forehead. "I didn't know what to say at first and then I blurted out the only thing I could think of. I said that I had an unusual form of asthma."

Jack was now laughing out loud. "I'm sorry, Mona," he said. "I don't mean to laugh, but from my perspective it is rather comical."

Mona couldn't be mad at him. Jack was right. The situation was a joke. She gave him a soft friendly elbow to the ribs. "You are really enjoying this, aren't you? Well then, listen up and I'll tell you what happened next. Do you know that Elijah came *this* close to calling an ambulance," she said, holding up her hand and gesturing with her thumb and forefinger. "It took some convincing to keep him from dialing 911."

"Oh Mona," said Jack, realizing that maybe he was being a little too insensitive, "I'm sorry I laughed. I can see that this is very confusing and difficult for you. In all the time I've known you, I've just never seen you like this before. You were always so sensible when it came to men."

Mona looked him in the eye, "I know I was—and especially around those ridiculously pumped-up rock stars. What's happening to me, Jack? I've gone over it again and again in my mind. I mean, this has to be just some sort of mid-life crisis. Right, Jack? It's just a foolish passing thing. Other women bleach their hair and buy a bright white convertible. I—well, I get a silly schoolgirl crush on a rock star. In my head, I know it's just a phase—just a stupid annoying inconvenient phase."

"If it's only a passing phase that will fizzle out, then why not just stick with it for now," Jack said, looking directly into Mona's eyes. "To be perfectly honest, since working with Elijah, you have been different. These past couple of months, I have never seen you more vitalized and excited about life and work. This whole experience has given you a fresh new perspective—a new energy. When you think about it, you have to admit, this has been good for you, Mona— very good."

Mona sighed and looked down at her hands. "I can't argue with you. It's all been exhilarating—wonderfully exhilarating! But I'm afraid that it's becoming too intense. Where is it going to end? How do I stop it when it gets to be too much? You know me, Jack—always having to be in control. I'm a chronic control freak and now I feel as though all control is slipping away. If I go any further, will there be any way back?"

"So then, let it go!" said Jack, surprising Mona. She thought for sure he'd try to encourage her to get control of the situation. "Just let it all go and use all this newfound energy to take Elijah's career to new heights. Everyone has their own magnum opus, Mona—everyone—no matter how small or insignificant it may seem. This may be yours. Remember why we picked up Elijah to begin with. Stuart told me to. And look what's happened. We defeated Dick Hinken, for God's sake—the most powerful man in the industry! And now there is no more he can do to us. Because Elijah has been successfully resurrected, Hinken can no longer try to harm him or us. Those are the Bloodline rules.

"We've come this far mostly because of you. You can't walk out now. I need you. Elijah needs you. Maybe the whole world needs you depending on where this thing goes. Please tell me that you'll stay on this job—at least a little longer." Jack tightened his arm around her shoulder. "And if you find yourself doing or feeling something that frightens you, come and see me—talk to me. That's what I'm here for."

Mona rested her head on his shoulder. "Oh Jack, you make it sound so simple."

"Perhaps you are just making it too complicated."

Mona sighed. Could Jack be right? Perhaps this was not as problematic as it seemed. Doesn't a mid-life crisis involve creating drama for drama's sake? That's what it could be. Just an attempt to fulfill a silly mid-life need for drama. *Perspective is all I need. You're a mature woman. Get some perspective.* "Alright," said Mona, willing to give it another try. "I'll continue to work with Elijah—for you, for Stuart, and for the world, if that's what it's about. I'll try to use this energy the way you say. Maybe I'm over-reacting anyway. Perhaps the whole thing will just blow over, and all this fuss I'm making will be for nothing. The last thing I want to do is to let you down. You've been so kind to me over the years." She raised her face and kissed him on the cheek.

"Mona, I'll always be there for you, and I would never ask you to do anything that I thought would cause you any harm."

"I know you wouldn't," she replied. "I just have to stop making such a big deal over what is obviously a small blip in my life. Most women go through some sort of mid-life crisis and get over it just fine. This time tomorrow I may look at Elijah differently. As quickly as these feelings came, they could easily disappear again."

"You're probably right," said Jack trying to reassure her.

Mona smiled a little. "Could I just ask you one thing?"

Jack gently rubbed her arm and answered, "Anything, my dear."

"Would you mind if I took the afternoon off to go look at convertibles? Something new, fast, and bright white might just help to get it all out of my system."

Jack began to laugh again. "By all means—why not leave now. Just for God's sake woman, don't come back here as a bleach blonde. I don't think my old heart could take that."

* * *

The ringtone chimed out *Ride of the Valkyries,* making Minton pause at his keyboard. This was the all-important client phone and the first time it rang since the job began. He reached over to pick it up, but before he could touch it, Todd swooped in and grabbed it, giving Minton a look to remind him that talking to clients was not his place.

"Good day Your Majesty, this is Mr. Todd," he answered. Minton looked at him questioningly. Todd ignored him and turned the other way to concentrate on the call.

"Yes, Your Majesty, we are very close. The entire process is very complicated and very delicate, but I assure you that we are almost there. My staff has informed me that it will only be a matter of weeks now."

Minton looked at his computer screen, and grinned. It was definitely only weeks away.

"Uh, that is an unusual request, Your Majesty. It would require much more time, planning, and effort on our part then…. How much? No… I mean yes. It is definitely doable for that amount."

Hearing that there was even more money involved, Minton turned from the computer and waited for the conversation to end. He was eager to find out just how much they were now talking about.

"Yes. Thank you, and goodbye, Your Majesty. I appreciate your business and guarantee that you will not be disappointed." Todd hit the *end* button and set the phone back down on the desk.

"Your Majesty?" queried Minton. "Who does our client think he is, the king of the world?"

Todd leaned in to have a look at Minton's computer screen. "For all I care, he can wear a feather boa and call himself queen of the world. As long as he pays us, he can be anybody he wants. Now, he's made a special request. And of course, it's going to mean more money—a lot more."

Minton's eyes lit up. "What's the request?"

"He wants as many people to witness it as possible. Also, he wants to watch and record the death for his own pleasure."

"Owww, he is a little freak, isn't he?" said Minton, scratching the back of his head and sending a few dandruff flakes onto his shoulders. "But how exactly are we going to accomplish that?" One of their first rules was to always be as discreet as possible. It lowered the probability of error. Doing it in front of an audience would be a big change to the way they usually operated.

"It'll definitely be more complicated, but this guy is the best paying customer we've ever had and now he's even better," said Todd. "And I intend on giving His Majesty whatever the hell he wants. Will this weevil be able to handle something this big?"

Minton giggled. "Are you kidding? He's my little king of the weevils. He'll be prepped and primed and ready to go anywhere we send him. A couple of days ago, I emailed him a photo of myself wearing only white panties while sitting on my pink canopy bed. He's hooked."

Todd laughed a little. He was feeling slightly giddy thinking about all that money. "Just as long as it wasn't really you in the photo," he joked.

"Do you want to see the picture? It's a good one. Some teenage girl posted it on a networking site. I don't even have to purchase these things anymore there's so much of it out there. Have a look."

"No," replied Todd. "Just tell me that we are only weeks away, and that there are no signs of anything going wrong."

"Everything is copasetic. I don't think the dude has stopped jerking-off since he's seen the newest photo of the lovely Britney," Minton snickered.

"Keep me informed of anything that might be a problem—no matter how small. We can't afford to mess up this job."

Minton grinned and looked at Todd. "I have calculated this with absolute precision. Nothing is going to go wrong." He then looked back at the computer screen and began to laugh hysterically. "Oh, this is my lucky day! My prince charming has just proposed to me. Oh yes, yes Prince Charming, of course I will marry you, you miserable disgusting but entirely useful little weevil," he said, as his fingers wildly hit the keys.

12

Mona stood outside of Elijah's door with her laptop in hand. *Why must he insist on meeting here*, she thought, hesitating to knock. She didn't want a repeat of the embarrassing incident last time. Being in his apartment—in the same place where he ate, slept, and showered, just made her think things she didn't want to think about. She had tried to set up the meeting at the office, but he insisted. He said he was too tired to go out after just returning from making a number of appearances in Los Angeles, and she couldn't very well argue with him. After all he was scheduled to fly out again the next day.

Use this energy for work, use this energy for work, she thought over and over again in her mind. If she could just harness it— control it—not let it control her, then things would be just fine. All it would require was a little willpower.

Mona zipped her loose-fitting hoodie a little higher. She had intentionally put on the unsexiest clothing she could find. There was nothing to make you feel less appealing than gray sweats and clunky white running shoes. She felt fat, dumpy and safe.

Taking a deep breath, she raised her hand and knocked on the door. It did not take long for Elijah to open it.

"Mona! Come in." He seemed genuinely glad to see her.

Mona stepped across the threshold and into the hallway. Elijah closed the door. For a moment, they just stood silently close together in the entranceway. Mona tried not to look into his eyes and cleared her throat. "So, should we get to work?" she asked.

"Sure, come on through," he said, gesturing towards the living room.

Mona walked ahead of him and into the room. There was a gas fireplace on one wall flanked by two large windows. In front of this were two sofas facing each other and in the middle a coffee table.

There were no chairs. She knew that if she sat on a sofa, he would likely sit beside her, as he did last time. This was not good. It was important to keep a reasonable physical distance. Choosing what she believed would be the safest alternative, she sat down on the floor at one end of the coffee table. Although there was a rug, it was still not very comfortable.

"Wouldn't you rather sit on the sofa?" asked Elijah.

"Oh no," she answered, "I'm perfectly comfortable down here. My yoga instructor advises sitting on the floor as often as possible. It's good for the posture." The truth was that years ago Mona had tried yoga, but after only one session, came to the conclusion that her joints were just not the yoga kind. She never ventured to try it again.

Elijah remained standing. "Would you like anything? Coffee, tea, wine?" he asked.

"You have wine? Have you started drinking again?" Nothing like a stern motherly role to help feel secure and in control.

"No, of course not," answered Elijah, who seemed a little insulted that she should ask. "I keep it only for friends."

"And you don't find it tempting, having it just sitting around like that?" Playing queen of the nagging-sweat-pants-mothers would certainly keep her safe from temptation.

Elijah was no longer feeling insulted. Now, he just laughed at her persistence. "You'd think that would be the case, but actually I find it repulsive—for me anyway. I know others enjoy it."

His laughter almost made her smile, but Mona had to be strong—to be focused. She thought about the wine. Maybe it was a good idea—just to calm her nerves. "Okay, a glass of red, if you have it, would be nice."

While Elijah was off getting the wine, Mona took out her laptop and set it up on the coffee table in front of her. She was still waiting for the itinerary document to open when he returned with the glass of wine.

Elijah handed her the glass and she quickly took a larger sip then she intended. "You are thirsty," he said, which made her feel a little self-conscious.

"It's good wine," she responded, setting down the glass on the table. She stared at her computer screen and said, "Now, I just wanted to go over a few things regarding next week. Wednesday, I had to do a little rearranging. I hope that's okay with you." Mona tried not to look at Elijah and to concentrate only on the screen in front of her, but she kept thinking about how good he looked in what was obviously a new shirt. She reached over to her glass and took another long drink.

"Let's see what you've done," said Elijah, who suddenly moved onto the floor beside her to look at the itinerary. Mona found herself taking in a sudden breath of air and hoped that he hadn't noticed.

As Elijah sat close beside her and studied the schedule, Mona tried hard not to think about how his leg was touching hers. If she moved it, would it look obvious? If she kept it there, was that even more obvious? Quickly she reached over and grabbed her glass of wine again. Only after she swallowed the last drop did it suddenly occur to her that this was the last thing that would help her situation.

"I can't see a problem with any of it. It looks good," Elijah said, turning his head towards Mona. He was now close enough that she thought she could feel his breath on her face. She kept her eyes firmly glued to the screen. *Focus control, focus control*, she repeated in her mind as she scrolled down the page pretending to be searching for something.

Much to Mona's relief, Elijah moved over a little so that they were no longer so close, and no longer touching. "Mona," he said in a serious tone, "I'd just like to say, thank you."

"For what?" asked Mona, as she continued to stare at the screen.

"For all that you've done for me. I was not an easy assignment by any means, but you still stood by me. You picked me up when I was ready to fall apart. You really kept me going, and I just wanted to say, *thank you Mona*."

Mona looked over at him but tried not to look directly into his eyes. "I did what anyone would do in my position. I just did my job."

"No, that's not true. You did more. I know the business. I know how it works. And it wasn't just business with you. You really took care of me. You honestly made me feel as though I mattered—as though I could make a difference. That's not business. That's friendship."

Mona laughed nervously. "And they always say never mix business with friendship."

"Well, I think it's *never mix business with pleasure*, but either way they are so wrong," said Elijah. "My early career was all about business. Just squeeze as much money as you can out of it, and then try and squeeze some more. That's what really did me in—the emptiness, and the times when I felt like I was just helping to support evil."

Mona looked at him. "Evil?" she asked. "What do you mean evil?"

Elijah leaned back against the sofa and looked at the table in front of him. "Do you remember the children's charity I was helping to promote when my career was beginning to slip?"

"Yes," replied Mona, "it was a very successful group, and still is."

Elijah continued to stare at the empty table. "Initially, I thought that this would be a real turning point. My agent and the record company suggested I go with it. By that time everything around me seemed so meaningless that I thought, *great*! I'd do something worthwhile—try and bring meaning into my life again. My record company was associated with this group and I believe that they still are. Anyway, as I became more involved, I started to feel that something was not right. Do you remember the man who founded it?"

"Yes, of course. He died only a few years ago."

"He did—thank God," said Elijah, confusing Mona who knew the man was well revered, and that the charity still carried his name. She waited to hear more.

"I saw things—suspicious things," said Elijah. "Eventually, I knew what he was—what he did to children."

Mona thought back about the man and how she had met him once. At the time, there was something about him that made her uncomfortable, but he was so highly regarded that she had simply dismissed those feelings.

"I was horrified!" continued Elijah. "I tried to say something, but they denied it all—said it was just my paranoia caused by too many indulgences. I knew I was right, but I was also naïve enough to believe that they didn't see it too. It was then that I began to push for some type of investigation. That's when my career co-incidentally began to really go downhill."

"You think that was when they decided to end it for you," said Mona.

"So, you know that it was intentional." Elijah was surprised that she had heard about the human sacrifices.

"I have learned a little about the way the Bloodline does things, and you were definitely a sacrifice."

"Oh Mona, that makes me admire you even more. To think you would take me on knowing that," said Elijah, wanting to hug her but not sure how she would take it.

"Don't be too quick to admire me." Mona could feel his warmth and sincerity, and it was throwing her off-balance again. "It was really Jack," she said, trying to regain control. "He was the one who decided to sign you up. I didn't want anything to do with you." Only after she said it, did Mona realize that the wine had gone to her head, and now she had blurted out something that could damage their working relationship.

Elijah surprised her when, instead of being hurt by what she had just said, he laughed and said, "Well, I do appreciate your raw honesty."

Now she felt bad. "I'm sorry, Elijah. I'm sorry I said what I did. Yes, I was hesitant, at first—afraid really, but that's not the way it is now. You impress me Elijah—your courage, your tenacity, your art." Mona had not meant to go over the edge like that. She felt like a pendulum swinging between extremes. *It must be the wine. Why did I drink that glass so quickly?*

"Well, thank you," said Elijah, sincerely.

Wanting to get back to the original topic, Mona asked, "So you think they got rid of you because of that guy. Wouldn't they be thankful that you were trying to save them possible future embarrassment?"

"No, they weren't afraid of the truth getting out. They knew they could keep it all hush hush. This charity was just too much of a cash-cow for them. It was also very politically useful. They had complete confidence in their ability to lie their way out of anything. It was me they decided to get rid of. I was the one threatening to upset what they had going. Also, he was considered purer Bloodline than me and even may have had some kind of physical marks that they considered powerful. I suppose you've heard of the marks?"

Mona nodded her head.

"I suspect this because they went well beyond simply seeing him as a valuable asset to the company. Often, they seemed to worship him as though he were a god," added Elijah.

"What do you mean by worship?" asked Mona.

"It wasn't just one thing. It was about the way they treated him, talked about him, and even marketed him. They presented him as superhuman in such a way that it made me wonder if many of them really believed it. Also, there were times when I couldn't help but feel that they were intentionally bringing him children—like some sort of sacrifices to their god—bringing their offerings to their god so that he would keep making money for the organization."

Mona knew there were many awful things going on, but she had always tried to block that part out of her mind. *Stay focused on the small details and don't look up too much* was her motto. It was difficult to hear Elijah say what he did.

"I think about them, Mona. Every time I see his face, which they still use in their campaigns. I think about all those children. Where are they now? How do they cope seeing their abuser still exalted as a hero? It's not right and it bothers me. Sometimes I wonder if there was more I could have done—I should have done."

Mona could see how upsetting this was for Elijah. "He's dead now," she reminded him. "No matter how many times his face shows up on billboards or television, he's dead. His victims will at least know that he can't hurt any more children. That's something Elijah. Don't feel bad. You couldn't have done more than you did."

"I hope you're right," he said, still feeling the guilt.

"I know I'm right," Mona reached over and took his hand to reassure him. "And you know what? You were right too. The best business is business between friends, and I do consider you my friend. So, what do you say? Should we get back to business, my friend?"

Elijah smiled, "I suppose I have a very busy week ahead of me, so we had better."

Mona let go of his hand and went back to the computer screen to open another document. *There now, we are friends, just business friends. Problem solved. All it took was a little time, patience, and communication.* She was relieved that her feelings were now firmly in check. With their relationship clearly and neatly defined, there would be no more emotional rollercoaster rides. From this point on, it would be easy. She could now focus completely on the work ahead.

* * *

Britney:
Good news! I think my socialist parents have finally decided to leave for Europe in 2 weeks.

AlienKiller666:
Alright! What day should I arrive?

Britney:
Not exactly sure yet.

AlienKiller666:
It will take me a few days to get there, so I need to know ahead of time.

Britney:
Don't worry. I'll let u know.

AlienKiller666:
I just want to hold you in my arms.

Britney:
I want that too. I have that naughty picture u sent me. It's hidden in my panty drawer.

AlienKiller666:
You know that I will marry you.

Britney:
I know u luv me. Do u know I luv u?

AlienKiller666:
As sure as I know anything, I know it. And all I want is to show you how much I luv you!

Britney:
It won't be too much longer. Patience is a virtue.

AlienKiller666:
But I think of you day and night. All the time!

Britney:
Do something to try and relax.

AlienKiller666:
I go out shooting. That helps.

Britney:
That doesn't help me. Imagining u shooting a gun. What a turn on!

AlienKiller666:
I'll bring a gun if you like.

Britney:
U better. My parents would freak if they found out. LOL

AlienKiller666:
Your parents don't understand.

Britney:
They don't understand me, but u do. We r soulmates.

AlienKiller666:
Yes, soulmates!

Britney:
Gotta go out for lunch with the parents.

AlienKiller666:
To the same restaurant?

Britney:
Yah.

AlienKiller666:
Let me know if you see that Jack again and if he does anything else.

Britney:
I feel so safe with u.

AlienKiller666:
There's nothing I won't do for you.

Britney:
I know. That's why I luv u.

AlienKiller666:
Forever?

Britney:
Forever and ever and ever and ever……

13

Mona sat at her computer going over the most recent sales number. Elijah's single had already reached platinum and his album was not far behind. She leaned back in her chair and took in a deep breath. To go from where he was only a few months ago, to this! What an incredible experience!

Someone knocked on the open door and she looked up to see Jack standing there. It was unusual for him to show up at her office.

"May I come in," he asked with a smile.

"Of course, Jack. Is everything all right?"

He walked in and sat down in the chair on the other side of the desk.

"I just wanted to see how you were doing. After the talk we had the other day, I still had a little concern."

"Oh that," said Mona, "That's all past now. Elijah and I have established ourselves as just friends. It's a working friendship."

Jack leaned his arm on the desk. "So, you are completely over your crisis. Those feelings you had are now gone."

"Well, I wouldn't exactly say gone. Let's just say they have been transformed—transformed into manageable feelings of friendship. Don't worry, Jack. I have it all under control again. Have you seen the sales numbers for today?"

"I'd assume they are good."

"Good? They're amazing! I can't believe how right you were about Elijah."

"You mean how right Stuart was."

"Yes of course. Stuart. Do you think he could be the one?"

"Stuart?"

"No, Elijah. Do you think he can awaken her?"

"He came to us for a reason. If that is the reason, then we are very blessed."

"Do you ever imagine what it would be like?"

"Before he…." Jack paused, wanting to choose his words carefully, "before he left, Stuart said that her awakening would bring balance and harmony to the world. It would change everything."

"That's a nice thought."

"It's more than a thought, Mona. It's the future. Stuart believed it and I believe it too."

"Should we say something to Elijah? Should we at least acknowledge his dreams?"

Jack sighed, "You know the rules. There can be no interference. We can't risk upsetting the balance of how things will go."

"Right—*obey the prime directive*. But who made that rule anyway?"

"I assume it was handed down over the years."

"I don't like it!" declared Mona. "Who knows why such a thing was decided in the first place. Perhaps Elijah should be told that his dreams have important meaning. Right now, he thinks that he is all alone in believing in them. That can't be good. It's not good for anyone to be alone, Jack."

Jack leaned back in the chair. "They say that if this rule is broken it could disrupt the entire world to the point where there would be no going back. There would be no fixing it. Do you want to take that risk?"

Mona thought for a moment. "I suppose not," she replied, but despite what her head told her to say, her heart secretly answered, *Yes, I would take that risk. I would gamble it all.*

* * *

Elijah tried on the new outfit that had been sent over for him that morning. In two days' time, he was scheduled to make one of his most important appearances so far. It was an interview with Catherine Parmlet, one of television's leading journalists. She would certainly be asking him the hard questions and delving into his past. It would not be an attack like they tried on the Hailee and Haley Hour, but it would be challenging. Elijah wanted to make sure his clothes were just right.

As he stood in front of the mirror trying to see himself from every possible angle, someone buzzed from the street. He walked to the hall and switched on the video surveillance. It was Mona. "Door's open," he said, pushing the lock release.

He opened the apartment door and waited. It did not take long before Mona appeared in the hallway. "Perfect timing," he said. "I need to know if these pants make me look fat."

"Shouldn't that be my question for you?" she laughed, as she entered the apartment and shut the door behind her.

"Your people sent me this ensemble," said Elijah, twirling around. "It's for the Parmlet interview. What do you think?"

"It looks great," she quickly answered, and then moved her eyes over to the copy of Dürer's *Adoration of the Magi* hanging on the wall behind him. "Is that new?" she asked, wanting to change the subject.

"Yes," Elijah answered. "Do you like it?"

"It's not very traditional, is it?

"Truth is rarely traditional."

Mona looked at him curiously. She was just about to ask him what he meant by that, when he said, "Enough about art. Come in and sit down," Elijah headed for the living room, and Mona followed.

Making sure Elijah sat down first, Mona was then able to select a spot on the opposite sofa. The thick oak coffee table made a perfect safety barrier between them. *Of course we are just friends, but it is still good to keep a distance,* she reasoned.

Mona reached into her purse and pulled out a black velvet box. "I've brought something for you," she said. "It's something to wear for the interview and also a little present from the company— every rock star needs some sparkle." She opened the box and inside was a well-crafted gold chain with a large, but not ostentatiously large, gold cross. In the very center of the cross, there were two narrow rectangular diamonds inlayed horizontally and parallel to each other.

"For little ole me? Aww shucks," joked Elijah.

Mona rolled her eyes. "Come on now. Every rock star must have a little something that says, *oh baby, I got what you need.*"

Elijah laughed. "Well, thank you. I'm sure it will mesmerize Ms. Parmlet."

Mona handed the box to Elijah who took a closer look. He brushed his fingers over it. "I like it," he said. "It's something I likely would have picked out for myself."

"And that's always the sign of a good gift," said Mona.

Elijah looked up at her with a sudden serious look on his face. "I had that dream again—last night. It was more vivid than usual. It was so intense."

Mona wanted to confess to him that it was not just *his* dream, but instead she asked, "Did you feel good about it?"

"Yes and no," replied Elijah. "When it happened, it was amazing. But when I woke up, there was almost a physical pain running all through my body—a pain that came with knowing it was just a dream. The feeling has faded away now, but at the time it was a lot to deal with."

This is becoming so difficult. I want to tell him everything but I promised Jack. I can't break my promise. "We all dream, all of the time," she said. "Many people will dream the same dream over and over again for their entire lives."

"Not like this. This is different, Mona. I wish I could explain to you how, but it is different. These dreams don't come from my head. They come from…" Elijah hesitated.

"They come from where?" asked Mona.

"Alright I'll say it. I feel that they come from God."

Mona was silent.

"I know I sound crazy, and don't think that I haven't gone over this thing again and again in my mind. *Old rock star loses marbles*—it happens all the time. But it doesn't matter. Every time I convince myself that it is all in my imagination, something happens to convince me otherwise. For years, I've tried to run away from it, but it keeps catching up to me."

Mona could see that Elijah was confused and hurting. She wanted to tell him. She wanted to tell him the truth right there, but she kept hearing Jack's voice asking, *Do you want to take the risk of destroying the world?* Instead, she got up and moved over to sit beside him. At the very least, she could try and bring him comfort. "Tell me about your ideas of God," she said.

Elijah laughed. "Really?" he asked. "That's usually the last thing people want to hear. What exactly do you want to know?"

Mona was just looking for something to talk about—something to get his mind off of the dream, and something to keep her from accidentally blurting out the secret. "What is God to you?" she asked.

Elijah gently set the black velvet box on the table. He leaned back into the sofa, looked into Mona's eyes and smiled warmly. "God is everything," he said. "And even as I say that out loud, I know those three words will never be enough to describe what really is. I mean, how could I do God proper justice working with such primitive tools—with only the inadequate simple babble of spoken-language at my disposal? It's like—like trying to build a magnificent cathedral when all you have to work with is a prehistoric hammerstone. But that's all I have. So, working with this pathetic tool, I'll try as best I can to build a somewhat recognizable cathedral."

"God is everything," he repeated and then paused for a moment to organize his thoughts. "There is no thing that God is not," he continued. "You, me, this table." He knocked three times on the polished oak surface. "But it is far from simple. God is Love—is Life—is Safety—is Father—is Mother—is the only real Power—God is—God is Home. Yes, I think maybe that explains it best. God is Home. You know when you are in a crowd and suddenly you see a friend among the throng of strangers; or you know how your own bed feels when you come back after a long journey; or you know what it's like when you see your own front door after having had a horrible day—well, that's home. God is like that except even more—God is more home than you could ever imagine. God is Home, and Home is God."

Mona just stared blankly at Elijah. "Sorry," he said, realizing that he had gone further then he intended. Elijah knew that people didn't enjoy it when he talked like this. He was usually alert enough to keep it under control and not let himself go. What came over him to make him speak so freely? "I know, I know," he said, trying to salvage the moment. "This is the part where people tell me to shut up. So go ahead. Say it. *Elijah, be quiet and stop pontificating.*"

Mona did not say a word. Instead, she continued to silently stare at him. Elijah wondered if what he had said was really that awful. He was preparing to say something funny to try and smooth over the situation when suddenly, she threw herself upon him with such force that it pushed him down into the sofa. Mona was now on top of him, her lips madly pressing into his. In an instant, her closed eyes flashed open and she could see him looking back at her in surprise and confusion. *What am I doing?* Unable to think straight, she barely managed to pull her lips away, but she could not keep from holding him down beneath her body. Completely at the mercy of passion, she was just able to whisper, "Do you want me to stop?"

Elijah stared questioningly into her eyes. He then smiled and with a single sudden turn, he flung her over, switching their positions. Now he was on top. "Do you want me to stop?" he asked.

"No," she breathed. "Don't stop. Don't ever stop."

14

It was a strangely quiet afternoon, as Jack sat on a bench in Central Park. Such a beautiful sunny day, and yet there was almost no one in sight. Why would the park be so empty today?

Jack looked down at the group of pigeons that bobbed and begged at his feet. He usually tried to avoid these *rats of the sky*, but today he was happy for what little company there was. Even these dirty greedy creatures were better than being alone.

When a single jogger suddenly ran past him, the birds instantly took off in a flurry. He watched as they vanished into the sun. When he turned back to look in the direction of the jogger, he too had disappeared. Jack was now alone.

At least there is green, he thought, looking at the nature surrounding him. Jack usually came here when he had to make a difficult decision, or just needed a little breathing space. Today, he came because he couldn't stop thinking about Stuart. Stuart seemed to be increasingly on his mind these last several weeks, and it was beginning to interfere with ordinary life. The last thing he wanted was for it to stop, but at the same time it was not easy to live with these intense emotions.

"Jack, Jack—Jack Sprat!"

Jack looked to his right and saw a dirty raggedy man coming towards him. He reached into his pocket and prepared to hand over the twenty dollar bill he had stuffed there earlier. Much to his surprise, the man did not ask for money, but instead sat down on the bench beside him. "I know you," he said with a yellow smile. "Jack Sprat the record man!"

Jack responded with a quick smile and then held out the twenty.

"Don't want your money honey. Render unto Caesar what is Caesar's, Jack the giant killer."

At this point Jack knew that he should leave. This man seemed to be suffering from a mental illness and it was best not to engage him in conversation. He should just say goodbye and then quickly walk away.

Just as he was preparing to go, the man began to wave his arms like a conductor and happily sing:

Jack Sprat, Jack Sprat
Jack Sprat could eat no fat
No no fat for Jack
Jack Sprat.

Jack couldn't help but laugh. Perhaps this man was no threat after all. Patting his stomach he smiled and said, "If only that were my problem, I would not have to watch my waistline so closely."

The man laughed too. "Jack Sprat eats lots of fat," he sang, and then kept repeating it over and over.

Jack watched as a single pigeon flew down and landed near the bench. The man stopped singing and began to speak to the bird. "Oh, sweet angel! Beautiful angel from Heaven, tell me the secrets of paradise." The pigeon just blankly stared back at the man and waited in the hope of some breadcrumbs.

Suddenly turning back to Jack, the man asked, "Jack Sprat, do you believe in God?"

Jack did not have to think about his answer. He answered it in the same way he always answered that question. "Does God believe in me?"

The man began to laugh. "That's a good one, Jack Sprat—a good one! Does God believe in me? What does God believe in? Yes, what does God believe in? Oh God, oh God, oh God!"

Suddenly the man had stopped laughing and his face was now sunk down in sorrow. "Do you know what happens when God cries?" he asked, turning his face towards the sky.

Jack began to worry at the change in the man's tone. If it was headed towards a psychotic episode, he did not want to find himself in the middle of it.

"When God cries," the man continued," his children fall as teardrops from His eyes. They roll down His face, fall through the sky and then—WHAM!—they hit the ground! Oh, why do they make God cry? Why? Why? Why?"

The man suddenly began to rock back and forth, wailing like a woman in mourning. "Owwwww," he cried, his arms now stretched towards the sky. Jack knew he should get up to leave, but was afraid that it might make the situation even worse. He looked both ways along the path, but there was no sign of anyone. He was alone with this unbalanced man.

Still with his face turned towards the sky, the man called out, "I was there! Oh, I was there! I was there the day God cried and his children fell down, down, down to the earth—the beautiful children of God in all their beautiful colors and shapes and sizes—down, down, down." He started to rock even faster.

"Toadman came. Toadman came and made God weep. Ohhhhhh! Noooo! No Toadman, please no! Toadman came and the children of God fell from the sky!"

Jack readied to make a move to try and get away when the man suddenly shouted, "JACK, THEY KNEW!"

Against his instincts, Jack found himself turning his head and looking directly into the man's blood-shot blue eyes which were filling with watery fury. "They knew!" he hissed. "They knew the Toadman was coming, and they let him come! Oh, wicked men! Oh, evil men!" he cried. "They opened the door and let the Toadman through!"

The man then went perfectly silent and just stared at Jack. Jack still wanted to leave. He desperately wanted to get up and go back to the safety of his office, but he had made the mistake of making eye contact. He was now being held in place by the dagger in a madman's eyes.

The man suddenly began to speak again, but this time in a low raspy whisper, "Oh Jack!" he said, "Jack Sprat, listen. Listen to me. The Toadman is coming again. He's coming again, but this time he's coming for *you*!"

Jack could no longer think about fleeing. His mind was now left dangling from the precipice of those fateful words. *He's coming for you. A madman's spell—forever frozen in time by a madman's spell. He's coming for you, Jack Sprat.*

"Jack!" a woman's voice suddenly called, instantly breaking the trance. Jack was now able to turn his head in the direction of the voice. Mona, looking a little concerned, was walking quickly towards him.

"Mona!" he said, relieved to see her. As she came closer, Jack felt a sudden surge of strength and an impulse to protect her against any harm. He turned his head, ready to get rid of the madman with some polite but firm words, however the man was gone.

"Susan told me you were in the park and I thought you might be here. Sorry to frighten off your friend," said Mona, sitting down close beside Jack.

"Well, I'm very glad you saw him too. I was beginning to wonder if I had imagined it all."

Mona laughed. "Imagination can't out-weird New York City."

"I suppose not," replied Jack, who was trying to quickly push all the man had told him out of his mind. *They were just the words of a mentally ill person, stop holding on to them.*

"Jack," said Mona, her voice now taking on a more serious tone. "I wanted to speak to you face to face about something. It's about—well—something has happened with Elijah."

Jack was suddenly concerned that something else had gone wrong with Elijah's career. He was also secretly glad for any possible crisis that could take his mind away from what had just happened. "Please don't tell me it's another paparazzi moment," he said.

"Oh no!" exclaimed Mona. "It's nothing like that. No, everything with Elijah is just fine. He's right on track. It's just that…umm…something happened between Elijah and me." Mona knew she sounded like a guilty school-girl and hated it. She was a full-grown woman—a mature middle-aged woman. She should not be finding herself in this ridiculous position.

"Oh, I see," said Jack.

"This is crazy!" said Mona, more to herself than to Jack. "You know that I've never been like this before. I've always been sensible—practical—in control, and I've been around a lot of them. Rock stars have never tempted me—never! Now, look what I've done. What's wrong with me, Jack?"

"If you don't mind me asking Mona, what exactly did you do?" asked Jack, wanting to make sure that she was not blowing the situation out of proportion.

Mona almost started to giggle. "Everything worth doing," she quickly replied. *Damn it, what am I turning into?*

Jack started to laugh.

"It's not funny, Jack," she snapped. "I didn't want this to happen. I thought I knew what I was doing. I thought I had everything under control, but then he started to say things and…" Mona didn't finish.

"What things?" asked Jack. "What did he talk about that made you, Mona the steadfast, lose all control?"

"Oh, it's just so silly. It was God," she answered. "He talked about God."

Now Jack started laughing again. "It's likely a good thing that you have always avoided church," he teased. "You could cause quite the scandal in the pews."

Mona couldn't blame him for poking fun. The entire thing was a big joke. "Oh Jack, what am I supposed to do now?"

"Well, what does Elijah think of what happened."

"I don't know," Mona replied.

"Did you not find any time at all to talk?" laughed Jack.

"I left while he was sleeping and I haven't answered any of his calls. Right now, he's already on his way to Los Angeles again."

"That's not very nice, Mona," Jack said, realizing that he was sounding more like a stern father than her friend.

"He's a rock star, Jack. What would I be to him? It was just a—a thing. It was nothing, and now all I want is for you to give Elijah over to someone else and just *please* let me fly off to Paris like I wanted to do before this whole thing ever started. I've made a fool of myself and now I just need to get away!"

Jack was silent for a moment. He could see how torn Mona was. Putting his arm around her, he mischievously asked, "So how was it?"

Before Mona could stop herself, she blurted out, "It was amazing! I don't know what it was—electricity—a fiery energy of some sort. But it was incredible! Like nothing I experienced before. And now I'm wondering why I just told you that. It's not like me, Jack. That's not who I am!"

Jack held her tighter. "You need to stop thinking so much. Just relax and let the tide take you. Answer Elijah's calls or at least send him a message promising to meet with him when he gets back to New York. It's not fair to treat him like that. You've been in this business long enough to know that not only do rock stars have feelings, but sometimes very intense feelings. At the very least, give him a chance to explain what he's thinking."

Mona rested her head on Jack's chest and wrapped her arms around his pudgy middle. It felt good to feel his breathing and to know that he was there for her. "I don't know why I'm acting like a stupid teenager. I'm sorry, Jack. It's just that something in my head keeps telling me to shape up and get control, and right now I feel so out of control."

"Und how doez dat make you feel?" asked Jack, pushing his glasses down his nose a little while doing his famous Freud impression.

This made Mona laugh. Jack always had a way to make her laugh when laughing was the farthest thing from her mind. "Well Doctor," she answered, "the truth is that it feels good—real good—maybe too good. And that's scary."

"Und vhy pray-tell iz dat?" asked Jack.

"Because it may not last, and that frightens me."

"And is that enough to throw it all away?" Jack asked seriously.

"No. I suppose not," Mona replied. She then added, "He's not even my type, Jack."

"I thought tall, dark and handsome was every woman's type."

"Not this woman. You know that I've always preferred men more—well, more like you."

"Gay ones? No wonder you're not married."

Mona gave him a playful swat. "You know what I mean—traditional, down-to-earth, reliable—like you."

"And who is to say that Elijah isn't all of those things and more. You can't cling to your daddy for the rest of your life."

Just then two young men came walking along the path. One looked at Jack, pointed and exclaimed, "Hey man, you're Jack!"

Thrilled to come across a real live celebrity in the park, the second waved and called out, "Hey Jack!"

Jack smiled at them both and gave a little wave with his free hand.

"Should we go talk to him?" asked the second youth, seemingly oblivious that Jack could actually hear him.

"No man, have some respect. He's with a chick," the first one answered.

As they continued on down the path, Jack could still hear them talking about him.

"Man, I thought that guy was gay."

"Guess not, dude."

Jack smiled and stroked Mona's hair. "Now look what you have done, Bethsheba. You have ruined my *spotless reputation*."

Mona laughed. "And what did you teach me? Whatever you do, always leave them talking. And they are definitely talking."

"And you have always been an exceptional student," said Jack. "But now you're falling behind in your studies. There needs to be some talking between you and Elijah. If, after you speak with him, you decide that Paris is the best place for you, I will purchase the airfare myself. If, on the other hand, you realize that your place is to stick with Elijah, I will do everything I can to support your decision. But you cannot simply run away. I won't allow that."

Mona took her head from Jack's shoulder and sat up straight. "You're right. I need to act my age and face him. But be prepared to shell out for a first-class ticket to Paris, Jack. I'm sure that once I talk with him, we'll both just laugh about what happened, admit our mistake and then we'll go our separate ways."

Just then, Jack saw a robin flutter down and rest in a nearby shrub. This made him think of Stuart again. "Perhaps," he said smiling. "But I won't be too fast to reserve your seat. After all, *we that are true lovers run into strange capers.*"

"Are you talking Shakespeare again?" asked Mona.

"Do you find it annoying?"

"I should," she answered, "but for some reason it reassures me."

"It reassures me too. Now, shall we return to the office and get some work done," said Jack, getting up and offering his arm to Mona.

Mona smiled and happily put her arm in his. Together, they headed off down the path leading out of the park.

From behind a tree, a raggedy man watched intently as they walked into the distance. Under his breath, he whispered over and over again,

> *Jack be nimble*
> *Jack be quick*
> *Jack beware the devil's trick.*

15

Elijah sat in the luxurious hotel room that had been booked for the interview. There were four different cameras set up to capture four different angles. Across from him was an empty wing chair identical to the one in which he was seated. This was the interviewer's chair.

Staring at the empty chair, Elijah worried that he would not be able to do this. Catherine Parmlet had a reputation for asking no-nonsense and in-depth questions. She was unrelenting and would definitely bring up his past. Was he really prepared to be truthful about it? Also, would being truthful destroy everything he had recently built up? He had considered all this before and thought he was well prepared for the interview, but now his mind was beginning to fill with doubts.

Catherine was standing on the other side of the room receiving some final touch-ups from her personal make-up artist. Elijah looked over at her knowing that very soon she would sit down and the questions would begin. What was she planning to throw at him? To add to his worries, he kept thinking about Mona. Why did she leave in the middle of the night, and why won't she answer his calls?

It seemed to take forever as he watched Catherine finally walk over and take her seat across from him. Her smile seemed genuine, but this was show business, and Elijah knew that appearances in this world could be very deceiving. Was she a responsible and fair journalist as her public believed, or was she really a monster planning to rip him apart? Of course, he knew the truth was somewhere in between, which was somehow even more disconcerting.

"Alright Elijah, are you ready to begin?" she said, while adjusting her tailored suit.

"Yes, I'm ready," he replied, trying not to show that what he really meant was *I'm not so sure about this*.

Catherine then focused on the producer who was signaling down to airtime. Quickly turning to the camera, she warmly smiled at her invisible audience and chimed, "Welcome to another evening of Focus Upon Conversations. Tonight, I am pleased to have as my very special guest, singing sensation Elijah. Once known as the Techno-pop King, he has reinvented himself and surprised everyone by becoming the best-selling artist of the year. His album *Love Rising*, which is also the title of his hit single, has recently gone platinum—which I might add is no easy feat in today's digital world." Gracefully turning towards Elijah, she gave him her most professional smile. "Good evening, Elijah."

"Good evening and thank you Catherine, for having me on your show."

"The pleasure is all mine. Now, before we get into all the amazing things that are happening in your life currently, let's talk about your fast rise to stardom in the early 1980's. Can you tell us what it was like to go from being an ordinary Midwestern boy to the Techno-pop King virtually overnight?"

Elijah had come prepared to talk about everything, including the past, but now he found himself hesitating to answer. Was the world really ready for the truth? Didn't they just want to hear the same old story they had come to expect? He knew the story Catherine was alluding to. *Elijah, the Greek tragedy. The victim of fame and fortune. Self-sacrificed on the altar of Hubris.* But that wasn't the truth. He really wanted to tell the world everything that was real, but would they reject him if they knew? Should he bow to expectations and just give the crowd what they want? Was truth ever a possibility in show business?

"I was very young," he began. "Only nineteen—and a small-town boy at that. I hadn't seen much of the world at all, and suddenly to have all of this coming at me was a little confusing and overwhelming—at first." Elijah did not want to add the '*at first*' because this was not the truth. There was no first and no last. It never stopped being overwhelming or confusing. He had gone over those years again and again in his head. Even when it seemed to have stopped, the truth was that it hadn't. It kept coming, but he just stopped noticing it as much.

"I can imagine that it must have been a very intense experience. How did you deal with it when you first found yourself thrust into the spotlight?"

Elijah could see she was working up to a proverbial fall and would be hoping to wring some ratings-making emotion out of him. He didn't blame her though. That was her job.

"When you are young, you tend to be more accepting of things or perhaps it is more accurate to say that you are more cut off from things. So, you blindly accept whatever comes your way. You are not fully connected to the world as yet. You simply don't have the capacity to see it clearly. It takes a long time to gain maturity and a better understanding of how you work within the world and how the world works within you."

Catherine, for a brief second, just stared and smiled politely. It was then that Elijah realized he had veered way off her course. She was expecting a simple easy-to-sell narrative and he was just not providing one. He began to worry that by not fulfilling her expectations she would become angry and aggressive. If she could not have an American fairytale, she might go for a bloody horror story instead. He prepared himself for the next question.

"So, you were in your early twenties and riding high. You had fame, money—everything people dream of. Elijah, when did it all go wrong? The tabloids reported that you were living a risky lifestyle with drug use, alcohol and women." She leaned in towards Elijah. "Can you tell us just what happened during those years? When did you reach your rock-bottom moment?"

Suddenly, Catherine stopped looking at Elijah and turned towards a camera to her left. She smiled warmly and said, "And Elijah will be answering that question right after this short break." The make-up artist rushed in to reapply Catherine's lipstick.

Elijah felt very alone as he sat quietly waiting. He tried to focus on how he would answer the questions about his past. There was no way he could play the role of the prodigal son when it just was not the truth. But how do you convey the truth when it was so complicated? How can anything as multi-layered as a man's life be summed up in only a few words?

Like a tiny electric jolt, Elijah felt a buzzing in his jacket pocket. At first, he tried to ignore it. The last thing he needed right now was a distraction. But at the same time, he knew he couldn't help checking. Taking out the phone, he looked at the message. It was Mona! Mona had finally called! He quickly opened the text.

Mona: Sorry I didn't call earlier. We will talk when you get back.

Elijah smiled. It felt so good to finally hear from her. He glanced up at Catherine who gave him a look that more than suggested he should put the phone away. Instead of putting it back in his pocket, he quickly texted his reply.

Elijah: Can't wait!

Knowing that the smart thing would be to put the phone away immediately, Elijah remained staring at the screen—just hoping she would say more. He wanted her to say something that could give him some support and encouragement. *Please Mona. I need you.*

As he continued to stare at the dark screen, he heard the producer sternly warn, "Ten seconds, Elijah."

He knew it would make him look like an arrogant jerk if they came back from commercial and the phone was still in his hand. That's what would be talked about in tomorrow's news. Not anything he said. But he couldn't let it go. *Come on Mona!*

Suddenly, the phone vibrated. Elijah quickly opened the message.

Mona: Me too!

Elijah sighed and slipped the phone into his pocket just as Catherine began speaking to the camera.

"And welcome back. Tonight, we are talking with singer-songwriter Elijah. Now Elijah, before we went to break, I asked you to tell us exactly what went wrong in your early career. How did you go from being the Techno-pop King to a virtual nobody overnight?"

Elijah thought about what she was expecting—thought about what they were all expecting. She wanted Achilles to weep and tell the story of his flawed heel. *Go ahead American hero. Tell the tale of how you were not strong enough—how you lost everything because you turned your back on motherhood and apple pie. You'll be safe as long as you stick with the same old story.* But then he thought about Mona.

"Actually Catherine, in a strange way everything went very right."

Catherine was obviously confused by his answer and laughed nervously as she asked, "What do you mean that everything went right, when it is very clear that everything went very wrong, Elijah?"

"Oh no," said Elijah confidently. "What went wrong was nothing to do with me—not the core me. The world went wrong. The world was upside down and that's how I found myself—upside down. We were all upside down."

"Could you please explain what you mean by that?" asked Catherine, who was now genuinely intrigued.

Elijah looked her straight in the eye and said, "There was a peculiar turn that happened at that time. Call it a cosmic turn if you like. Our human values that we had spent thousands of years developing were suddenly thrown away—all the values that offered us balance and meaning and hope. We lost it all. Greed became good. Fashion became menacing and militaristic. Humanity became just another product to be marketed. The music became an assembly-line product. And what music somehow slipped past the assembly-line inspectors was either the voice of anger and fear, or of mourning what was lost. The world had gone mad—stark raving mad. And if things had gone right for me, then I would have been mad right along with it. I would have gone along with the new rules. I would have been a part of that world. But I wasn't. Within all that seeming chaos, I somehow kept myself. And when I fell out from the world, I fell out from the madness. The fall was not a defeat, but a victory. I fell out from the madness and towards sanity. It's just that it's not simple, fast or easy to finally reach the bottom of understanding and balance. But I did make it. That's what you see reflected in my new music. Everything in my life has been part of the necessary journey to reach this exact point. Catherine, we are all in the same boat. Our individual journeys are what make us who we are. And who we are is within our journeys—journeys that make us change—make us become. So here I am now sitting before you—a man unceasing to become."

Catherine stared in silence at Elijah for a moment. She then turned to the camera and said. "And on that very profound note, we must again break for a word from our sponsors."

When the producer signaled that they were off the air, she leaned in closer to Elijah. "Well," she smiled, "you surprised me. I wasn't expecting anything so—well—so enlightening. I suppose I bought into those leather pants jokes like everyone else. After the break, I'm going to ask you about your new album and in particular about your song *Love Rising*. I just wish we had more time for you to perform. I'd love to see that. Next month, we'll have you back and I'll personally make certain that there is time for a song. What do you think?"

Elijah couldn't believe what he was hearing. Very few guests ever got booked on the Catherine Parmlet show twice in the same season. "That sounds like a great idea. I'd consider it an honor to return. Also, I'll be performing at Radio City next week if you would like tickets."

"I'd love tickets!" said Catherine, clapping her hands together.

Elijah felt his phone vibrate again. "Pardon me a moment," he said, as he took it out to check the message. It was another text from Mona.

Mona: When you fly in tomorrow, come straight to my place.

Quickly, he typed his reply.

Elijah: Will be there!

"Ten seconds, Elijah. Are you almost ready?" said the producer, her words no longer a stern warning but now a gentle reminder.

"Ready like you would not believe," Elijah answered, slipping his phone back into his pocket.

* * *

Mona set down the phone and turned up the volume on the television. She had been watching the live interview when she finally couldn't take it any longer. She had to text him. Of course, this was impulsive craziness and she wasn't even sure if he would be able to answer. But seeing him on the screen, looking like he did, instantly drained her of all willpower. She needed to reach out to him and couldn't hold back.

When she read the words, *Can't wait,* a fire ran down her back. Did he really mean it? Was he just being polite? No, polite was *see you soon. Can't wait* was something entirely different.

Hearing him so eloquently explain himself to Catherine left her feeling weak with admiration. At that point, all she could think about was how much she wanted him there with her—not sitting in a room thousands of miles away talking to some other woman. That's when she found herself texting him again. *This is more madness. Don't push send!* But she pushed the button anyway.

"What have I done?" she said out loud to herself right after. "This is childish." But when he responded, and she saw his words, the fire ran through her body again.

Mona watched the show to the very end. She felt so proud. Elijah had managed to impress the great Catherine Parmlet. He had given the kind of interview that would be front page news tomorrow. There would be no stopping him now.

Leaning back in her chair, she thought about what would happen when he returned to New York. Now, he would be coming straight to her place. She needed a plan. There were things to be discussed. That's of course the only reason why she invited him. They needed to talk—a nice rational discussion between two professional adults. Feelings aside, it was time to get serious about her job and Elijah's future at Einhorn.

Mona could see her cloudy reflection in the blank television screen. "Hello Elijah," she said to her darkened image. "Did you have a good flight? Wonderful! I appreciate that you could take this time to meet with me. I thought it best if we start by agreeing that what happened between us is something that is best forgotten. After all, we are both mature adults who understand that these things can sometimes happen. Anyway, let's put it behind us and talk business. We have a great many serious things to discuss…"

* * *

As Jack watched the interview, he knew he should be feeling at least a little anxious. It was true that a bad interview with Catherine Parmlet could end a career instantly, but he wasn't worried at all. He had faith that Elijah would do him proud.

His eyes never left the television screen as he picked up his low-calorie beer from the coffee table and took a small sip. It was amazing to see how Elijah was completely charming Catherine. This was a woman who in no way was easy to enchant. He had seen her

116

take apart confident self-assured men. Yet here she was continually melting with every word Elijah said.

"So, tell us Elijah, was your song *Love Rising* inspired by anyone in particular?" Catherine asked, leaning in flirtatiously.

Elijah smiled at her and answered, "Well, I guess I would have to say *yes* to that."

"And is it anyone we know?"

"It is not even anyone I know," he answered, laughing a little as he said it.

"What do you mean by that?"

"It is a woman from my dreams—perhaps I should say from all of our dreams. *Love Rising* is about all the things we ever really hoped for. You know—real things—peace, happiness, love. Isn't that what any of us really want?"

Jack smiled. "Yes, the woman of our dreams," he said to himself. "Hopefully she is not far away."

16

Mona was wrapped in only a white sheet with her head resting on Elijah's bare stomach. She stared up the slope of his chest and into his handsome face. "We were supposed to be meeting to talk," she said.

Elijah reached down and ran his fingers through her hair. "This is talking," he smiled. "It's just a different kind of talking."

Mona laughed. "Stop making it seem so simple. It's not simple."

"Nothing in this world is simple, but some things are just meant to be enjoyed and not over-analyzed."

Mona sat up and looked directly at Elijah. "I just want you to know that this…this is not the kind of thing I usually do. I don't…I've never had a work-related relationship before—if you can even call this a relationship."

"So, if it's not a relationship then what is it?"

"I don't know—perhaps just a moment of ridiculous uncontrolled passion."

"Then that would be two extremely long moments of ridiculous uncontrolled passion."

Mona sat back against the pillow and looked at the opposite wall. "Alright then, it's *two* moments of ridiculous uncontrolled passion."

Elijah ran his hand down her arm. "Looong moments," he added.

Mona sighed. If he wasn't going to be sensible, she would be the one who would have to get things back on track. "Your career is on fire, Elijah. The last thing you need is someone like me. You're a hit again. You need to find someone that could be part of that lifestyle—someone more like—like you."

Elijah folded his arms on his chest. "Are you trying to get rid of me?"

"No," Mona answered. "Of course not, it's just that how can this really go anywhere? You're a rock star and let's face facts, you'll get tired of me. This is just a…a *thing*. It's an easy *thing* to have happened with us working so closely together. But it's just a *thing*."

Elijah was hurt by what she had just said. What did she think he was? "So, perhaps I should date what exactly? And don't even try and answer that question as though I'm some sort of child. I know what you mean. You think I should get a young Bloodline bimbo—perhaps one who's had some plastic surgery early in life to make her look more symmetrical. A girl who has been prepped and primed for Bloodline breeding. And the paparazzi would adore us—and follow us everywhere. And when and if we eventually produce a spawn, we'd dress it in the latest fashion and parade it through the most exclusive shops, so that they'd take our pictures. Is that what you think of me? Is that what you think I want?"

Mona immediately felt bad. She put her hand on his folded arms. "I'm sorry I said what I did. I….maybe it's more about me and my own insecurities. I'm not a young woman anymore and you're a superstar. Maybe I'm afraid of the risks—of being hurt—of losing you."

Elijah unfolded his arms and pulled her closer to him. "I'm not a young man anymore, and I'm very happy about that. And before you say that it's different for men, I know that society's rules are very different. But I'm not the kind to be bound by any rules. I refuse to be. And I'm strong enough not to need a certain kind of woman to placate my ego. I want a real woman, not a fashion accessory to impress the other boys. When we first met, I knew that there was something there, but I wasn't sure what it was. As I got to know you better, I got to see the real you, and that's when I began to realize why I felt so drawn to you. You are a superstar, Mona. Maybe not in this world with all its faults and follies, but in another world—the real world I see whenever I look into your eyes. That's why I could never resist you even if I tried. And that's why I want you and only you."

Mona wanted to argue with him. She wanted to say that it was all too much, and that she would be catching the next plane to Paris. She wanted to say that she would be staying in France and never coming back. She wanted to simply stand up and walk out forever. Instead, she remained right where she was, leaned into his body and pressed her lips tightly to his.

* * *

Minton was lying back in his chair with his feet up on the desk. He was passing the time reading a Hollywood entertainment magazine. The latest celebrity scandals and outrageous rumors were making him burst out into fits of laughter. He loved this stuff.

Mr. Todd, who heard Minton's annoying laughter before he even opened the door, was now coming down the basement steps. "What are you doing?" he asked sternly. Lately, he had begun to really worry about Minton becoming too smug. Once they lose all fearful respect, such men are both no longer useful and a liability. At that point, steps would have to be taken.

"Oh, I'm just waiting for my fiancé to show up," said Minton chuckling. This increasingly jovial attitude was getting on Todd's nerves.

"I need you to keep that fish dangling a little longer," said Todd. "I've come up with a plan that will more than satisfy our client. The Treble Clef Music Awards is next month. It's televised internationally so our client will be able to tune in. Millions of people all over the world will be watching and Jack is guaranteed to be there. I read this morning that one of their biggest organizers, Dick Hinken, died yesterday. This could really be to our advantage. If things are a little more chaotic than usual, it should make getting the weevil inside that much easier."

Minton put down the magazine and sat straight up in the chair. "Old Dick Hinken finally bit the dust? I didn't even know he was sick. So, I guess those rumors about him being a zombie weren't true after all," he laughed.

"This is huge, Minton. Are you certain the weevil can handle it?"

"No prob! This makes for an even better play. He's already chomping at the bit. A little more time will aggravate him even more. I'll just say that my dear old daddy sprained his ankle and his European trip has been postponed by a few weeks. This'll make weevil-boy even crazier for the lovely Britney—crazy enough to kill real good."

"Okay. Just be sure to keep him under strict control. We don't need him going off half-cocked."

"I know how to play 'em Mr. Todd. He'll be primed and ready when the time comes."

120

Todd was relieved that Minton was still calling him *mister*. He did not really want to lose such a useful rat-catcher, and getting rid of him would not be any easier than replacing him. He turned to go and started up the basement stairs. Before he had even reached the second step, Minton called out, "Wait, I just want your opinion before you leave."

Thinking it must be something important, Todd looked back at Minton who smiled and said, "I'm trying to pick out a dress. Which one do you like? I'm partial to the cute strapless number."

Todd could see on the computer screen was a wedding dress catalogue page. Minton burst out laughing. "Gotcha!" he exclaimed.

Son of a bitch! Todd then turned and headed up the basement stairs.

* * *

With umbrella firmly in hand, Jack stood in the pouring rain. He didn't really want to attend Hinken's funeral, but he had no good excuse to miss it. It would look bad if he didn't show.

He had been sitting in his office and reviewing the DVD of Elijah's Radio City performance, when the call came in. It was from an old friend of his—a singer who was still under contract with Hinken's company. "Hinken's dead," he said simply. "His heart gave out while he was on the toilet. That's where his wife found him."

At first, Jack couldn't believe it. Hinken was one of those larger-than-life guys who seemed like he would go on cheating death forever. Guys like that just don't suddenly drop—and on the toilet of all places. Until he saw the report on television, it didn't seem real. The report never mentioned how Hinken was found.

Jack stood in the large circle of people as they all watched the black steel coffin lowered slowly into the grave. The group made for an eerily somber sight with everyone dressed in black and carrying big black umbrellas. It reminded Jack of those strange old 1960's horror films he once loved to indulge in.

The only person not dressed in dark clothing was the bishop, who stood front and center in his gold and white mitre and robes. A long lanky man in a black suit held the umbrella high over his head. Jack imagined what it would be like if the umbrella slipped and knocked the mitre off of the bishop's head. Could the pretend mourners stop themselves from laughing out loud?

121

He looked down at the bishop's feet and could see that the mud from the grave had soaked up into the white robe, staining it a foul brown. Would it ever be possible to make it clean again? Even in death, Hinken left his blot behind.

"Ashes to ashes, dust to dust..."

Jack did not want to listen anymore. This line always made him think of Stuart's memorial service. He hated to hear it. It made him imagine the explosion—the fire. Those words had the power to make him cry all over again. The last thing he wanted was to be seen crying at Hinken's funeral.

"Well Jack, they are finally burying the old dog. I was beginning to think that the crazies were right and he really was a zombie."

Jack had not noticed Benton Billington standing beside him before. Next to Hinken, Benton was the biggest music producer in the industry, and a well-respected person of the Bloodline. He was also known to Jack as a fringe member of the Underground.

"The Underground will be relieved," said Jack.

Billington would have laughed out loud, but he was at a funeral so he discreetly chuckled instead. "The Underground?" he said. "What Underground? Don't tell me you still believe in that stuff, Jack? The real Underground was pretty much axed to death in 1980. Today the Underground is in deep mourning. They lost their meal ticket. The truth is that they have been well in with Hinken for years. There's no God anymore, Jack—no God but mammon. Sure, there are a few little guys at the bottom fighting the good fight, but they don't realize that the ones at the top are lying to them—manipulating them. I'm surprised you haven't figured it out by now, but I suppose that being outside the Bloodline, in some ways you're just a pawn like any other."

Jack did not say anything. For years he suspected, but he just did not want to believe it. He still wanted to believe there were good people at the top fighting for good things. Now that Billington was coming out and saying it to his face, there could be no more denial. It was true. The only real Underground was in the past—kept alive only in his heart. Jack felt the cold dampness creeping under his clothing and reaching his skin. The Underground was a sham and he was alone.

"Do you know what they are saying?" Billington asked.

"No," said Jack. "What are they saying?"

Billington started chuckling again. "They are saying that you killed him," he said. "Little old Jack the giant killer."

Now Jack stood in stunned silence. *What was he talking about?*

"That's right," said Billington. "They are saying that you killed him by raising Elijah from the dead. Somehow by doing that, it made things in the universe align and WHAM—down goes the king pin. Like we used to say in the old days, isn't that a gas! Doesn't it make you laugh, Jack? There you are—the little guy who made it big—the odd man out—the one they tried time and time again to rein in and keep down, and now they are terrified. You're scaring the hell out of all of these superstitious Bloodline buggers!"

Jack looked at the coffin that was now deep in the dark hole. The rain had drenched and flattened the red, white, and blue flowers on its top. Suddenly from above was a blinding flash of light and then *BOOM*! Lightning hit close by! The bishop quickly instructed everyone to run for shelter.

* * *

The clock said 7:17 as Jack sat in his living room waiting for Elijah and Mona to arrive. Carefully pouring his beer into a glass, he couldn't help wishing that he had not taken out the keg system years ago. But unfortunately, after only three months of having the unit put in, he found he had gone up two pant sizes, and so had it promptly removed. However, tonight of all nights, he could really go for a freshly pulled pint.

Spending the entire afternoon at Hinken's wake had exhausted him. Although he had wanted to go straight home after the funeral, Benton Billington was insistent that he attend, and Jack knew that it would look bad if he didn't go along. As a result, he was forced to listen to seemingly endless tedious talk, including Billington's non-stop bragging about a twenty-three-year-old mistress he kept in Manhattan. The entire thing was very tiresome.

After he had arrived home, he phoned Mona right away to ask her to come over and sit with him. When she explained that she was with Elijah, he invited them both to come. Jack desperately needed his true friends around him. Learning the truth about the Underground had left him feeling like his entire world had been turned upside down. What had he been fighting for all those years? Had all his hard work been simply in vain?

Jack took a long sip of beer and leaned back in his chair. Just then, the room echoed with the beginning notes of *Für Elise*. He did not bother getting up to answer the door, knowing that Mona would let herself in. Sure enough, it was not long before both she and Elijah appeared in the great room doorway.

"Entrez-vous," said Jack. "Come in and sit down."

Mona quickly came over and sat on the settee opposite Jack. She suspected the funeral might have taken a toll on him. "Are you okay?" she asked him in concern.

"Now that you're here, I feel a good deal better," answered Jack, setting his beer on the coffee table.

Elijah said nothing but began to walk slowly around the room looking at the various works of art hanging on the walls. He stopped in front of the painting Stuart had given to Jack those many years ago.

"It's different, wouldn't you say," said Jack. He then turned to Mona and asked, "Would you like some wine? I have a lovely merlot I think you would enjoy." The open bottle and glass were already on the table. Jack began pouring the glass before she even answered.

"That sounds good, thanks," Mona said.

Elijah was still looking at the painting. "I don't think I've ever seen this before," he said. "But for some reason it looks familiar. Is it a copy of one in a museum or gallery?"

"No," replied Jack. "That is an original and the only one in the world. It was a gift from someone special."

"I like it," said Elijah. "I don't know why, but I like it."

"Would you like something to drink, Elijah? I have tea or water?"

"Yes. A glass of water would be fine, thank you." Elijah then looked at a framed tapestry that hung next to the painting. "I know this one," he said.

"Is that so?" said Jack, as he poured a glass of water from the pitcher that was on the table. "I had that one specially crafted."

Elijah marveled at the fine workmanship. "This is a copy of *Unicorn in Captivity*, except I see that your unicorn is not. In your copy, the fence isn't there and neither is there a collar around its neck. That's interesting."

Jack smiled and pushed back his glasses. "You're one of the first people to notice. I had it made that way. You see, Stuart always hated to see restraints on unicorns. He never liked the British Coat of Arms for that very reason." Jack suddenly realized that Elijah would not know who he was talking about so he explained, "Stuart was my dearest friend. He's been gone a long time now."

"The photo on your office desk—is that Stuart?" Elijah asked.

"Yes. I have another picture of him here." Jack picked up a framed photo from the table beside him and offered it to Elijah.

Elijah walked over and took it in hand. He looked at the smiling handsome young man in the picture. "I think I would have liked him. He has a kind face."

"I loved him, and still do," said Jack, surprising himself by this bold confession in front of someone other than Mona.

Elijah looked at Jack and smiled. He handed back the picture and then sat down on the settee next to Mona. Picking up the glass of water, he took a small sip.

Jack placed the picture back on the side table and then stared at his friends for a moment. *They look right together*, he thought. *Just like Stuart and me.*

Mona was not sure if she wanted the wine, but to be polite she picked up the glass and took a drink. Realizing what an exceptional vintage Jack had poured, she took another longer drink, holding it in her mouth a few seconds before swallowing. "Very nice!" she said.

"I knew you'd like it."

Mona then set the glass back down on the table. "When you called me, it sounded like you were feeling more than a little upset. Are you sure you're okay, Jack? I know that going to the funeral today would have brought back memories."

Jack picked up his glass and had another drink of beer before he replied, "It wasn't pleasant, but I got through it well enough. What was more upsetting was the news I received from Benton Billington."

Mona knew Billington very well and didn't like him one bit. If he had news to deliver, one could bet that it would never be good.

"What did he say?" she asked.

Jack looked over at Elijah and said, "Before I explain I should first ask Elijah if you have ever heard of the Bloodline Underground?"

"I've heard rumors here and there, but I wasn't sure how much of it was true," he answered.

"Well apparently, none of it is true," said Jack bluntly.

Mona was shocked. "What do you mean, Jack?"

"Oh Mona," he said, "it may have been true once, but I discovered today that it's now all just a sham. The Bloodline is the Bloodline and there are no rebels—no Underground—not anymore. The Underground was more or less absorbed years ago."

She could see how hurt Jack was. "I'm so sorry," she said. Mona never really trusted those people anyway and had wondered a long time about whether or not they were being honest. She had never confessed her feelings to Jack and figured it would be like salt in the wound to mention it now.

"To be honest, for a very long time I suspected the truth," said Jack. He took a long swig of his beer and then set it back down on the table. "But I suppose I just couldn't bring myself to admit it. I couldn't—for Stuart's sake. I wanted to believe for Stuart."

"So, you were a part of this Underground?" asked Elijah.

"Yes. Stuart and I were both a part of the Underground—when there still was one, that is. I feel like such a fool—being strung along for so many years—putting money into their lies. Who knows how this money was really being used."

Elijah understood just how Jack was feeling. His own experience, in many ways, had been similar. He too had been used and misled. Staring into his glass and swirling the water around, he said, "Jack, years ago when I started to see things more clearly, and began to realize how I was making music I didn't really want to make, I felt something like you do now. For a while, I couldn't help but feel shame and anger, and it really did a number on me. Finally, I had my epiphany and stopped blaming myself for being human. I was idealistic, like you, and wanted to believe in other people so badly that I was willing to let them take advantage of me. I simply didn't want to believe the truth. Don't blame yourself for being human and wanting to believe in the humanity of others. The blame belongs in other places."

Jack sighed, "So the fault lies not within ourselves, but in our stars."

Elijah laughed at how Jack had turned Shakespeare's words upside down. "Maybe sometimes that is very true. What I do know Jack, is that you have to believe in the bigger picture. So what if the Underground was put to an end by other people? It didn't end with you. In some way, didn't you keep it going? No matter how they deceived you and played you, you were still the Underground. And if you think that one man doesn't matter then think again. The greatest changes in the world have come about by the power of one. And now, you have Mona and you have me. Why can't we be the new Underground? What do you think? Shall we be the Underground II?"

Jack laughed. "Well since there are only three of us to start this new Underground, it would be much better if we were some sort of super humans."

"Aren't we that already?" Mona asked with a smile. "After all, we raised a man from the dead, didn't we?"

"Yes! Just look at how alive I am," Elijah said, jumping up, throwing his hands in the air, and then sitting back down.

"See Jack," said Mona. "This new Underground is more powerful than any other that went before. We can do anything!"

Jack looked at them both. There was a strange and potent hope in their humor. It felt as real as the hope he remembered Stuart having after he came back from America—the kind of hope that changes things. "Why not!" exclaimed Jack. "After all, we have nothing left to lose. Let's do it!" He then raised his beer as a toast. "To the new Underground!" he declared.

Mona and Elijah raised their glasses in kind.

"By the ever-under-estimated power of *the milk of human kindness*," said Jack, "we pledge to fight for the poor in spirit, for those who mourn, for the meek, for the persecuted and for those who hunger and thirst after righteousness."

"Hear, hear," added Elijah.

"To the Three Unstoppables!" declared Jack.

"Don't forget Stuart," said Mona.

Jack smiled and picked up the photograph. "No," he said, "We won't forget Stuart."

He then lifted his glass a little higher. "To the new Underground and the Four Unstoppables! All for one and one for all!"

Mona and Elijah both raised their glasses and then all three clinked them together. "To the new Underground and the Four Unstoppables!" they avowed in unison.

17

Lifting the bubbling eggs from the frying pan, Elijah carefully placed them on the plates alongside the crisp bacon and buttery toast. "Tomorrow, I go back on my rock star diet," he said. "But for today, we shall eat to our hearts' content." He set the spatula on the counter, and carried the plates over to the table, setting one down in front of Mona.

"Thanks," she said with a smile. "It looks delicious." It had been a long time since any man had cooked breakfast for her, and she had almost forgotten just how satisfying it could be.

"So how will we begin?" Elijah asked, as he sat down and picked up his fork.

"Call me traditional, but I like to start by dipping my toast in the yolk," Mona replied to his odd question.

Elijah laughed. "I'm talking about the New Underground. How should we begin?"

"I thought we were all just kidding around," said Mona. "You really want to start a new Underground?"

"If not us, then who?"

Mona looked at Elijah. She could see he was serious about this. It made her begin to worry. "Elijah, is that a good idea? The Bloodline is so powerful. You know what they can do."

"I know they think they are powerful."

Mona took a sip of orange juice. "We could lose everything. You could lose your new career. Is that what you want?"

"What I want is to set this world back on its axis, but I'll settle for any small victory. Mona, stop thinking about what we could lose and start thinking about what we could win."

Elijah got up from his chair and went over to the window. He looked up at the clear sky. "You see how the sun shines," he said. "There isn't even a single cloud up there. And you can actually see the moon glowing in that bright blue sky. The moon is wide awake with the sun. Does the Bloodline command the sun and the moon? This is a

128

new day, Mona. We have to seize it. I feel deep within me that this is the right thing to do. Just tell me everything you know and we can move on from there. I'm sure there are secrets that you haven't told me, and it's time I knew *everything*."

Mona didn't want to tell him what she knew. He seemed so passionate about this new Underground that knowing everything could put him in real danger. She didn't want that. She wanted only that he'd always be there for her. Was it selfish to not want to risk losing him?

When she remained silent, Elijah realized that he would have to persuade her. "Mona," he said, "this could be the most important thing we will ever do in our lives. Just stop and think about it a moment. I mean, does it even feel possible to turn back now? You must feel like me—like we have to move forward no matter what. Please tell me what you know!"

Mona stared at her plate. Over the years, she had done so much self-analysis that she knew her own weaknesses. She understood how she desperately held onto things in fear that they would disappear, and she knew it was this fear that was holding her back now. If she told Elijah the truth, wouldn't it change everything? Would he somehow just disappear forever, and she would be alone once again?

She looked up and across the table at Elijah's pleading eyes. In the bright morning sun, they sparkled like tiny lights. *What was that British word Jack used for decorative lights? Oh yes, he called them fairy-lights.* The first time she heard him use this word, she thought how beautiful and magical it was. Elijah's eyes were like that—wonderful entrancing fairy-lights—fairy-lights that seemed to be drawing her towards a new and mysterious world. Surprising herself, she suddenly blurted out, "There's a girl!"

"A girl?"

Mona knew she should consult Jack before going any further, but it was such a relief to finally say it out loud and share it with Elijah that she couldn't possibly hold back any longer. "Of course, she would be a woman now. There's a girl they sometimes call the Golden Grail."

"Why do they call her that?"

Running her finger along the edge of the table, Mona explained, "She has the proportions of the golden mean, but she also has the mark of the Holy Grail."

Elijah was confused, "What do you mean by the mark of the Holy Grail. Doesn't the Holy Grail simply refer to the Bloodline? Is there more to it?"

Mona was not surprised that Elijah did not know the whole truth. Jack had explained to her that only a select few were privy to the secret. The rest were given bits and pieces of information and sometimes even misleading lies. It was all about keeping power at the top. "It's in the skull," she said. "There is a small, indented area like a bowl in the crown of the skull."

Elijah was silent as he thought about what she had just told him. He sat back down in his chair. "Well, that could explain a lot of things—the Western Asian obsession for covering the head—the idea that spawned phrenology—the yarmulke, just to think of a few."

"I'd never really considered all that," said Mona. "But I suppose it fits."

"So, what exactly does this woman do?"

"As far as I know, nothing so far. She has to be awakened. They think it will happen with music. That's why so much of their focus is in the music industry."

"And do you believe in this woman?"

"Yes," answered Mona without any hesitation. "I believe in her because Jack does. And although Jack has never seen her, Stuart did. When he was still alive, Stuart found her."

"Where is she now?"

"I don't know," replied Mona. "Only a few elite ones in the Bloodline have this information."

"How do they expect the music to awaken her?"

"I'm not sure exactly and perhaps they aren't either. It's partly based on the story of the Baptism of Jesus. You know…when Jesus comes to John the Baptist and the Holy Spirit descends from Heaven. Something within the energy of John and Jesus coming together caused this—this thing to happen. They say that it can happen again with this woman."

Once more Elijah was silent while he thought about all she had told him. Of course, this had to be related to the woman in his dreams. It must be the same woman. It made sense.

"When I told you about my dreams, did you think that they were possibly connected to this woman?" he asked her outright.

Mona felt both guilty and worried. Would he be angry to know that she held back this truth? Would he walk out? Could she blame him? "Yes," she replied. "I'm sorry. I should have told you before. It's just that I still thought there was an Underground, and I was under strict instructions that the secret had to be kept for the greater good. I'm really sorry, Elijah. I should have listened to my heart earlier."

Elijah reached over and grabbed her hand. "It's okay. I don't blame you. It's not always easy to know what's right, especially in a world where there is so much lying and scheming. Just please, don't hide things from me anymore. We have to be honest with each other. Do you know if they've tried to awaken her?"

"Yes and no." Mona tried to think how to explain something that she was not so sure of herself. "They put out music to call her, but they keep a distance. No one makes contact."

Elijah leaned back in his chair and said, "I knew that they made music that was intended to change the cosmos in their favor, but I didn't think it was aimed at a specific person."

"Some of it is and some of it isn't. It depends on the specific belief systems of the producers at any given time and, of course, where they think the money is. I suppose for many of them God and money are now just one and the same."

Elijah tapped his fork on his plate in tiny perfect rhythm while he thought for a moment about everything he had just been told. Suddenly, he set the fork down and looked straight at Mona. "But if the Underground no longer exists, who is there to make the right choices—choices that will open the way for this woman?" he asked.

"That's a good question," replied Mona. "We should talk to Jack about that."

"Oh, I intend to," said Elijah.

* * *

Britney:
Good news. 13 days and they r going. Yippee!

AlienKiller666:
Your parents?

Britney:
Yah! Soon we will be together luver!

131

AlienKiller666:
I want you so bad!

Britney:
Good things come to those who wait. Don't u think I'm a good thing?

AlienKiller666:
You're more than a good thing.

Britney:
Bet u say that to all the girls.

AlienKiller666:
You are the only girl in the world for me. I knew one day the perfect
girl would come along and you are it!

Britney:
Ur so romantic! That's what I luv about u.

AlienKiller666:
I luv you too.

Britney:
No I luv u more.

AlienKiller666:
No I luv you more.

Britney:
Oh stop!

AlienKiller666:
Uh-oh some guy is at the door. I'm doing a little gun trading today.

Britney:
Stop trying to turn me on.

AlienKiller666:
I'll be back on-line tonight.

Britney:
I'm out tonight. Have to help Mommy shop for Europe. Be back tomorrow.

AlienKiller666:
Until tomorrow then.

Britney:
Tomorrow and tomorrow and tomorrow…

18

Jack sat in his living room, leaning his elbow into the soft upholstered arm of the chair. He adjusted his glasses, and looked over at Elijah and Mona, who sat side by side on the settee across from him. They had phoned him earlier saying they wanted to talk about something—something very urgent.

"Thanks for seeing us," said Elijah. "We need to discuss the New Underground."

Jack was surprised that Elijah was being so straight forward. "So, you were not just joking," he said. All night he had been thinking about their humorous pledges to be the new Super Underground, but he did not dare get his hopes up.

"It was no joke," replied Elijah. "This is very important to me, Jack. I'm taking it as a serious commitment."

"Alright then," said Jack. "Tell me what you are thinking?"

"Let me begin by saying that Mona explained to me about the woman."

"The woman?" questioned Jack.

"The girl," explained Mona. "The one Stuart found."

"Oh," said Jack pensively.

Mona now wondered if Jack would be angry with her for telling Elijah the secret without checking with him first. He had never been angry with her before about anything. She looked him in the eye and said, "With the Underground now finished, I didn't think it would be a problem. And I believe that Elijah has the right to know. After all, he's in it as much as we are."

"No—no of course not," Jack reassured her. "It's no problem. You can tell Elijah anything. After all, we are the New Underground, are we not?"

Mona smiled in relief. It was good to know that Jack thought as highly of Elijah as she did.

"I've been thinking about what to do next," said Elijah. "Now, this may sound strange, but I've had…dreams."

"I know," responded Jack. "Mona told me about them. It was one of the reasons I knew that I had done the right thing by signing you."

Elijah looked straight into Jack's eyes and said, "I want to find her. I want to talk to her."

At first, Jack did not know what to say. He understood what the rule had been from the beginning. But did this rule still apply now that everything had changed? After all, this was a new day—a new Underground.

"I don't know where she is," Jack answered.

"We can find her," exclaimed Elijah. "I know we can!"

Jack sighed. Which course was the right course? Would he be making a horrible mistake to violate the rule he had adhered to all these years? Needing to be certain that Elijah fully understood the risk, he explained, "They say that if someone interferes with her, it could cause a cosmic catastrophe. It is my understanding that they partially base it on the Bridegroom's words from the Song of Songs: *Do not rouse her, do not disturb my love until she is ready*. Given what I know, I'm unsure if finding her would be the right thing to do."

Elijah looked at the floor and thought silently for a moment. He then looked back up at Jack. "Years ago, I became involved in this group that practiced the worship of Mary Magdalene," he said. "I joined because I wanted to know more about her—who she was, what she stood for. But I found it disappointing. All their talk about the Sacred Feminine and the group prayer sessions just left me feeling unsatisfied. I wanted to know about the woman, not to indulge in religious rituals and belief systems. One day I realized that all I needed to know was in the stories that survived. And it was there that I found her true beauty. And when I looked around me, I saw her everywhere. You see Jack; her beauty is in everything—accessible to everyone."

When Jack just looked curiously at him, Elijah realized that he needed to explain things more clearly if he was to be fully understood. The problem was how to put something so elusive into words. He'd have to try his best.

"When I looked closely at the Bible stories," he continued, "I could see the society as it was—a society where the most vulnerable could be chased down and stoned to death by an angry mob—where a woman had no rights and at any point her husband could utter the word *divorce* sending her alone into the street and forever dividing her from children—where parents of the blind, sick, and lame were considered sinners responsible for their children's suffering. It was a horrible world, and yet out of it came this remarkable Man. I tried to imagine what it would have been like for Jesus to have to wander through such a world and look day after day upon this horror. It must have hurt. How could it not?"

Jack nodded. He had considered this before, but never really discussed it with anyone. It was somehow comforting to know someone shared the same thought.

"And don't you see Jack!" Elijah exclaimed. "That's the thing about Mary Magdalene. She saw an extraordinary Man, who had to walk day after day through this awful world where people constantly questioned, laughed at, and even laid traps for Him. When they surrounded Him, only wanting to try and chip off a piece of Divinity for their own, she was the one who cared about who He was in His entirety. She never denied Him His humanity.

"When the others took whatever He could give and then demanded more, she reached out to try and give back. It was never about the scented oil. That was simply a symbol. It was about giving and loving Him as best she could with what she had. When the rest wanted Him to amaze them with tricks—to be their circus clown, she was the only one who could see that sometimes He tired of trying to get His crucial message across. She was the only one who seemed to try to imagine how alone He was in a world that wasn't His world at all."

"What exactly are you saying?" asked Jack, leaning back into his chair.

"I'm saying that Mary Magdalene is the one we should be emulating—the one who refused to just take from Him—the one who was ready to give no matter what. And I think she would want us to find this woman—if anything, just to let her know that she is not alone."

Elijah stopped and took in a deep breath. He knew he needed Jack's help and was feeling desperate. He needed Jack to understand what he was seeing. The entire thing was so complicated and difficult to explain, that it made him wonder if his explanation was making any sense at all. What more could he say to make Jack understand?

Shifting forward on the settee, Elijah moved slightly closer to Jack. "In all these years has anyone ever worried about this woman even once?" he asked, "I mean, what exactly do those Bloodline people do—the ones who know about her? Do they spy on her? Do they cast lots among themselves for her DNA? What if the rule of distance is now only for their personal convenience? What if they even do things to ensure that she stays down—stays quiet? When you think about it, wouldn't the last thing they want be a new Messiah? A new Messiah could seriously dry up their cash flow."

Jack looked at Mona who looked back at him. It was clear from the expression on her face that she was on Elijah's side. He saw her reach over and take Elijah's hand in support.

Elijah continued to stare passionately at Jack. He had to get through to him. He had to make Jack hear him. "Tell me, what good reason do you have to believe the arguments of these Bloodline people—people who think that God is so pathetic, weak, and useless that some ordinary guy need only break one rule and the universe will shatter? You have true faith, Jack. I know this from the kind of person you are. And you know in your heart that what I'm saying is true. Perhaps there was a time when the rule applied, but not any longer. Times are different. Everything is different."

Jack looked in silence at Elijah. All these years, why did he never think of it? Of course they would not want a Messiah. Why would they? What use was a Messiah in their world? This was a long way from 1969. Everything was different, so why would the rules stay the same? Stuart believed in Elijah, and he should too. Perhaps it was time for a *brave new world*.

Without a word, Jack got up and walked over to the expansive bookshelf that graced the single windowless wall of the living room. He removed a large thick book and returned to the chair. Mona and Elijah looked at the old book he held in his lap. The faded jacket read, *Classic Fairy Tales for Children*.

"No one knows I have this information," Jack said. "When they asked me if I had read the pages or made copies, I lied and told them *no*. At the time, I wasn't sure if it was the right thing to do, but I did it anyway. After Stuart had given his life for what is written here, I knew I had to hold on to this information. I couldn't just trust it all to strangers."

Jack opened the front cover revealing that the book had been hollowed out. Inside were a number of papers folded together. He removed and carefully unfolded them. Elijah and Mona could see old type-written words on the yellowed sheets. "This is the genealogy that they wanted to keep hidden," said Jack. "It's her family history." He handed the papers to Elijah.

Elijah took them in hand. He looked at the first name on the page. It was a woman listed as born in Scotland. Her death was recorded in Nova Scotia. Then Elijah looked at the date of her arrival to America. The date was 1399!

"Go to the final page," said Jack.

Elijah quickly flipped to the last page. At the bottom was a first and last name. Beside it, etched in pen was an address in Canada.

"I copied out the genealogy before handing it over. Later on, I happened to be in a rather highbrow meeting and overheard someone mention the address so I scribbled it down. I don't know where she is now, but hopefully that information is enough for you to find her."

Elijah looked up and smiled happily at Jack. He then turned and kissed Mona on the cheek. "Rose," he said, showing her the paper. "Her name is Rose."

"Thank you so much, Jack," said Mona. "I know this is the right thing to do, and we won't let you down."

"I hope it's the right thing to do," said Jack, knowing that there was no turning back now.

Elijah stared at the papers and sighed. He then looked up at Jack and asked, "Why did you sign me when no one else would?"

At first, Jack was surprised by the question, then without hesitation he found himself answering truthfully. "Stuart told me to do it." Realizing that he had just shared his most treasured secret, Jack went silent. Should he say more? It sounded so mad to say it out loud to someone other than Mona.

"And would Stuart ever deceive you?" asked Elijah.

Jack was surprised again. Elijah was simply accepting without question the fact that he received messages from his dead lover. "No," he replied. "Stuart would never deceive me. He has always told me the correct way to go. Einhorn is Einhorn because of him."

Elijah smiled. "Then believe in him and believe in me. In your heart, you know this is the right decision. Just don't worry anymore about the rules and regulations of the world. Take a leap of faith Jack, and just jump."

Jack looked up at the painting on the wall as he remembered something Stuart had said to him on their last night together. He told him that whatever was to happen always take to heart the first line in the Book of Psalms: *Happy is the man who does not take the wicked for his guide*. He added that although it sounded simple, there was nothing at all simple or easy about it. It required a lifetime of work.

How many times had Jack dined and danced with the wicked, always thinking he had everything under control? Now he worried that perhaps unwittingly he had also sometimes allowed them to guide him. They made him doubt himself many times and now they were making him doubt Elijah. At that moment, Jack knew what he had to do. No more doubts. No more blind following of the wicked. It was time for him to stand up and reclaim himself.

"Whatever you need to find her, just ask," he said to Elijah. "Whether it's money or any other sort of resources, I will support you all of the way."

19

Minton quickly closed the computer window when he heard the sound of Mr. Todd's key in the lock. He did not want his boss to discover the kind of porn he was into. It's not that he felt shame. Minton had never felt shame in his life. It was just best not to give anyone with power too much information about your weaknesses. He pretended to stare in wait at his desktop background—a giant mosquito impaling the skin of someone's flesh.

"Is our weevil fully primed?" asked Todd, as his boots thudded against the old wooden stairs. There was a sense of urgency in his voice.

Minton swiveled his chair around to face Todd. "As primed as they get," he answered.

"Good." Todd approached the computer and looked at the screen.

"I'm just waiting for him to show," Minton explained. "He's a little late, but he should be here soon."

"There've been no problems with him—no signs of the hook in his mouth starting to loosen?"

"Oh, he is well hooked." Minton grinned and ran his fingers gently over the keyboard.

"I've made the special arrangements," said Todd. "He'll be able to gain access backstage at the Treble Clef Music Awards next Sunday. You'll be sure he's there and on time. It's the gray metal door on the south side of the building near the loading dock. I'll email a photo later today so that you can give him as many specific details as possible. This is much more complicated than anything we've done before. There's no way to add a back-up gunman, so we need him to be completely prepared. There can be no slip-ups."

"Understood," said Minton with a grin and a salute.

Todd didn't like this at all. He took the salute very seriously and was not impressed when non-military people made light of it. But instead of voicing his objections, he simply turned and left. It was important not to give Minton any hints about what had been on his mind lately. He was already working on finding a suitable replacement and had been considering a plan to get rid of him completely. It would, of course, be complicated. Minton was from a family of upper-class professionals who would be looking for answers when their darling boy went missing. Disposing of expensive garbage was never easy; however, there would be more time to tackle this problem after the job was complete.

* * *

"It's such a beautiful full moon," said Mona, as she lay curled up beside Elijah on her terrace lounger. The bright city lights had dulled many of the stars, but the moon was unstoppable.

"It is unbelievably bright tonight," said Elijah, stroking the nape of her neck.

Mona took in a deep breath of sweet summer night air. "I'll go tomorrow," she said. "You have a full schedule all next week and it's just not possible for you to take the time. Tomorrow, I'll fly to Canada and check out that address."

"Are you sure? If you would like to wait, then we'll go together."

Mona slipped her hand inside the warmth of his shirt. She could feel his heart pulsing against her palm. "There's no way either of us can wait that long. I'll be fine. I've been all over the world and have dealt with all sorts of people. This is no different. I'm just hoping that she is still there or someone is there who knows where she is. It was so many years ago when Jack wrote down that address. She would still have been only a child at the time."

"Do you know what you will say to her?"

"No," Mona answered laughingly. "Maybe there's not even any point in trying to think of something to say. If she is who Jack says she is, then shouldn't the words just happen naturally—like magic?"

Elijah laughed. "All my life people accused me of being spacey. It's good to have someone who can talk just as spacey as I do."

"Just two space cadets ready to launch. Well, there's the moon. Shall we go there?"

141

Squeezing her tighter, Elijah replied, "Is there any other destination?"

Mona kissed his neck. "When it beckons like that," she said pointing into the sky, "there could be no other place in this universe." Wrapping her arm tightly around him, she breathed, "Sing me a song to go with this beautiful night."

Elijah thought for a moment and then said," I have an idea for a song about you. Would you like to hear it?"

Mona sat up and looked into his face. "Of course I want to hear it!"

Gazing into her eyes, and running his fingers through her hair, Elijah began to sing:

My mistress' eyes are nothing like the sun
The sun is but a fleeting, fading star
Whereas her eyes are so much more
O' deep blue pools of infinitude
Give me to drink!
Give me to drink that I might taste
The untold pleasures of your Eternity.

By the end of the song, Mona was in tears.

* * *

Jack was sitting on a wooden crate outside of his mother's back door. The sun was shining and there was a little bird perched on the back gate. It felt good to be home again. He had missed it during all those years in America.

Jack's mother suddenly appeared in the doorway with a glass of milk and a plate of her special sandwiches. "I was thinking you might be hungry," she said, as she set the plate and glass down on the little old table nearby. Jack looked at her smiling face. It was so wonderful to see that face again after all this time. "Well, go on then," she said happily. "Try one."

Reaching over, Jack grabbed one of the sandwiches. He put it to his mouth and took a large bite. It had been so long since he had tasted food prepared by his mother that he had almost forgotten how delicious it was. "You make the best sarnies in the world, Mum!" he exclaimed.

His mother gently laughed. "Oh, Jack love, it's only a sarnie."

Jack could feel the warm sun on his face. He looked over again at the gate that led out to the back alleyway. There were now four little birds perched in a row. He silently pointed them out to his mother.

"Yes love, I see them," she said, softly smiling. "And they're gorgeous! You can show Stuart when he gets here."

Jack almost couldn't believe what he had just heard. "You mean Stuart is coming?" he asked excitedly.

"Oh, he just telephoned. He said he'll be here soon."

Jack was beginning to feel overwhelmed with emotion. *Stuart had finally phoned! He said that he would be coming! At last, to see him again! But when would he arrive? Please God, let it be soon!* Jack turned to ask his mother if Stuart had mentioned what time he would arrive, but she had already disappeared inside the house. Just then he was sure he heard a knock on the front door. *Could Stuart be here already?*

He jumped up from the crate, but before Jack could even get inside the house, he heard the loud ringing of the telephone.

Brrrrrring…Brrrrrring!

In an instant, Jack's eyes flew open. *Stuart?* For a moment, he was not sure where he was, but it quickly came flooding back to him. He was in his own bed.

Brrrrrrring…Brrrrrrring!

The phone on the nightstand was ringing. Checking the alarm clock, he could see that it was only 5:33 a.m. Who could be calling him at this hour? He picked up the phone.

"Hello," he said sleepily.

"Jack, you old dog! Guess what! You've won!"

"Who is this?" asked Jack, preparing to just hang up on what he suspected was a crank call.

"It's Benton, old man. I know it's a little early, but I wanted to be the first to congratulate you. So, congratulations!"

Jack was getting very annoyed. "What are you talking about?"

"You won the big one! The biggest honor in the music industry—the Lifetime Achievement Award! It'll be handed out to you at the Treble Clef Awards. How'd you do it, Jack? You must have scared the shit out of those idiots with your Elijah hat trick. Maybe I should try something as crazy. I'm green with envy."

Jack wanted to feel excited about the award, but he kept thinking about Stuart and the dream. More than anything he wanted to get back there. If only that fool Billington hadn't phoned, would he have gone to the door and found Stuart standing there, waiting for him? *It was just a dream,* he tried to remind himself, *it was just a dream.*

"So do you now expect me to thank you for waking me up?" Jack asked.

Billington laughed a little too loudly into the phone. "Just wanted to share this moment with you, old man," he answered.

"Well, thank you then," said Jack, not meaning a word of it.

20

Mona pulled up to the curb and parked the rented sedan. As she opened the door and stepped out onto the sidewalk, a small three colored dog came suddenly running up from behind a white picket fence. Its high-pitched angry barking startled her, and for a moment, she considered getting back into the car. Mona looked at the tiny canine and laughed. *Imagine coming all this way and then being scared off by you,* she thought, as the tiny sentry continued to try and ward her off.

Looking up and down the old tree-lined street, it seemed this single yappy beast was the only sign of life. It was then that Mona noticed how strangely still the air was. There was not even a hint of a breeze. The thought entered her mind that perhaps everyone had disappeared. Long ago they had evaporated like water drops in sunlight. Only this peculiar silly little dog remained to guard everything left behind. She knew this could not possibly be true. All of the homes were well-kept. People must still live behind those walls.

Mona noticed how the aged sidewalk under her feet had more than a few cracks. Here and there weeds were growing up through the openings. It certainly seemed like a place that had been lost—a street completely forgotten within a bustling town. She stepped on one of the weeds, crushing it into the concrete.

The quaint looking gray stone home in front of her had the number 331 in big brass letters beside its blue painted door. Seeing this number glistening in the sunshine made her heartbeat just a little faster. Could she really be this close? The next house would have to be it!

For a few seconds, she could not move as she wondered what she would say. Would this woman know why she had come? Would she recognize Mona as a friend or dismiss her as a crazy lady? She wasn't sure what to expect. Was any of this really real at all? *Jack and*

Elijah believe, she reminded herself. *If Jack and Elijah believe, so do I.*

Moving past the expansive yard, she headed to the next house. There were beautiful red roses in full bloom growing up the porch. *This has to be it*, she thought excitedly. Trying to prepare herself mentally, she started up the walk to the front door. When she noticed the black house number nailed on a white plaque, she stopped. It read 335. This did not make any sense. Where was it? Where was the number 333?

Retracing her steps, she returned to double check the previous house. No, it was definitely 331. Mona stood confused and wondering what to do next. The place could not have just disappeared. She had an address and the existing house numbers corresponded to a missing building.

Mona looked carefully at the wide space between the two houses. It was a thick deliberate tangle of trees and garden. The owners had let it grow up in such a way as to give it a natural appearance while still maintaining it with limited tending and sculpting. The result was a kind of purposeful chaos. She stared at the blue morning glories that snaked up a pine tree and over some thick bushes. It was then that she noticed a peculiar area that seemed a little less tended than the rest. There was something about it that didn't seem like it was part of the gardener's design.

As she moved closer, she saw something peculiar hiding behind one of the bushes. Peering through the leaves, she could see what appeared to be an old field-stone pillar—the same kind of old-fashioned pillar that would support a fence and front gate. In that instance, it became clear to her that there was indeed another property here. Mona pushed aside a tree branch, and leaned in. A secret narrow footpath was winding its way through the underbrush. She slipped behind the foliage and began to follow the trail.

The vegetation was thick at first, but not far in, the area opened up. It was obviously an old 'T' shaped lot with narrow access at the road, but wider in behind. Also, the place was definitely large enough for a house, but where was the house? There appeared to be nothing but thick weeds and underbrush.

As Mona examined the area, she could see why the little footpath existed. It led directly to a large maple tree and a well-worn area littered with garbage, alcohol bottles and an old backseat from a car. It was clear that teenagers were using this empty lot for their secret parties.

Without thinking about it, she picked up a large stick from the ground and began battering down some of the tallest weeds. Even though she knew this was a silly thing to do, she still wanted to find something—some remnant of this place being more than it was now. Even a small sign would be better than nothing at all.

Swinging the stick like a sickle, she moved forward bending the weeds over at their stems. As she came upon a thick group of tall thistles, she gave an extra hard whack. The stick made a loud cracking sound as it suddenly broke against something hard. Moving in closer, she could see, behind the thistles, the remains of a very old field-stone wall. It was short and mostly hidden by weeds and brush. Her eyes followed its direction and saw what appeared to be a large rectangular shape. It was a foundation! This was the house—or what was left of it. So, there was a number 333 after all!

Mona stared for a moment at the ruins. All the way here—in the plane—in the car—she had been so excited that this would finally be it. After all this time, it would be she who would find the mystery woman and be the first to come face to face with her. Jack would be so proud. But now it seemed the entire quest was a failure. There was no house—no woman—no nothing.

The intense emotion she began to feel surprised her. Why should she feel this sad? As the tears started to well up in her eyes, she wanted only to sit and rest for a moment. Looking around for a place, she at first considered the old car seat, but then thought better of it. Who knows what went on there? It was then that she spotted a limestone boulder that was flat on top. She walked over and sat down. It was surprisingly comfortable.

As she sat, she stared at the place where the house used to be and tried to imagine what it must have been like. Was it carefully crafted from wood or from stone? How many rooms did it have? What kind of drapes hung on the windows? Did one of the windows look out onto the rock where she was now sitting? She closed her eyes and tried to see Rose at that window looking out and knowing that someone—that Mona had come to find her.

Mona opened her eyes and sighed at the empty space in front of her. Now, she would have to phone Elijah and tell him the bad news. This was the last thing she wanted to do, but she knew he'd be wondering—and waiting. She looked down at the ground and began to stir the dirt with her foot. Loosening some pebbles from the earth with her shoe, she kicked them around and then out into the weeds. It was then that she spied something small and white that had been hiding underneath one of those pebbles. She reached down and dug into the dirt with her fingernail. Scooping up the little object, she held it between her thumb and forefinger. At first, she wasn't sure what it was because of the dark earth that clung to it, but as she scraped away the soil, it became clear. It was a doll's shoe—a tiny white fashion-doll's shoe! Accidently finding this odd treasure made her laugh out loud, and a new sense of hope washed over her.

Mona stared at the little shoe she now cradled in her palm. *This must have belonged to Rose. That little girl must have played with it—putting it on and taking it off of her doll's foot maybe hundreds of times—and then one day losing it completely.*

A moment ago, Mona had all but given up. Now this one small sign was filling her with renewed determination. Taking her phone out of her pocket, she quickly called Elijah.

"Mona!"

There was obvious anticipation in his voice. "Don't be discouraged," she said.

"You didn't find her, did you?" It was clear from his voice how disappointed Elijah was feeling.

"No, I'm afraid not. The house is gone. It's been gone for years. But chin up! I did find Cinderella's slipper."

"What do you mean?"

Mona laughed. "It's a tiny white doll-shoe. Nothing but a tiny shoe, but isn't that how the Prince found Cinderella?"

"So, we are going to believe in fairy tales now?" he asked jokingly. Mona could hear from his voice that she was sending him the hope she intended.

"Let's just keep believing in everything with a happy ending, shall we?" she answered.

"I'm alright with that," said Elijah. "Anything with a happy ending will be our story."

"Good. I'm glad we are now on the same page," said Mona, as she watched two chickadees fly into a nearby tree and stare at her. "So where do we go from here?"

Mona had already begun to consider their next step. "We'll start with what we have," she said, "which is quite a lot when you consider that we have both a first and last name and an old address.

I'll just hire a private investigator. Don't worry Elijah. They can find anyone nowadays. It's not as easy to hide as it used to be."

"I'm sorry Mona, but they are signaling me that it is time to go—the show's about to start."

"Relax and have a good time on the show. I'll fly back tonight and we'll talk some more."

"Sounds like a good idea. I love you, but I have to go now. Bye," he said quickly, and then hung up.

Mona was surprised. She had not been expecting those three words. Of course, she wondered privately about whether or not it was love, but she didn't want to think too much about it. Now that he had said the words aloud and they were out there, she couldn't ignore it. Did he really mean what he said or was it just one of those meaningless things rock stars say when they are preparing to perform?

Not wanting to over-analyze the entire thing, she quickly tucked the little shoe in her pocket and headed back to the place where she had parked the car. There was work to be done if they were ever going to find the mystery woman, and for now, she should concentrate on only that.

* * *

Britney:
Something awful happened.

AlienKiller666:
What?

Britney:
I'm so scared!

AlienKiller666:
What happened?

Britney:
It's that queer Jack again.

AlienKiller666:
What did he do?

149

Britney:
I was in that restaurant with Mommy. He was there. I'm so scared! I
don't know if I should even talk about it.

AlienKiller666:
Tell me!

Britney:
He was sitting at a table that was very private. Nobody could see him.
Except where I was sitting, there was a mirror. I could see him in the
mirror. It was horrible!

AlienKiller666:
What was horrible?

Britney:
I was just sitting there and happened to glance in the mirror. That's
when I saw him change.

AlienKiller666:
What do you mean?

Britney:
No, it's too horrible!

AlienKiller666:
You have to tell me what happened.

Britney:
I couldn't believe it! Sitting right there, his face changed into this
hideous reptile creature. Our suspicions were right. He doesn't just
work for aliens. He is one!

AlienKiller666:
What exactly did he look like?

Britney:
He looked just like those alien pictures u sent me. Only it was worse
because it was real. I was so afraid.

AlienKiller666:
Did your mother see?

Britney:
No she was sitting opposite me. She couldn't see.

AlienKiller666:
Did you tell her?

Britney:
No way! She wouldn't believe me. She's not wise to the world like
u and me.

AlienKiller666:
Are you alright?

Britney:
No! That's not the worst part.

AlienKiller666:
What else happened?

Britney:
He saw me in the mirror too! He saw me because he looked right at
me and sneered just before he changed back. I'm so scared! What will
he do to me for seeing him shape-shift?

AlienKiller666:
I need to get to New York as soon as possible.

Britney:
Would u really come? I'm so frightened!

AlienKiller666:
Don't worry. I will pack the car now and be there as soon as I can. It
will take a couple of days. I wish I could be there faster but can't take
my guns on a plane.

Britney:
U don't know how much better that makes me feel. My parents would
never believe me. I'm so glad I have u. I luv u so much.

AlienKiller666:
I luv you too and no filthy alien is ever going to so much
as threaten my woman.

Britney:
I luv it when u call me ur woman.

AlienKiller666:
You know you are. I will do anything to protect you! Consider that
fat queer, dead meat!

21

Jack was at his office desk going over the itinerary for the awards night. As the recipient of the music industry's most prestigious prize, he luckily would not be expected to announce any of the winners as he had done in previous years. Instead, he could spend the entire evening lounging in a comfortable seat and enjoying the show. There would be no worrying about whether or not he would read the words on the teleprompter correctly, or having to try to salvage some lame joke written by one of their bad writers. In the end, there was only the matter of his acceptance speech, and Jack loved to make speeches. This was something he was very good at.

"Perhaps I should start with a quote from Shakespeare," he said out loud to himself. He then stood up and boldly declared,

The man that hath no music in himself,
Nor is not mov'd with concord of sweet sounds
Is fit for treasons, stratagems, and spoils.

Jack tried to imagine what that moment would be like when he received the award. Thinking about standing on that stage in front of the best of the best, he ran his hands over his chest and down to his stomach. The new exercise program and healthier diet were starting to pay off. He had already lost a little weight. *I wish I had a proper mirror*, he thought to himself. There was a mirror in his private washroom, but it was unfortunately too small to see his whole body.

Jack walked over to the large glass case holding Stuart's unicorns. Because of the way the light came through the windows at that time of day, his reflection was clearly visible and he was able to see most of his body. For a moment, he just stared at his other self as though meeting a stranger. Was that really what he looked like? So squat, so square and now so old. "Where have you come from, old man?" he asked his reflection. "Have we really traveled this far? Do you know something I don't? If you do then tell me what it is. Tell me all of your secrets so that I might convey them to the world."

His other self remained silent and only stared back at him with the same puzzled look. Just then Jack noticed an odd blur on the shoulder of his reflection. He checked his own shoulder, but there was nothing there. He looked back at the reflection and saw what now appeared to be a hand. Removing his glasses, he held them up to the light and checked for smudges, but the lenses were perfectly clean. He quickly put them back on and stared again at the reflection. The hand was still there only this time it was more vivid. It was really there!

Jack stayed perfectly still and stared at the hand for a few seconds. It did not move. He felt a sense of amazement, but not fear. His instincts told him there was no reason to be afraid.

Then, out of the corner of his eye, Jack saw something else in the glass—something over his other shoulder. At first, he wasn't sure what it could be. It was fuzzy and difficult to distinguish. But slowly it came more and more into focus. Jack quickly realized that it was a face. It was as if there was someone standing behind him with a hand on his shoulder!

As the image came into perfect focus, Jack suddenly became weak in the knees. *This wasn't just any image. It was Stuart!*

"Oh Stuart," Jack breathed. "It's you! It's really you!"

After all these years, there was Stuart—looking alive and well—smiling so warmly the way he always did. Jack could see him! He wasn't asleep. He wasn't dreaming. Stuart was really there!

Reaching out, he tried to touch Stuart's face, but as soon as his fingers hit the glass, the apparition instantly disappeared.

"No!" he cried, pressing on the cabinet with his palm. "Don't go! Don't leave me again! Come back, Stuart!"

Jack took two steps back, never taking his eyes from the glass. Surely Stuart would return. He stared hoping—watching. As the minutes ticked by, the tears began to roll down his face. All he could see in the glass was his own reflection—the reflection of a sad crying old man. "Stuart will you not come back to me," he pleaded. "Please. I can't lose you again!"

Eventually, Jack had to admit to himself that whatever had happened was not going to happen again. All the waiting and begging in the world could not change it. Feeling light-headed and weak, he dragged himself over to the armchair and plopped down. *I saw him! I really saw him!* Running his hand through his hair, he began to sob. "Oh Stuart, what does any of this mean? Are you trying to tell me something? Please come back. Please!"

* * *

Elijah rested his head upon Mona's breast. "Remind me again that I must have hope."

She put her hand inside his shirt collar and gently stroked the nape of his neck. "You must have hope. We have to both keep our hope alive."

They were lying together on the guestroom daybed in Mona's condo. Through the skylight above them, they could see the stars in the night sky.

"What did you tell Jack about not finding the woman?" Elijah asked.

"I told him everything. I always tell him everything."

"It's a special thing isn't it—I mean between you and Jack."

Mona laughed, "Are you trying to imply something?"

"Of course not. I just thought how nice it is to have such a close friend. I wish I had a friend like that."

"Well, you have me, don't you?"

Elijah got up on one elbow and smiled at her. "Yes, I have you. I'm so happy I have you." He then gently kissed her mouth.

Mona wanted to discuss their relationship and had been looking for the right opening. Could there be a more perfect time to ask him? "Elijah," she said, while caressing his arm, "do you remember what you said to me on the phone?"

"When?" he asked.

Oh God why am I bringing this up? "It was when I was in Canada. Do you remember?"

"Is this about my request for you to bring back maple syrup?"

"What? No. When did you…" Mona looked at his face and saw him smiling mischievously.

Elijah sat up and pulled Mona up with him. He wrapped his arm around her and asked, "You mean when I said *I love you*?"

"Yes," Mona answered.

"Didn't you like me saying that I love you?"

155

"Oh no! No. It's not that I didn't like it. It's just that I wasn't sure…" Mona couldn't finish the sentence. *Please don't start sounding like a needy woman.*

"You just weren't sure if I meant it," said Elijah. "Of course I did. I wouldn't have said it if I didn't mean it. I don't play those sorts of games. Mona, I love you, and that's the way it is. There's really not much either one of us can do about it."

Mona took in a deep breath. He loved her. It was such a relief to hear him say it, but it was also so frightening. Doubt had sometimes been her comfort. Whenever her feelings became too overwhelming, she could always raise doubt in her mind to quell them. *Of course it's not love. It's just a passing thing. Just a bit of fun.* Now the doubt was gone. There was no more convenient denial. He loved her and there was nothing either one of them could do about it.

All of a sudden, Mona felt the full extent of her powerful feelings bubbling to the surface. She had never felt anything like this before. It was like being swept up in a hurricane with the wind turning you in endless circles and the lightening crackling so close as to send tiny electrical surges all through your body. So overpowering was the intensity of it all that she couldn't help feeling the urge to run straight out into the street and as far away as she could. It was too much. She needed to regain control. Where was the ground?

"I do love you," Elijah whispered into her ear. "I think I loved you from the first moment I saw you, even if I didn't realize it at the time."

Mona wanted to catch hold of all the things that were wildly racing through her mind. She wanted to grab these thoughts— thoughts that could explain everything. She wanted to tell him how she had known all about love. How she had been in love before—how she had experienced and understood all kinds of love—and how she had never before felt a love that could so fiercely consume her the way it did now. But she didn't say any of those things. Love had left her nearly speechless. Instead, she just barely managed to whisper, "I love you too."

* * *

Jack was late by the time he reached the restaurant, but he had called Benton Billington from the cab to tell him as much. Because they were only meeting over drinks his tardiness should not be an issue. And it was true that Billington spent the better part of most days sitting around in restaurants, anyway.

As he entered, he could see Benton at his usual table—the best in the house. He was talking to an attractive twenty-something woman who was standing opposite him. Just then, he looked up and saw Jack. With an expression of relief, he waved him over.

By the time Jack had reached the table, the woman was already walking away. She looked back with longing. It was obvious she wanted to meet the famous Jack, but Billington must have said something, in no uncertain terms, to get rid of her.

"Hello old man," Billington chirped, reaching over, and shaking Jack's hand. "I'm glad you could make it on such short notice."

"Who was the woman?" asked Jack, as he sat down on the expensive padded chair.

"Oh her? Can you believe it? She sashays over and I'm thinking *hello honey*, then she bold-as-brass tries to set me up with her mother. What does she think I am?"

Jack laughed, "Probably an old man."

"When you are filthy rich, my friend, you are eternally young in the eyes of women—or in your case the eyes of men." On the table was a very expensive bottle of scotch and an empty glass. Billington already had a full glass in front of him. Without asking, he poured one for Jack. "Money is the only fountain of youth."

Jack smiled politely and took a very small sip of the scotch. He would have preferred a beer, but asking for one could get too complicated with a man like Billington. He was the sort who believed that he knew what other people wanted and needed. Try and do the smallest thing that could disprove this belief, and he would fight you tooth and nail until you simply tired and gave in.

"So, Jack, now that old Dick is food for the worms, there is some restructuring going on." Billington swirled the scotch in his glass. "Thought you'd like to know just how much you are confusing them."

"What do you mean?" asked Jack, who suspected that there may be some secret discussions concerning him.

"Jack the giant killer—that's what I mean. They say that you wasted Moby Dick." Billington burst out laughing.

Jack took a longer sip of scotch. "That's ridiculous," he said.

"Tell it to those superstitious Bloodline bastards," responded Billington. "And I know…I know, I'm one of those bastards, but I'm not superstitious. I'm an atheist all the way."

"Which may in fact make you far more radical and dangerous than any religious nutter."

Billington did not like what Jack said, but there was no point in getting into it right now. There were more important things to discuss. "Anyway, what you need to know is that they are looking to promote you—to give you an actual ranking within the Bloodline."

"And how do they propose to do that?"

"They've been combing through your family history and think that they have found a remote Bloodline connection on your mother's side."

Jack was surprised, but not about a Bloodline connection. Long ago he came to the conclusion that a complicated web of connection likely stretches to everyone on earth, although the established Bloodline would never accept this as the truth. They would never let go of their sense of privilege.

What surprised him was that they were considering admitting him to what was essentially a very exclusive club. It wasn't the kind of club to accept a man who came from the poor streets of Liverpool. If it were true, this was a major change to the system. Jack had mixed feelings about the entire thing.

"So, what do you think?" asked Billington. "Not exactly King of the Bloodline but they might make you a Duke."

Jack felt disgust at the thought. He knew that Billington was only speaking figuratively, but for him to raise that word at all was troubling. *Duke* was a word that rarely came up in conversations, but when it did, it was like a knife through his heart. Now, Billington had said that this is what Jack could become. He took another sip of scotch even though he knew it would not comfort him.

"You, old man, are on the cusp of greatness. So, what do you have to say about that?"

At first, Jack said nothing, and he could feel Billington becoming a little annoyed with the silence. Finally knowing he would have to say something soon, he answered, "I…I doubt that they are serious about this. Elijah did not make a comeback solely by my hand. There were many others who contributed. My assistant Mona was instrumental in his recovery."

"That doesn't matter. What matters is what those stuffy old codgers believe, and they believe that you are *the man*."

Jack shifted uncomfortably in his chair as he considered what this could mean. Could you really change a system from within, or would the system inevitably change you? Would the change be so gradual and veiled that you wouldn't even realize it until it was too late? Would he just be another fool selling his own soul for the illusion of gaining the world? He looked Billington in the eye and said, "Like you were saying, such a thing would be very unusual. I think I'll just wait and see if they approach me with an offer before I jump to any conclusions."

"Go ahead and doubt, but they will be coming, and with an offer you won't be able to refuse. I just wanted to be the first to welcome you to the VIP room. You should have a good friend going in. Someone to help you get oriented. And I just wanted you to know that I'm here for you, Jack," said Billington.

So that is what this meeting is really about, thought Jack. *He wants to ensure he can control me—keep me in my place.* "I have always been the kind of man who knows how to rely on the support of good friends," Jack replied.

Billington grinned a sloppy scotch grin. "Jolly good old man!" he exclaimed, without a thought that this expression might be offensive or condescending. It also never crossed his mind that Jack might not consider him a friend.

* * *

"Okay, my boyfriend's almost here. He stopped by an internet cafe to send me his love."

Todd cringed. He wished Minton would stop referring to the weevil as his 'boyfriend.' "You need to be sure that there are no signs of wavering or of him being too far gone to carry out the job properly?"

"No siree. I worked him into a perfect place—not all the way crazy, but just crazy enough to execute with passionate precision."

"Good. This one can't go wrong."

"You mean like what happened in Alabama?"

"I told you never to mention that again!" Todd was becoming angry. "Those people were not our fault."

"Sorry, I forgot." Minton had not forgotten. He just always enjoyed getting under his boss' skin. After all, it was what he did best.

Just then Todd's phone played *Ride of the Valkyries*. He gave Minton a look that said, *keep your mouth shut. This is important.*

Taking his phone from his pocket, he answered, "Hello Sir." He then turned in the other direction so that he would not have to look at Minton during the conversation.

"Yes, I understand, and I assure you that there is nothing to worry about. The chess pieces are in place and you will get the show you ordered."

Minton, who was well trained in voice analysis, was surprised to hear a new nervousness in Todd's tone. This was unusual. Although he was always stressed when it came closer to the extermination, Todd had only ever sounded like this once before. That same change in his voice happened the one time he tried to hide money from Minton to keep a larger percentage for himself.

There must be more money coming from somewhere, thought Minton. *But the client has not made any new requests that could up the price. Also, the agreed upon cost was already well beyond what the job was worth. Could it be a third party? Was there someone else wanting Jack dead? With someone that high profile, it wouldn't necessarily be unusual for another client to happen to come forward with an order. After all, people are very vindictive, jealous, and territorial animals.* He wondered just how much could possibly be on the table. There'd be no point in confronting Todd outright because he'd only deny it. Minton knew he'd have to investigate carefully to find out more.

"I am happy to hear that Sir and thank you again." Todd put his phone back in his pocket.

"Is he worried that we won't be able pull it off?" asked Minton, all the while thinking about how Todd had not addressed the man as *Your Majesty*.

"He's just not exactly the trusting type."

"Who is?" Minton looked straight into Todd's eyes.

Todd looked over at the small dirty basement window and replied. "Only the suckers and that's what keeps us in the game."

22

Jack was sitting at his desk when Mona came flying through the door. "I just received a call from the private investigator!" she exclaimed with excitement.

"Did he find her?" Jack eagerly asked. It still seemed so unreal that they were actually looking for her.

"He says so. She has the same name. It must be her Jack. It has to be!" Mona, who was carrying her laptop, now set it down in front of Jack and pulled up a chair. "I was just on the phone with him," she said. "He was at her house with a hidden camera and is now returning to the hotel room. He'll be uploading a video shortly. We'll be able to see her, Jack! We'll be able to finally see the girl Stuart found!"

"Where's Elijah?" asked Jack.

"Oh, I wish he were here. He's out of town doing another interview. I can't wait to tell him!"

Jack could see how excited Mona was, but he learned a long time ago to be cautious about raising one's hopes too high. High expectations could be far too emotionally taxing.

Mona typed in the URL and logged into the site. She quickly scrolled down the page and then back up again. "It's not here," she said, not hiding her disappointment. She took a deep breath and reminded herself about the importance of patience. "He said he would upload it right away. Don't worry. It should show up soon."

"Did he tell you where he found her?" asked Jack.

"Somewhere in Alaska of all places. I definitely never would have thought of looking there."

This didn't sound right to Jack, but he did not say anything. Until he knew for certain, it was best to let her believe what she wanted.

Mona clicked the refresh button. "Still nothing," she said, as she began to tap nervously on the desk.

"Do you have a dress for the music awards?" Jack asked, wanting to alleviate the pressure of waiting with a little chit chat.

"Oh, you know me. It's always a lastminute thing—a scramble for what to wear."

"I'm certain you will want to ensure you look your best beside Elijah," Jack said, hoping she would take the hint without feeling insulted.

Suddenly, Mona was no longer thinking about the video. Why hadn't she thought about Elijah and the awards? With everything that was happening, she had not put these two things together. Was she to be his date for the evening? They had never really been seen out in public as a proper couple. Would it be better if they just went separately? Being seen with her could possibly slow down his career. Although she was never short of admirers, she was not exactly the kind of beauty that steps out onto the red carpet.

"I don't know if it's a good idea for Elijah and me to go together," she said.

"Why not?" asked Jack, who was annoyed that she would even think of trying to hide the truth about her and Elijah. Even though show business was full of illusions and half-truths, there were some things that Jack felt should never be compromised. Important personal relationships were at the top of his list. After all he went through with Stuart, he knew there was a steep cost to hiding love.

"Wouldn't it just complicate things? It could even jeopardize his career. If he shows up with just a plain woman from the record company, some people might say that he is desperate for a companion—especially if he shows up with a woman in his own age group."

Jack laughed and put his hand on her arm. "Don't underestimate yourself. You'll look wonderful walking down that red carpet with him. But I will not argue with you. Ultimately, it's Elijah choice as to who will be his date. If he wants you by his side, there is nothing you can do. You must go." Jack was confident that this is what Elijah intended anyway.

"Well, I don't know if I have to do everything Elijah wants, but I'll agree to it if he says he wants me there."

"Oh, I am quite sure he wants you there," said Jack.

Mona didn't wish to talk about it anymore. What if he didn't want her there? Doubt was creeping in and she found herself feeling a little angry. This is precisely why she hadn't been in a serious relationship for years. She just couldn't stand all of the wondering and uncertainty that goes along with romantic love. Better to date a down to earth man you could love, but never fall in love with.

Clicking on the refresh button once more, Mona was thrilled to see the video appear on the page. "Fantastic!" she exclaimed, as she clicked play.

At first, they were confused when all they could see was a car steering wheel. A man's voice then said "Good morning, Mona. As you can see, there is a small camera hidden in the lapels of my coat. Everything that I will see, you will see. You will also, of course, be able to hear conversations. This is a part of the true virtual experience our company is committed to delivering to our clients."

Mona looked at Jack. "It's a top-notch investigation company. They promised a platinum service."

"I will now be approaching the house," said the voice in the video.

For the first time, they had a shot of the house. It was an opulent large white home with green shutters on the many windows. A long veranda spanned the front of the building. "It's beautiful," said Mona.

Jack stared at the house as the man in the video approached the door. He did not feel right about it but said nothing. It was best to wait for positive confirmation.

A hand could be seen ringing the doorbell and then there was a long pause. Eventually the door opened and an Indigenous woman appeared on the threshold. Jack's heart beat a little faster. Maybe this was her.

"May I help you?" she asked.

"Courier service! Is your name Rose? If it is, I have a special package for you."

"I'm not her, but I can sign for it and will see that she gets it," said the woman, holding out her hand.

"Oh no! It's a prize and I'm under strict instructions to deliver it to her hands alone. Is she home?"

"Just one moment," said the woman and closed the door.

Soon the door opened again, but this time it was a dark haired European looking woman. "I am told that you have a package for me," she said curtly.

"And I assume that you are Rose," said the detective. "Well, your favorite author Gunsten Grimm was so thrilled with the lovely things you had written on his fan club website that he has sent you, as a surprise, a special autographed copy of his new best seller."

Mona glanced for a moment at Jack. She could see the look on his face, and it was not good. She paused the video.

"It's not her, is it?"

"No," said Jack. "She's all wrong and her features do not even begin to fit the golden mean."

Mona looked like she was about to cry. "Damn it! This guy is the best there is. If he can't find her, where do we go from here?"

Jack put his arm around Mona and she leaned her head on his shoulder. "Maybe it's just not meant to be," he said. "Maybe they were right after all when they said that she must find her way on her own. Perhaps we are overstepping the mark."

"But Elijah seemed so sure about it." Mona sat straight up again. "I'll talk to him. He might have an idea."

"You do that," said Jack, trying not to show his own deep disappointment. "In the meantime, I have an acceptance speech to write, and don't forget about buying that dress. It should be quite a night."

* * *

Leaning back in his chair, Minton was beginning to fall asleep. Just as he had almost slipped into unconsciousness, he was jolted awake by the sound of *The Ride of the Valkyries* ringtone. He looked over at an old tin filing cabinet in the corner. On top of it was the client phone. Todd had gone out for lunch and carelessly left the phone behind. This was the opportunity Minton had been waiting for.

First, he looked up the stairs at the door, half expecting Todd to come running down, but there was no sign of him. Minton moved quickly over to the cabinet, reached up and grabbed the phone. "Hello," he answered.

"Mr. Todd?" asked a man on the other line. Minton immediately noticed that this man was not British. He grinned at his luck.

Knowing that impersonating Todd over the phone could cause too many complications, he decided to take a more straight forward route. "No sir. I'm afraid Mr. Todd is unavailable at the moment," he explained. "I am his executive assistant Sam. May I be of service to you?"

For a long moment, the other end of the phone was silent. Finally, the voice said, "I think I'd prefer to speak directly with Mr. Todd. When will he be available?"

This has to be the third-party guy. "Is this regarding the Jack of Hearts?" he asked outright.

"Yes," was the reply.

Minton clenched his fist in victory. *I just knew he was hiding another client. Todd baby, you slipped up this time.* "Do you have any concerns, sir? Because I assure you that we will be fulfilling our contractual obligations to your fullest satisfaction."

"And I'm expecting nothing less. But what you can do now is pass on this message to Mr. Todd. Tell him that everything is set. The ducks are all lined up for the big night. I've done my part, now he had better do his. For the amount I'm paying for this job, I expect nothing short of total success. Got it?"

"Yes sir. We give you our iron-clad guarantee. Would you like Mr. Todd to call you back?"

"No. There will be no further contact. Just be sure he gets the message."

"I certainly will, sir. Is there anything else I can do for you?"

The man laughed, "Other than remove that fat, queer, limey stain from my city? No that's all I need. Just tell Mr. Todd that Mr. Billington will be expecting his money's worth."

* * *

Mona closed her eyes. It felt so good to be held tightly in Elijah's arms again. She never wanted him to ever let go. "I missed you," he whispered into her ear. "Please come with me next time. I know it sounds silly, but even a day apart is becoming too long."

Taking in a deep breath, Mona relished this moment. She had been thinking of nothing else since he left two days ago. Now they were back together. Their bodies were pressed so firmly against each other that she could feel their hearts beating together like ancient drums playing one song. Strange and beautiful images flowed through her mind and it seemed like the entire world had just disappeared from underneath them. They were flying.

Suddenly, there was the sound of voices and she opened her eyes. In her eagerness, she had forgotten they were still standing in

165

her open doorway. Down the hall, three men were staring curiously at them. Quickly pulling Elijah inside, she then pushed the door shut.

"I promise that I'll try to be there with you next time," she said. "I don't like being away from you either."

For a few moments longer, they remained in a silent embrace—both of them reluctant to break the spell. Finally, Mona said, "We can't stand here all night. I ordered some food and it's been staying warm in the oven too long already."

Elijah smiled and kissed her gently on the mouth. "I'm very hungry," he said smiling. "I just couldn't eat that disgusting food on the plane."

"Well, I have a feast fit for a king," she said, taking him by the hand and leading him to the dining table. She had set a formal table complete with lighted candles and roses. "Sit here," Mona pulled out a chair for him.

"It's beautiful. Thank you," said Elijah, as he sat down.

"I'll just be a moment," Mona said, then disappeared into the kitchen.

Elijah looked at the lovely table in front of him. Everything was very carefully arranged and thought out. She had put a great deal of effort into every detail. Had anyone ever done something this nice for him before? Perhaps it just seemed so wonderful because it was Mona who had done it.

Mona returned with two covered china dishes in hand and then went back into the kitchen for two more. Once everything was on the table, she began to remove the covers, "Voila!" she exclaimed, as she revealed the delicacies hidden within. "I did consider taking credit for the cooking too, but I knew, even if you believed me, I couldn't hide the truth for long. Eventually you'd figure it out when I burn the breakfast toast."

Elijah wrapped his arm about her waist. "You can tell me whatever you like and I'll believe it. Tell me you flew to the moon and prepared it there, and I'll just say *how wonderful*!"

"That is the hokiest thing anyone has ever said to me," laughed Mona, as she sat down. "If any other man had said that, I would have run a mile. What is it about you, Elijah? Why are you so different?"

"I don't think I'm that different," he replied.

Mona leaned her elbow on the table and looked into his eyes. "You are very different."

"I am very hungry. Do you want to begin or should I."

"You first."

Elijah began to eagerly spoon the various foods onto his plate. "I'm glad to see you're not feeling down about the private investigator," he said.

Mona had phoned him right after she left Jack's office to tell him about what had happened. "I'm not sure what we should do next. You still believe that the right thing is to find her, don't you?" she asked.

"I never wavered," said Elijah, taking a large bite-full from his fork. "Oh, this is so good!"

"It's from one of my favorite Manhattan restaurants. I want to take you there one day."

"And I want to go," said Elijah, taking another bite. "So, how was Jack about it? I know that this situation must be very emotional for him. It must bring back memories of Stuart."

"He seemed all right, but I don't think he had raised his hopes—not like me. Jack's gotten smart over the years and takes things more in stride. At least that's what he tells me."

"But he's still okay with us going ahead and finding her?"

"Of course," she answered. "Sometimes he doesn't seem completely sure that we can do it, but he's always willing to support us in our efforts."

"Good," said Elijah, in between bites. "We need Jack on our side."

Mona stopped for a moment just to watch Elijah eat. He seemed so happy and vibrant as he savored his food. What a difference from the melancholy man she had first met only months ago. This man had a determination and drive that amazed her, and she knew she was partly responsible for this transformation.

Elijah looked up and saw her staring at him. "I'm sorry, am I being rude?" he asked, suddenly aware that maybe he was eating a little too zealously.

"Oh no," said Mona. "I just like watching you eat."

Elijah smiled at her. "Well since I like eating, this relationship should work out just fine." He then reached over, grabbed a serving spoon, and piled more *magret de canard aux pommes* onto his plate.

As Mona watched him, she wondered if now might be a good time to ask him a question that had been on her mind for a while. It was something she had wondered about from the beginning. "Elijah," she said. "Why did Danny Green bring you to Einhorn?"

Elijah took a drink of the sparkling water then replied, "I suppose he felt that he owed me a favor."

"A favor for what?"

"I just helped him out one day. It's not important. It was an accident. It's not like I intended to help him." Elijah kept eating.

Mona could see he was a little reluctant to talk about it. "What happened?" she asked.

"I was just in the right place at the right time, and I was able to help out."

"Okay, vague again. So, tell me exactly what happened."

Elijah looked at Mona. He could see from her eyes that she would not let it go until he told her the whole story. He sighed and set down his fork. "About a year ago, I was staying at a cabin resort in the Finger Lakes area. It was just supposed to be a quiet place to go and clear my head. I'd been thinking a lot about the dreams I was having and about getting back into singing. I needed a serene setting to try and understand all the things that were going through my mind.

So, one morning I'm out at the crack of dawn down by the lake, (I love walking in the early morning when everyone else is still asleep), and as I walked around a cluster of bushes growing close to the bank, I saw something fall from the dock into the water. At first, it wasn't registering what it was, but then I realized that it was a child. I was seeing a small child disappearing under the water. Without thinking about it, I ran over and dived in. The water was dark and I wasn't able to find her, but then my hand touched a small arm and I quickly grabbed her and brought her to the surface. I climbed onto the deck and immediately began CPR.

"That's when I heard the parents shouting as they ran down from their cabin. I glanced up but continued to try and revive the child. By the time Danny Green and his wife arrived, she had begun to breathe on her own again. Apparently, she had just wandered away from the cabin while her parents were still sleeping."

"You saved a child's life!" said Mona. "Why didn't you tell me this story before?"

"I didn't want to sound like I was trying to impress you. Like I said, I just happened to be in the right place at the right time."

Mona reached over and took his hand in hers. "You saved a little girl's life," she said. "That's big news, and you should feel proud of yourself."

Elijah smiled at her. "I'm proud that you're proud."

Was there anything this man could say that would not make her fall more in love with him? "You had just better save room for dessert," she smiled. "I bought the most decadent chocolate cake ever made. It's from a small mom and pop bakery miles from here. And I promise that you have never tasted cake before until you have tasted this one."

"Now you're tempting me not to finish my dinner," said Elijah. "I knew you were a temptress the first time I laid eyes on you. If I had not been so blinded by your seductive powers, I would have been able to run away then. Now it's too late. There's no hope for me. I'm hooked."

Mona softly laughed. She then suddenly stood up, and dramatically swept her hand in the air as she declared, "Then, thank God for merciful blindness! The night is young, my beloved, and I think I am already *drunk with love*."

23

Britney:
Hi! Where r u?

AlienKiller666:
Almost in city limits. Can I come to your house?

Britney:
No. My parents have left for Europe and I'm staying with Auntie Barbara. I'm too scared to stay alone.

AlienKiller666:
Don't be alone! As long as someone is with you, you'll be safe. Aliens are careful about witnesses and arousing suspicion. The more humans around, the better. Their powers are weakened by strong human presence.

Britney:
U know everything!

AlienKiller666:
I've been studying their patterns long enough. One day I'll write a book.

Britney:
A book? Wow! Ur amazing!

AlienKiller666:
What's the name of the restaurant where it happened? I'll stake out the place and learn Jack's movements. I'll track him like an animal and then ambush him.

Britney:
That's good but I have a better idea. I read in the paper that he will be receiving an award at the TCMA. With all of those people around, wouldn't his powers be at the lowest point with an increased human presence. U always write about that in ur blog.

AlienKiller666:
Good point. But security will be too tight.

Britney:
My uncle is a sound man for the show. During the day there will be lots of people going in and out. Let me ask him a few questions about the ways in and get back to u. I'm sure u can get in with my help.

AlienKiller666:
Do you really think it's a good idea to do this in front of all those people?

Britney:
But u know when aliens die they transform back into their reptilian shapes. If Jack does this on international television, it would expose them all. U would be a hero to the world!

AlienKiller666:
I never thought of that.

Britney:
Sure u would have. U think of everything. I'm just here to support u in every way.

AlienKiller666:
You're right. I would have figured it out had I known about the TCMA. Thanks for telling me.

Britney:
Where will u be staying?

AlienKiller666:
I'll find a place. I'm a trained survivalist.

Britney:
I wish we could be together tonight.

AlienKiller666:
I wish that too.

Britney:
After u finish off Jack, we can be together every night. It'll be wonderful!!!

AlienKiller666:
Can we meet somewhere in the meantime?

Britney:
No. It's too risky. I don't want to be out alone on the streets with Jack still around. He might already know where I'm staying and could be watching the house right now.

AlienKiller666:
I don't want you to take any risks.

Britney:
Oh u luv me don't u!!!

AlienKiller666:
You know I do.

Britney:
I'll send u something special tonight. It's a picture of me wearing a little something I bought for our first night together. I shouldn't really show it to u now but I'm too excited.

AlienKiller666:
You're driving me crazy.

Britney:
O, I've only just begun….

* * *

As Jack relaxed on the park bench and soaked up the afternoon sun, he was surprised to see Benton Billington come strolling along the path. This was the last person he expected to run into in Central Park. Billington had always complained that the park was just a foolish waste of prime real estate.

At first, Jack thought that Billington had not spotted him and he would be able to enjoy the beautiful afternoon without interruption. But as Billington got closer, Jack saw him grin and wave. *So much for peace and quiet.* Jack politely waved back.

"Jack old man!" called Billington, boldly striding over, and plopping his large heavy body down on the bench. For a moment, Jack wondered if it would break under the force. "Looks like fate has brought us together once more, but then again, I don't believe in fate. Believing in fate is too much like believing in God."

"*Men at some time are masters of their fates,*" said Jack.

"My words exactly!" exclaimed Billington, not really understanding or caring what Jack had just said. "You're a smart guy, Jack. That's why you're at the top."

Jack didn't like the conspiratorial tone of Billington's voice. Just what exactly was it he supposed to be at the top of? If Billington was there too, it had to be the top of a steaming manure pile. "I'm at the top of nothing," he said. "Just an ordinary man trying to make my way through this life. Just like that man over there." Jack pointed to a crumpled-looking man pushing a shopping cart filled with filthy bags and boxes.

Billington burst out laughing. "And that's why they love you, Jack. Humility! A rags to riches story, but no Citizen Kane. Not for you, Jack. You held on to your Rosebud and never let go. You're the stuff heroes are made of."

Jack was feeling like he had seen far too much of this man over the past few weeks and began to consider how to politely excuse himself. The direct approach was likely the best for such as Billington. "It has certainly been a pleasure bumping into you like this, but I have a full schedule of meetings this afternoon and should get back to the office."

Before Jack could make a move, Billington grabbed him by the arm and held him in place. "I want Elijah, old man, and I'm willing to pay a good price for him."

Jack just looked at Billington in shock. He could see from his face that this was no joke. Billington wanted Elijah. He wanted him desperately. "First off," said Jack, "I don't traffic human beings. And second, his contract is not for sale."

Billington's grin got wider. "Oh, come on, Jack! How long do you think this guy can go for? He's already well past his best-before date. How many years has he got before he falls and breaks a hip? I'm offering you a great deal of money—far more than he's really worth. I wouldn't even bother, but it's just these damn Bloodline fools and their superstitions. They are beginning to believe that he can do magic. That's what I'm paying for—only illusions—illusions that could go up in smoke tomorrow. But I'm willing to take that chance and to pay big for them. Don't be an idiot and hang on to something that will soon fizzle out when you can cash in now! You're not young anymore. You're getting near the end of your life. While you're still able, wouldn't you like to retire to some beautiful paradise island somewhere? Lying back on a beach—every desire you have being fulfilled by a different young Adonis every day. Think of it Jack! Life is short and you have to get out while the going is good, old man. This is the chance of a lifetime."

Jack just looked at Billington in amazement, and then began to laugh out loud.

Assuming that this meant Jack was ready to cut a deal, Billington grinned and said, "I knew that a man like you would recognize a good opportunity when you see it. Believe me, Jack, from here on in life will be a dream. When should I send my man to meet with yours and go over the details? And I'd like to personally meet with Elijah today, if he's in town. If not, as soon as he returns."

"Never!" exclaimed Jack.

"What! You're joking right?"

"No Benton. I am very serious."

"Well, what do you want? Don't try to drive the price up without even knowing the number I'm offering. It's a nice number, Jack."

"There's no price. Elijah is not and never will be for sale."

"Come on Jack! What's your game?"

"No game. He's my friend and I don't throw my friends to the dogs."

Billington tried not to let Jack see his anger, but he could not hide the raging red color of his face. He chuckled nervously and said, "I'm surprised at you, Jack. How the hell you ever got to be at the top is a mystery. I've crushed so many weak men like you that I've lost count over the years. Maybe you do have some secret magic."

Jack stood up and looked down upon Billington. "Perhaps I do. Now if you will excuse me, I'm ever so slightly late for a meeting."

Benton Billington watched as Jack walked down the path and disappeared among the joggers and women pushing baby carriages. *Low-bred queer*, he thought to himself. *You'll get yours alright, and Elijah will be mine!*

* * *

"I want to take you out one day—maybe dinner and dancing. We spend too much time in this place," said Elijah, referring to Mona's condo.

Mona was pouring herself a glass of wine in the kitchen while Elijah leaned up against the counter beside her. "But it's so peaceful here—no cameras—no gawkers," she said. "You know that as soon as we go out that door and are seen together, it gets complicated."

Elijah moved over behind Mona and put his arms around her waist. "I really don't mind complicated. There has never been anything about my life that has not been complicated. I'm used to it."

Mona didn't want to say what she was really afraid of. If they took their relationship public, could it mean the end? There would certainly be people who would have a lot to say about it. People who would not think Mona was good enough, young enough or pretty enough. It could change everything. She didn't want to risk that. Not yet anyway. "So far, no one has really identified us as a couple. To the world, we are simply business associates. Do you really want the hassle of our relationship being in the spotlight?"

Elijah gently turned Mona around to face him. His arms remained firmly around her waist. "What's the matter?"

"Nothing's the matter," she said. "I'm just being practical. You have a very successful career—a career and an image to maintain. I don't know if that image can include someone like me?"

"Didn't we have this conversation already?" Elijah was beginning to wonder why she always seemed to doubt his commitment. He had tried so hard to show her that he was not just another stereotype. "I'm not interested in image. I'm not interested in being a cookie cutter rock star. I came back to singing because I want it to be real this time—not singing and dancing to someone else's tune. Not following the lead of fools. I want to show my raw heart to the world and you, Mona, are very much a part of my heart."

Mona rested her head against his shoulder. "Are you sure about this? I don't want to ruin things for you."

"Oh Mona! Why do you talk like that? Everything would be ruined without you. Next week it is *you* who is going to be walking with me down that red carpet at the Treble Clef Music Awards, and I hope you have started planning for it. It's my life and you are the most important person in it. You make me feel like I'm not alone, and I've never felt that before. If you're not there to support me, there'd be no point in going at all. We'll make it our stepping out place. After the whole world sees us together, we'll be able to go wherever we want without worrying about it."

"I'm sorry," she said and then kissed his neck. "I didn't mean to play the businesswoman role with you. It's just all been so wonderful, and I guess I'm afraid that any little change could make it all fall apart."

Elijah ran his hand down the side of her face. "Nothing's going to ruin it because there's nothing strong enough to ruin it. Don't you feel it? Nothing can come between us."

Mona knew he was right, so why did she fight so hard against it? It made no sense to keep pushing him away.

Just then, she understood what it was—what it had always been. Her two old enemies fear and pride were still holding her down—still keeping happiness at bay. Why hadn't she recognized these devils and their sabotage? Slowly turning her face towards his, she said, "Yes, I feel it. Nothing can ruin what we have, and I promise I won't try to fight it anymore. I surrender." She then gently placed her hand on his cheek. *With all the billions of faces all over the world, what is it about this one that can make me feel more light and alive than I had ever felt before?* Staring into his eyes she asked, "Elijah, where was I before you came into my life?"

Slowly running his hand up her back, he replied, "I think maybe you were just waiting for me." He then gently cupped the nape of her neck and brought their lips together.

24

Jack stared into the mirror. He was hoping to have lost a little more weight before the awards, but each year it was becoming more and more difficult to take the pounds off. Still, he had to admit that the tuxedo did flatter him. Standing in front of the looking glass, he couldn't help but feel a sense of his old debonaire youthfulness.

Straightening his black silk bowtie, he smiled at his image and whispered, *"We are such stuff as dreams are made on."* He had come such a long way to get to this evening and was determined to feel proud of all he had accomplished. Receiving the Treble Clef Lifetime Achievement Award was something he never dared to even dream about before. It just wasn't a possibility in the world as he knew it. They simply didn't hand out such a prestigious award to people who were not of the Bloodline. Jack had changed all that and not just for himself. This was a precedent setting moment. This would alter everything.

As he continued to admire himself in the mirror, Jack suddenly noticed something over the left shoulder of his reflection. It appeared to be a strange bright white mist rising and swirling about as if struggling to take shape. He quickly turned to look behind him, but there was nothing there. Turning back towards the mirror, he froze in wonderment at the sight before him. It was Stuart! Stuart was standing right beside him, just the same as he had in the unicorn case. This time, however, the reflection was perfectly clear. Stuart was real and alive!

"Stuart!" Jack cried, as he reached out his hand towards the mirror. But he didn't dare touch it. He was too afraid that if his hand should touch the mirror, it may cause Stuart to disappear just like he did in the unicorn case. "Stuart," he said. "I don't even care why you are here. Just to see your face again. Oh, sweet torture!"

Jack was trying hard to hold back the tears. Tears would make it more difficult to see clearly. Perhaps if he never flinched—never moved from that spot—never even so much as blinked, then Stuart would stay forever. Jack would gladly never move again if this were possible.

Don't say anything more, he thought to himself. *Don't break the magical silence of this moment.* He watched in amazement as Stuart turned his head. His lips were now near the left ear of Jack's reflection. Jack did not know what to think, but as he stood there mesmerized by the image, he suddenly became aware that he could feel something in his ear. It was like someone's warm breath. He could feel what he was seeing in the mirror! He could actually feel Stuart! *Is this true? Is this imagination? Is this how senility starts?*

It was then that Jack heard Stuart say, "Keep Elijah close tonight."

That voice! The one he had so often worried he might never hear again. That voice—so crystal clear! So real! Not sounds in a dream, but a real voice! Stuart's voice! It was all too much for Jack. His legs gave out and he collapsed on the floor.

Jack did not know for how long he was on the floor. Had he lost consciousness? He wasn't sure. As soon as he could, he quickly got up, picking up his glasses that had fallen beside him. He put them on and stared into the mirror. His heart sank. Only his own dazed reflection looked back at him. Stuart was gone.

Despite his instincts telling him it was pointless, he waited and watched. It would just be too tragic if he looked away and then Stuart came back. Maybe calling his name would make him return. "Stuart!" he called. "Please Stuart please! Please come back!" Jack waited, but there was no sign. He leaned his head up against the cold mirror. "You are not coming back, are you?" he whispered, finally admitting to himself that Stuart was gone again.

Jack walked over to the bed and sat down. He stared at the mirror and tried to collect his thoughts. To see Stuart and to hear him as if he were really there was incredible! It brought back everything that was good, but at the same time reminded him of everything that was lost. There was heaviness in his chest, and for a moment he almost wished he were having a heart attack. Anything to see Stuart again. How would he get through the evening after that? Jack put his hands over his face and began to sob.

* * *

"Jack! Jack! Where are you?" called Mona, who had let herself in. She had hurried to his place after receiving his desperate phone call. *Please Mona! Come over right away! I need you.* Such a thing was not like Jack at all.

She ran through the rooms looking for him. When she could not find him on the lower floor, she began to ascend the stairs. "Jack!" she called again.

"I'm here," said Jack, in a voice that didn't quite sound like his own.

Mona went into Jack's bedroom. He was dressed in his tuxedo and sitting on the bed. He did not look at her, but instead was staring across the room at a mirror on the other side. Mona had never seen him look like this before. She was worried.

Walking softly over to him, she sat down on the bed. As she gently took his hand, she asked, "What's wrong Jack?"

Jack still did not look at her. Instead, he simply pointed at the mirror and said, "It's Stuart!"

Mona looked at the mirror in confusion. *What was he talking about?*

"You'll call me crazy, but it *was* Stuart. I saw him there," Jack said. "I saw him. There, in the mirror. As clearly as I see you now."

Mona looked across at their reflections in the mirror. With Jack in his tuxedo, and her in a blue satin evening gown, they looked a strange ghostly *Theatre of the Absurd* pair eternally sitting on a bed and staring.

"He was there, Mona," said Jack, trying to keep convincing himself as well. "I'm not going mad."

"Oh, course not," she said, gently rubbing his back. "If you saw him, he was there. After all, you've seen him before in your dreams. Why shouldn't you see him when you're awake?"

"Then why am I struggling to believe it," said Jack.

Mona thought about it for a second and then answered, "Perhaps it's both shock and pain. All these years, you have dreamed of him and believed in those dreams without question. Now that somehow Stuart has come into your waking life, maybe it's harder to believe because it is just so painful to see him again. It brings back all the pain you felt when you lost him."

179

"You may be right."

"Of course I'm right," Mona said, giving his hand a gentle squeeze. "But at the same time that it is painful, it must feel wonderful to have seen him again—to know that he is somehow coming closer to you."

"That's not the first time it's happened either," said Jack. "I didn't tell you about it before because...well, I'm not sure why I didn't, but it also happened last week in my office—in the glass of the unicorn cabinet. I saw him there too, although it was not so vivid—not so real."

"You see," said Mona. "That proves it. He's coming closer. Somehow it is really happening."

Jack began to smile a little. "Do I dare hope? To catch glimpses in dreams was nothing compared to seeing him right there!" He pointed at the mirror, and his reflection pointed back at him.

Mona was happy to see that she had already begun to raise his spirits a little. She could not begin to imagine how painful it must be to go through something like this. "And surely, he must have been trying to tell you something—something more important than anything he has ever had to say before," she added.

In the deluge of emotion, Jack had almost forgotten about what Stuart had told him. "Oh yes!" he exclaimed. "The first time he did not speak to me, but this time he did say something. He told me to *keep Elijah close by tonight*."

Mona felt the hair rising on the back of her neck, but she was not about to let Jack know. "It must be an important message for him to appear like that."

"Yes, you are right," said Jack, as he began to think more deeply about it. "But what exactly does he mean by it? After all, we will be arriving altogether, and I will be sitting beside both you and him all evening. What more can I do?"

Mona considered Stuart's words carefully. "I think we have to follow his instructions as closely as possible. He said 'close by' so we should do just that. Wherever you go, be sure to take Elijah with you—whether it's on stage when you accept your award or even to the washroom. Keep him close by at all times."

Jack started laughing. "You know that will most definitely cause some people to start gossiping about my relationship with him."

Mona was glad to hear him laugh a little. "So be it. I think it's more important to follow Stuart's instructions than to worry about what people will say. They'll be saying enough when I show up on Elijah's arm. What's a little more gossip?"

Jack looked over at Mona. How wonderful it was to have such a dear friend—someone who was always on your side. "And you look beautiful, by the way," he said. "I'm happy to see you going as Elijah's date otherwise you would have been mine, and that would not do such a lovely lady proper justice."

"Thanks," said Mona, blushing just a little. "Don't take this the wrong way, but I'm happy too—that you're not my date this time."

"No offence taken," smiled Jack. "It's time you grew up, but still, it is a little sad—like watching my own daughter leave the nest."

"You know that no matter what happens, I will always be there for you," said Mona.

Jack put his arm around her. "I know," he said. "That's why, when I need help, you are always the first person I call."

* * *

Mr. Todd was pacing back and forth along the basement floor. Minton had never seen him this anxious over a job. All this nervous energy was beginning to eat into his own confidence, and he didn't like it. "This weevil is going to come through with flying colors," he asserted. "He's one of the best we've ever had—crazy as they get, but incredibly focused. That's a rare combination."

"Why haven't we heard from him yet?" asked Todd.

"It's still too early. He has the phone I sent to the motel. He sent me his love this morning, sweet thing."

"Would you stop saying things like that! It's repulsive!"

Minton could see just how unnerved Todd was getting. This was a good opportunity. His guard would be completely down. Now was a good time to hit him with the truth. "No problem, sir. Oh, by the way, Billington called the other day."

Todd looked up at the dirt covered basement window. "Billington? Who's Billington?"

"You know who he is, Mr. Todd. But I don't blame you. Of course I would have done the same thing. It's our shared philosophy, isn't it? The strong shall eat the weak. It's this belief that binds men like us together. We both know we are the chosen among men and belong on top. We are also willing to do anything to make that

181

happen. Two superior animals like us are bound to try and take a bite out of each other once in a while. It's in our nature."

"Okay, so you know about Billington. What did he say? Is it all set?"

Minton grinned. "Of course. The ducks are all in a row. That's what he told me."

Todd breathed a sigh of relief. He was worried when he thought Billington hadn't phoned back. "Don't worry," he said. "You'll get your fair share."

"Worry is the farthest thing from my mind right now," said Minton, as he leaned back confidently in his chair. Before he could say anything more, there was sound of the *Bridal Chorus* ringtone. "Alright! There's lover boy now." He took the cell phone out of his shirt pocket, read the message, and then began to quickly text his reply.

* * *

Elijah sat quietly in the back of the stretch limo and considered everything Jack had just explained to him. As absurd as the whole thing sounded, he believed in what he had been told. If Jack said Stuart appeared in the mirror with a message, then it had happened. He had to go with his gut instinct, and his gut told him that what Jack saw was very real. Taking in a deep breath, he said, "I won't move from your side, Jack."

Mona, who was sitting close beside him, reached over and grabbed for his hand. She could not help but feel a little nervous and worried for the safety of two men she loved. Somehow, they were going into danger tonight. She could sense it.

"Who knows?" said Jack. "It may not even be about *the crack of doom*. Perhaps it is merely about allowing ordinary events to unfold in a certain way, which is what most of Stuart's messages have been about."

"Yes," said Mona, who wanted so much to believe that Jack was right—that there was nothing to worry about. "Maybe it's not such a big deal, but only has to do with some type of mundane metaphysical alignment."

Elijah couldn't help but laugh. "A mundane metaphysical alignment? Perhaps I should make that the title of my next album."

Mona gently nudged him playfully in the ribs. She loved how he had a way of lightening her mood whenever things became too heavy and was grateful for it now.

"Whatever it is," said Jack, "it is best that we follow Stuart's instructions."

"Consider me your shadow," responded Elijah.

The limo slowed, turned, and then stopped. Jack looked out the window. "It seems that we are next. Are you ready?"

Elijah smiled at Mona. "As ready as I'll ever be."

With that, the door opened and Jack stepped out of the car and onto the red carpet. There were furious flashes of light as photographers scrambled for a prize picture of the man of the hour.

Next was Elijah, who then held out his hand and helped Mona out of the car. Lights flashed all around them, and screaming female fans began to call out Elijah's name.

Elijah could feel Mona tense up as they stood together on the red carpet. *She's still nervous about us being seen like this.* He leaned over and whispered into her ear, "You look so beautiful tonight. I can't wait for this thing to be over so that we can be alone."

Mona smiled and blushed. "Stop trying to embarrass me in front of the crowd," she whispered back.

"I'm trying to relax you," smiled Elijah. "Let's enjoy this."

Elijah offered his arm to Mona. She smiled and accepted. On her other side, Jack did the same thing. Now the three stood, side by side, linked together. The flashes of light never stopped coming.

We are a wall, thought Elijah, as the three walked arm in arm towards the brightly lit entrance way.

* * *

AlienKiller666:
Are you there?

Britney:
Yes! Where have u been?

AlienKiller666:
First, I couldn't find the hiding place under the stage. Then there were too many people around and no chance to slip in unnoticed. Then

somebody thought I was there to help with the set-up and I had to carry boxes of wine.

Britney:
Ur a perfect spy!

AlienKiller666:
I know. Can't believe I did all that. Your uncle was right about the secret crawl space. I'm under the stage now. It's pretty dark and cramped but I can hear everything going on above.

Britney:
U need to stay there, until it is time. I'll send u a text to let u know when target will be on stage.

AlienKiller666:
I still can't believe we are doing this. It's like a dream.

Britney:
A wonderful dream!

AlienKiller666:
The dream I always wanted to come true!

Britney:
Ur my dream come true!

AlienKiller666:
Can't think of that right now. Have to get psyched. This may not be easy and that shit reptile could have a trick up his sleeve. I may not come out alive.

Britney:
No! Don't say that!

AlienKiller666:
It's true. We have to face facts. I might die tonight.

Britney:
Stop talking like that! I luv u so so so so much!!!!

AlienKiller666:
It's no longer just about you and me, baby. I need to do this for the future of the world. If I go down, it won't be without killing him first. Don't worry about anything. You'll be safe no matter what. I'll make sure of it.

Britney:
Ur my hero!

AlienKiller666:
I'm gonna have to say bye for now. I need to prep. It takes some time to achieve that perfect deep focus. A warrior has to hone his mental powers before battle.

Britney:
I don't want to say bye but I know u have to do what u have to do. I luv u, my brave brave soldier!

* * *

"Let's try and avoid the mingling charade for now, shall we" said Jack, who wanted to keep focused. "I'd rather we just headed to our seats."

"That's fine by me," said Mona, who didn't want to face prying questions from the media or gossipy celebrities. She knew they'd be fishing for anything they could about her relationship with Elijah. From the looks she was getting, it was clear that people were now fully recognizing that they were a couple.

An usher led them to their seats, which were of course front and center. This was the first year Jack had found himself in the first row of the TCMA, and he had to admit that it felt very good. He looked at the huge elaborate stage in front of him. The art-deco design bordered on gaudy and, to Jack, it resembled an over-the-top set from an old movie about Atlantis. *They've really outdone themselves this year. All it needs now is a mermaid riding through on a dolphin's back,* he laughed to himself.

"Elijah, you take the seat next to Jack," said Mona. "It's not the traditional seating arrangement, but we don't want to take any chances."

The three of them sat down and Jack stretched out his legs in the wide-open space in front of him. "This feels good," he said to Elijah. "No bobbing and weaving trying to see past the oversized heads of those pop stars this year," he laughed.

"I'm not sure if I should be insulted or not," said Elijah. "Don't I fit into the pop star category?"

"Not the big-headed kind," Jack replied. "You are a new breed, my friend."

The room was now quickly filling up. Famous musicians, singers and producers waved to Jack as they made their way to their seats. He had always been popular, but not to this extent. People who had once looked down on him as just an ordinary guy with extraordinary luck were now looking up at him as a man truly capable of exceptional things. It was a pleasant change, but at the same time Jack wasn't feeling entirely comfortable with his new status.

Shifting in his chair, Jack tried to mentally prepare himself for the unknown. He couldn't help wishing that Stuart would have been more precise in his warning. Ghostly warnings were, of course, never straight forward, or simple in books or movies. They should, at the very least, be straight forward and simple when occurring in real life.

Suddenly, something hard and cold latched onto his shoulder with a force that was almost painful. "Hey old boy! How are you feeling tonight?"

Jack turned to look at Billington who was grinning from ear to ear. "Ready for your moment in the sun, old man?" he asked, now taking his hand from Jack's shoulder. "This should be quite a night for you, Jack my man."

Beside Billington sat his wife of many years. Jack ignored Billington's question and greeted his wife instead. "Hello Dorothy," he said. "How are you this evening?"

"Oh Jack! We are so excited for you! Aren't we Benton?" she chirped, her strange mask-like face barely moving after years of cosmetic surgeries.

"We certainly are," said Billington. "This night will be one for the history books." He then reached over and placed his hand on Mona's bare arm. "Hello Mona. Blue satin—nice choice! You look stunning tonight."

"Yes, she does," said Elijah, who had immediately decided that he didn't like Billington or his tone.

"And our prodigal son… Even though we both recognize who the other one is we've never been properly introduced, have we? I'm Mr. Billington, but please feel free to call me Benton."

Out of politeness, Elijah extended his hand. "How do you do," he said, barely glancing at the man. Billington's hand was cold and clammy.

"So, Elijah, you and Mona…well, well who would have guessed? Not a bad catch, Mona. There could be some interesting articles in tomorrow's paper."

"She's a remarkable woman and I simply could not resist," said Elijah, who then turned completely around to face the stage. Mona took his hand in hers and held it tight.

Billington turned his attention back towards Jack. "So, Jack, have you prepared one of your groundbreaking speeches for tonight? They've come to expect a lot from you. I can hardly wait, myself," he said.

Jack just wanted the man to shut up and go away, there was enough to think about tonight without this fool going on and on. However, he knew that it would be best if he was civil. Turning around and looking the man dead in the eye he answered, "They don't call me the Grand Master of Pontification for nothing, old man."

Billington began to laugh heartily. He clapped his hands together and exclaimed. "Oh yes—the Grand Master! That's funny! I can hardly wait to see you up on that stage, Grand Master."

* * *

Minton descended the basement stairs carrying a tub of fresh hot popcorn and some soda pop in a large paper cup.

"Where did you get that?" asked Todd.

"Down the street, at that little movie theatre," Minton replied. "They didn't mind selling it for take-out."

"Why would you bring even the smallest degree of attention to yourself? You know better," scolded Todd.

Minton smirked and replied, "It's no big deal. We're out of here soon anyway. The van's packed and we're ready to roll right after the show is over."

Todd did not respond. He knew now that this would have to be the last job with Minton. The man had broken ranks once too often, and when this happened there was no going back—there was no

187

possible way to bring him back into perfect line again after he had gotten into a habit of defying authority.

Minton sat down in his chair, grabbing the remote from the desk in front of him. He leaned back and turned on the brand-new flat screen television. Quickly, he switched over to the station where the TCMA red carpet event was being broadcast.

In the center of the screen was a beautiful young singer being interviewed by an entertainment reporter. The singer smiled with camera-savvy sweetness as she discussed her very expensive and very revealing virgin-white gown.

"What do you think…real or fake?" asked Minton, as he stuffed popcorn into his mouth.

Todd sat in another chair far away from Minton. He did not respond.

"Her tits! Real or fake?" Minton asked again, determined to force Todd to answer his question.

"I only care about one thing and that is getting the job done," Todd curtly replied.

"All work and no play makes Jack a dull boy," said Minton. "And oh look! There's our man now. All dressed-up for his exciting night—smiling for the camera—never suspecting. You know, the funny thing is that I always liked that guy. He was one of those few nice guys you see up there at the top. What a shame. I'm gonna miss him."

"That weevil had just better not miss," said Todd.

"Not my lover boy. He's miss-proof. I guarantee it." Minton stuffed a large handful of popcorn into his mouth.

Choke, you dog, thought Todd. *Choke and save me the trouble.*

* * *

In the darkness he silently prayed:

O' Thor, great god of thunder. Give me strength. Bestow upon me your power to destroy mine enemy. Through me, let your hammer fall on his head and smash his worthless reptilian skull into a million pieces. O' Thor, it is time the world knows your full glory. That you should be restored to your rightful place as a god among gods. I, your humble servant, am here now to do just that. I will be your great and

188

noble warrior. I will put an end to the filthy reptilian race. I will raise up the name of Thor once and for all. For you are my god, and I am loyal to the end. O' Thor, accept this sacrifice of my blood to prove my loyalty to my one and only god.

He then reached down to his leg and pulled something from his boot. There was a click as he opened the switchblade. Turning on his cell phone for light, he then held out his left hand in front of him, gritted his teeth and with three quick sharp movements carved a thunderbolt into the underside of his forearm. The blood slowly seeped out and dripped down, disappearing into the darkness.

O' Thor, god above all others, I am a sacrifice to you. I am your warrior. I am one with you, oh lord. Take my blood, my offering and pour into me the strength that is you and you alone. I am your holy hammer.

He set his cell phone down beside him and began to rock back and forth, back and forth. In his head, he hummed a heavy tune.

Thor's song of war—a song sent from heaven only to the most worthy. I am he. I am the worthiest among men. The worthiest. The worthiest. I am the worthiest among men.

As he bellowed the song in his mind, the noise above him became barely audible. His self-induced trance-like state had now dampened the sounds of one of the most celebrated shows on earth.

* * *

"It's almost time, Jack," whispered Elijah into his ear.

"Are you ready?" asked Jack.

Elijah's gaze remained firmly fixed on the stage. "Yes, I am," he answered with confidence.

A ruggedly handsome man with honey brown skin and tight shining African curls stood at the microphone. This year's TCMA's host was none other than Magnus Tabor. For many years, he remained America's favorite dashing hero, but he was now getting older. Things were changing. It seemed there was an onslaught of new vibrant young actors and he was worried that he was headed for Hollywood-has-been-land. Being asked to host the TCMA was a wonderful surprise, but it could also possibly be a sign that the community considered him finished and were simply allowing him to exit with dignity. He couldn't remember the last time an interesting script had come his way. Magnus also happened to be an old friend of Jack's.

The crowd listened intently as he began his introduction to the Lifetime Achievement Award. "Leonard Berstein once said, *music can name the unnameable and communicate the unknowable.* This is so very true. Where language fails us, music takes up the cause. It is a powerful weapon in the war against our limitations and deficiencies. It imparts knowledge and makes us better, more intelligent people. The Treble Clef Lifetime Achievement Award represents the highest honor of our industry. It recognizes those few individuals who have proven time and time again their almost supernatural talents in gifting to the world some of the greatest music ever heard.

"Tonight, I have the privilege of giving this award to a man who I have personally known for a very long time. His amazing contribution to the music industry is unprecedented. Arriving in New York over thirty years ago, this self-proclaimed *ordinary guy from Liverpool* turned the American music industry on its ear. He challenged the status quo and redefined music production forever. Known the world over simply by his first name—and in fact, I'm not even sure anymore if he has a last name," there was a short pause while the audience laughed, "Here tonight, I have the great honor of giving the Treble Clef Lifetime Achievement Award to someone who I also have the great privilege of calling my dear friend, none other than our beloved magic-music-man, Jack!"

The audience burst into wild applause as Jack stood up. He signaled to Elijah, who also stood, and then both men began walking up the steps towards the stage.

25

"Will there be anything else, Your Majesty?" asked the servant with a bow.

"No, nothing. I will watch a little telly to help cure my insomnia. You may go now," said the man who was propped up in his bed by an excess of pillows.

"May I switch the television on for you, Your Majesty?"

"I said, go!" It was almost time.

"Yes, Your Majesty," answered the servant, as he walked backwards with his eyes down. He reached behind him, opened the door, and slipped out without turning around.

Happy to finally be alone, the man pressed his head further into the gray satin pillowcase. He picked up the nearby remote and clicked on the television. Mr. Todd had been precise in his instructions as to when he should begin watching. The program was, of course, also set to record, but he wanted to see it at the moment that it happened.

"Very good timing, Mr. Todd," he exclaimed, as he excitedly began to watch the introduction to the Lifetime Achievement Award. When the Magnus Tabor described Jack as *an ordinary man from Liverpool*, he cringed and added, "A common bourgeois curse is what you are! May you rot in your poor man's hell!"

"…. none other than our beloved magic-music-man, Jack!"

The man watched eagerly as the camera turned on Jack. "Go on. Go on," he hissed. "Step up to your death my old enemy."

* * *

Underneath the stage, he laid in wait. No longer able to feel the pain in his arm, he was now feeling only embodied with a new sense of power and determination—a pure power that could only come directly from the Hammer of Thor. The blood sacrifice had worked.

Suddenly the cell phone vibrated. He picked it up and looked at the message.

Britney:
NOW MY LUV!

Dropping the phone on the floor, he swiftly kicked it into the darkness. "I am Son of Thor!" he hissed and began to crawl his way out of the dirty hole.

* * *

"Yes, I am definitely going to miss him. Poor old Jack," said Minton, as he set down the cell phone and then took a long swig of soda. He let out a loud burp. "Excuse me," he said with a laugh.

Todd watched the television screen closely. There was an incredible amount of money riding on this job plus his reputation. He couldn't help worrying that the weevil would lose his nerve and not be able to shoot straight. It had happened before, but at least he was always able to have a back-up sharp-shooter nearby. This time there was no such luxury. Everything rested on the skills of this one patsy.

As he watched Jack go up the stairs with Elijah, he became even more worried. *Why was he not going alone?* From his time on the battlefield, Todd knew how the smallest unforeseen thing could change everything. Elijah was more than a small thing.

* * *

When Jack reached the microphone, Magnus handed him the elegant crystal and gold Treble Clef statue, and then followed with a proper Hollywood bro-hug. "Congratulations friend," he said, as he moved back to give Jack the stage.

Jack smiled and looked out at the crowd. Every person in the room was now standing and cheering wildly. Perhaps for the first time in his life Jack was speechless. Over the years, he had received plenty of applause, but this was somehow different. This was the type of acclamation reserved for heroes. It was amazing!

As he stood there frozen by the level of emotion in the room, Jack suddenly felt a gentle hand pat his shoulder. In all the excitement, he had almost forgotten about Elijah standing beside him. He was now reminded of the speech he had to make.

Twice Jack tried to interrupt the roaring crowd to start his speech, but they would have none of it. He looked over at Elijah, who looked back with a smile and a shrug. Could the adulation go on forever? Jack was beginning to feel a little embarrassed by it all.

He tried a third time. "Thank you, thank you," he said, raising his hand for silence and the crowd began to calm. "Thank you. This is such a great honor."

The crowd was finally quiet except for the odd stray *hurrah* or shrill whistle.

Taking in a deep breath, Jack began his introduction, "First, I would just like to say that this has been an incredible year." He then reached over, took Elijah by the arm, and pulled him a little closer. "It has been full of unforeseen successes and brilliant surprises. But the main reason for Einhorn's amazing success over the past few months has been due to this extraordinary performer and artist I have with me tonight. So, I have asked Elijah to join me on the stage because without him, I truly do not know if I would even be accepting this award this evening—an award that I believe he deserves as much as I."

Elijah looked honestly embarrassed as the crowd burst into applause once again. When they quieted down, Jack was more than ready to give the speech he had so carefully prepared. He opened his mouth and let the words roll out like waves over the audience:

> *Since once I sat upon a promontory,*
> *And heard a mermaid on a dolphin's back*
> *Uttering such dulcet and harmonious breath,*
> *That the rude sea grew civil at her song,*
> *And certain stars shot madly from their spheres,*
> *To hear the sea-maid's music.*

He paused for a short moment to let the magic of the words settle and then continued on with his well-rehearsed allocution. "Those beautiful words were written hundreds of years ago by

William Shakespeare—words still relevant today—words that express so richly the true power of music. Yes, music is power—a power that can harness the very hearts of humankind and cause heaven and earth to dance in unison. Music is magic. It is all that is strange and all that is familiar. It is the rising and falling of God's breath. What a blessed life I have led, to live so long in the midst of this heaven. And although I am extremely grateful for the honor the Treble Clef Society has so graciously bestowed upon me of all people—just a simple short fellow with a funny accent—nothing could possibly compare to the gift that music has given—the gift it has given to all of us. I look back at my achievements, not as mine alone, but as a collective magnum opus. Einhorn records would not be what it is today without the hard work and dedication of thousands of people who are part of the Einhorn family. And then there are our millions of fans, who are like our extended family. One family bound together by music—one *very very* large family."

Jack paused while the audience laughed a little.

"If I were to thank everyone who deserved it, we would be here well into next year. Instead, I will simply say thank you to all of those who…." Jack stopped talking when he heard the gasps and saw the sudden looks of horror on the faces in front of him. Confused, he looked first to Elijah. They then both turned to look behind them. From the back of the stage, walking slowly forward was a tall pale thirty-something man. He was wearing camouflage pants and a plain army green t-shirt. His round head was shaved clean and his left arm seemed to have a large fresh wound covered in congealing blood. His unblinking eyes were fixed on Jack and so was the small semi-automatic weapon in his right hand.

At first, it didn't register with Jack and his mind raced to make sense of it. *This couldn't be real. No, not this. It had to be some sort of a surprise or trick—part of the show. But why would they do such a thing? No one would play a horrible trick like this. It would never be funny. And that man, he's no actor. No, this can't be. And yet it is. This is real!*

Although Jack knew that everything must be moving very fast, time seemed to slow to a crawl. Everything was now moving in slow motion. Jack looked to the right and to the left but could not see security anywhere. He looked again at the man who was coming closer. There was no possible way he could outrun the bullets from that gun. He felt helpless and trapped—unable to escape and with no rescuer in sight.

As the man drew ever closer, Jack saw a grin creep across his face and heard him say, "Prepare to die, alien queer!"

* * *

The gray-haired man sat up straight in his bed and stared eagerly at the television. Suddenly, out of the corner of his eye he noticed a shadow moving from the dark corner of the room towards him. Angry that a servant had returned to his room without permission, he yelled, "I did not call! Get out now!"

Instead of leaving, the figure came closer. "Did you not hear me? Deaf fool, get out!" the man screamed.

The figure did not say a word but moved ever closer. He stopped when he was in enough of the television light for the gray-haired man to see his face. "You are not a servant," said the man, now feeling fear and panic at a stranger having accessed his private rooms. For many years, he had had nightmares about assassins.

As he stared at the intruder, he began to realize that he recognized the younger man. "Wait, I know you," he said, trying to place a name with the face. "It was a long time ago. But from where do I know you?" Suddenly, it came to him like a bolt of lightning. "Yes, of course! But it can't be!" he exclaimed in shock.

"It is I," the figure answered.

"You are that…that person! But you are dead. My father killed you years ago. It can't be you."

"Do you remember my name? Say my name."

"No, this is a dream! This is not real! I have been drugged!"

"Say my name," said the figure, moving ever closer.

The man was beginning to tremble now. "Stuart!" he screamed hoping this would make this apparition disappear. Stuart stood in his place.

"Do you remember that day behind the chair?" asked Stuart.

The man immediately knew what he was talking about, but instead of answering, he put his hands over his face and yelled, "Go away!"

"Do you remember? Your father had been particularly cruel that day and you sought refuge behind that chair even though you were much closer to being a man than a child. I stumbled across you hiding and weeping, and so I sat down on the floor and we talked. Do you remember?"

"You are not real!" he yelled, taking his hands from his eyes, and looking straight at the apparition hoping that a direct approach would finally make him disappear.

Stuart stood strong. "Amongst the many things I told you that day, I emphasized that you must concentrate on the good things within yourself and not let others dictate who you are and who you will be. No one can possibly know you but you. Do you remember?"

Now, the man's fear was quickly turning to anger. *Who did this apparition think he was to come boldly into His Majesty's room and bring up the past?* "You weakened me, that day!" he screamed. "My father worked to make me strong—make me powerful! You told me things that made me feel better—things that would make me weak and useless!"

"Anger and frustration are not power," responded Stuart. "They are death."

"Liar!" screamed the man. He then looked at the television screen and could see the assassin holding the gun and walking up behind Jack. Smiling wickedly, he exclaimed, "Look there apparition! You are just in time to watch your beloved die. Like my father destroyed you, I am just about to destroy him!"

"But I am here," said Stuart. "I am not dead. Your father did not destroy me. True your father killed, but not me or anyone else. Your father killed himself and himself alone. Such as him have no real power. He was nothing."

"You are a completely mad apparition!" yelled the man, never taking his eyes from the television. It was then that he saw something on the screen that made his jaw drop.

"No man has the power of life and death over another," continued Stuart. "But every man has the power of life and death over himself. It is sad you have chosen your death. I am sorry, but the choice was yours and yours alone." He then turned and began to walk back into the shadows.

"No!" the man screamed after him. "I have power over whomever I choose! I can kill whomever I wish to kill! It is mine—all mine! You are nothing! I am every...."

* * *

As they stared in shock at the television, Minton's mouth fell open and some half-chewed popcorn rolled out and onto the floor. He looked over wide-eyed at Mr. Todd.

Todd looked back and yelled, "Get the rest of the stuff in the truck! We need to get out of here! Now!"

* * *

Jack watched as the man stepped ever closer. Having never been afraid of death, he was not afraid now. But still, he did not want to die here. He did not want to die in this way and in front of Mona and Elijah. He did not want to leave them behind like this.

In those long-drawn-out moments, the theatre was so silent. It was as if everyone had been frozen in time. Jack looked at the gun and wondered, not if, but when the trigger would be pulled. When it happened, would he know he had been shot, or would he die instantly? Where would the man shoot—the head, the heart? Either way it would ruin his tuxedo. As he thought about all of this, he realized how ridiculous the entire situation was and almost began to laugh.

Then, like a burst of rain in an empty desert, a strange, beautiful sound suddenly broke through the suffocating silence. It stopped the man in his tracks. At first, Jack could not understand what was happening, but then he quickly realized that it was Elijah. Elijah was singing *Love Rising*!

Time still continued to creep along as the man now stared curiously at Elijah, who released each perfect note into air as though he were releasing a magic dust—dust with the power to quell all horror and mesmerize the man with the gun.

Jack turned his head to look at Elijah, and as he did, time broke free. Without warning, everything was moving at an incredible pace—too fast for Jack's mind to grasp what was happening. The air was filled with shrieks and screams, the sound of running, grunts and shouts, a body-thump against the stage floor and worst of all, the single loud bang of a gun.

Jack was horrified to hear that last sound. He worried first about Elijah, but when he looked over at him, he looked perfectly fine. He then placed his hand on his own chest to check for wounds, but there was no wet sticky blood like he half-expected. He then turned his head back towards the gunman and was surprised to realize that the man was now being pinned to the floor by Magnus. Magnus, who was looking just like a character from one of his movies, had him in a classic action-man hold. Security was finally rushing in from all sides.

There was a great sense of relief in the room, as the security guards quickly took charge of the would-be assassin. They lifted him up from the floor in handcuffs. Before they had a chance to move off stage, there was a sudden strange animal screech echoing throughout the theatre. It immediately sent shivers through the crowd. Everyone looked in the direction of the horrible noise. There, pressed as far back into her seat as possible and screaming hysterically, was Dorothy Billington, her over-tightened face looking as hideous as the sounds coming out of her mouth. She was staring in horror at her husband beside her. Billington was slouched in his chair with his head to one side. His eyes stared out at nothing as a tiny crimson stream flowed from the tidy little bullet hole in the middle of his forehead.

26

Jack poured the boiling water from the kettle into the teapot. The steam billowed up as the Hollies played in the background. It had been a long night and he had barely slept, but still, he did not feel tired.

"Should I make you some breakfast?" asked Mona who was standing by the refrigerator. She and Elijah had stayed at Jack's place, not wanting to leave him alone after what had happened.

"Would you believe it, for maybe the first time in my life, I'm just not hungry," Jack smiled slightly. "But feel free to prepare something for yourself and Elijah."

Elijah, who had been standing beside Mona, moved over and placed his arm around Jack's shoulder. "Maybe you should sit down and let me finish the tea."

"Nonsense," replied Jack. "I am fine, and more importantly I am alive."

"And we are glad of that," said Mona.

"Both of you sit," said Jack, gesturing towards the table. "Let me finish the tea. After all, who knows tea better than an old Englishman?"

Elijah and Mona sat down while Jack set cups in front of them. He opened the fridge, took out the milk and placed it on the table beside the sugar bowl. "I suppose that is the second time I have cheated death," he said, opening a drawer and taking out some spoons.

"Are you referring to the close encounter with the Duke?" asked Mona.

"Yes," he answered, as he brought the teapot from the kitchen counter to the table. He began to pour the brew into the cups. "I stared directly into the eyes of that murderous swine!"

Mona turned and explained to Elijah, "The Duke was responsible for the death of Stuart. He also came close to having Jack killed."

"Close but no cigar," said Jack, as he sat down. "He did, however, die very shortly after our meeting. The Good Lord works in mysterious ways."

"He's not really dead though, is he?" said Elijah. When Mona and Jack looked at him questionably, he added, "I mean Stuart, not the Duke."

Jack smiled and sighed. "No, I suppose you could say that he isn't dead at all."

"It was Stuart who saved you," said Elijah. "Without his warning to keep me near, that man would have shot you."

"You both saved me," said Jack, as he patted Elijah's hand. "And I am grateful for the both of you—and of course for the help of good old Magnus."

Elijah shook his head. "I really didn't know what I was doing and have no idea why I started singing. It just sort of happened."

"There are no accidents in this world," said Jack, as he sat down. He then took a sip of tea and closed his eyes.

After a few moments of silence, Mona asked, "What are you thinking about?"

Jack opened his eyes and looked at her. "I was remembering Stuart, and the times we would just talk forever about all sorts of things. Sometimes when I'm alone, I'll talk as if he were really here. I know it sounds daft, but it has kept me going all these years."

"It's not silly," said Mona. "And it's especially not silly since you have seen and heard him. Maybe he hears every word you say to him. If he can tell you things, then he must hear you too."

"That is a beautiful thought," said Jack. Turning to Elijah, he then said, "You realize they will be coming for us in hoards. Wanting to know every detail—every thought—every feeling—every hint of a feeling. Are you ready for the media onslaught?"

Elijah laughed. "As my old grandma used to say, we'll be rolled in honey, covered in feed and then sent into the chicken pen."

Jack started laughing too. "I could not have explained it better. If you don't mind, I think we should do all interviews together. In fact, we should get Magnus to join us on the circuit. He's a real-life action hero now."

"Sounds like a good plan," replied Elijah.

"Would you like us to stay again tonight?" asked Mona. "I don't know if it's a good idea for you to be alone." Mona suspected that if a crazy killer had managed to get access to the TCMA, someone on the inside must have wanted Jack dead. She was worried there might be a second attempt on his life.

Jack smiled. "I don't think that will be necessary. Believe it or not, there is still the spirit of a strong young man underneath this aging facade. In the past, I've faced all types of threats and conflicts. The only difference this time was the public drama. Besides which, don't you two have some work to do? There is still the business of finding Rose."

Elijah could see that the last thing Jack wanted or needed right now was to be mothered. Trying to be as diplomatic as possible, he said, "Jack's right Mona. He'll be fine on his own. If there was any danger, surely Stuart would have sent another warning. The best thing we can do for him now is to keep searching for Rose."

Mona was still not sure. She wanted so much to protect Jack and keep him safe; just the same way he had done for her over the years. "I just don't feel right leaving you alone."

Jack affectionately placed his hand on her arm. "Please stop worrying," he said. "I'll be fine. I simply need to be alone right now."

Mona was still hesitant, but she realized that the choice was not really hers to make. Jack had a right to decide for himself. "Okay, we'll go home, Jack," she said. "But if you need anything at all, then call us right away. And I mean *right away*. I don't care if it's just a spider in the bathroom. Call us!"

Jack laughed. "If it is between me and a spider, I'm quite sure I'd win that fight. You need to start concentrating on where to search next. That's my biggest concern right now. If you can find Rose, it will help me know for certain that all we've been through has not been in vain. Keep your focus on what is important."

"I was thinking that maybe we should make the trip back to Canada and ask around her old neighborhood. We can knock on doors. Maybe someone will know something," said Elijah.

That sounded perfectly logical to Mona, and she wondered why she hadn't thought of it before. "Good idea," she said. "But maybe I should go alone again. After all, if a big rock star turns up at the door, it might be too shocking."

Elijah laughed. "Oh, I think that might make them even more talkative."

"You're probably right," said Mona. "The problem now is that your schedule is just too full. I'll have to move a couple of things around if we are going to take the trip."

Jack was leaning back in his chair and sipping the hot tea. It felt good to hear them getting back to business. There were no longer any doubts in his mind that this was the right course to take. He finally had complete faith, but now he mustn't let that close call undermine his confidence. "Just think how wonderful it will be when you find her," he said. "I know now that this is definitely what Stuart wants, and whatever Stuart wants, I want too."

Mona smiled at her old friend and wondered how he could be so strong so soon after a threat on his life? Jack's perseverance had always amazed her. Even the day his mother died, he was so brave. "Don't worry, Jack, we'll find Rose," she said. "We'll find her and nothing's going to stop us.

* * *

"Well, at least we don't have to worry about Billington being disappointed," said Minton as he turned up the van air conditioner. "Should we try to get a hold of the King of Fools once more? Why would he ignore your calls? Unless he is planning to quietly come after us for not coming through."

Mr. Todd, who was sitting in the passenger seat, had been trying to contact his primary client for a couple of days now, but with no luck. He knew the man would be furious and wanted to calm things before it became too much to handle. He needed to explain the next option and to get the ball rolling again. This had to happen quickly if he were to salvage his reputation. "I'll try him again," he said, taking out his cell phone.

Todd waited and listened as it rang over and over. Just as he was expecting the automated voice to once again tell him that the customer was unavailable and to try again later, someone answered. "Hello."

"Hello, Your Majesty. This is Mr. Todd," he said, ready to plead, grovel or do anything to make this right.

Minton glanced over at his boss and then looked back at the road ahead. *Finally, this moron is talking. He'll want a second shot, but where I am going to find such another perfect weevil? Oh, what went wrong my sweet psychopath? I thought I knew you and then at the last moment, you let me down. I suppose my happiness is something I will have to continue fighting for, so rot in prison dumb fuck. You are just one among the many forgotten.*

Todd silently listened to the person on the other line. As time went on without Todd saying so much as a word, Minton began to wonder just how long the King of Fools was going to berate him. Surely, he would have to shut up and let Todd explain eventually. He couldn't go on forever.

"Yes, thank you very much," said Todd. He then took the phone from his ear and hit the off button.

"So, what did he say?" Minton asked. "Did we get fired? Please don't tell me that ass wants the down payment back."

"He didn't say anything," replied Todd.

"What! Come on. What did he say?"

Todd turned his head and looked at Minton. "He said nothing because he's dead."

"Dead?"

"Apparently, His Majesty is dead. It happened that same night. He died of a stroke."

"Yee-hah, the king is dead!" shouted Minton. "We are the luckiest devils on earth. A job goes wrong and then both clients, who have the capacity to make our lives a living hell, kick the bucket. Can you believe it, Mr. Todd? We are golden. Nothing can touch us."

Mr. Todd smiled. "I guess we are pretty lucky at that," he said.

"That calls for a song," said Minton, who then began to tap on the dashboard and sing Yankee Doodle.

Todd was feeling so good that he even joined in at the line where Yankee Doodle stuck a feather in his cap. Suddenly, their song was interrupted by the ugly sound of a deflating balloon.

"Sorry," said Minton. "I guess that burrito I ate at lunch didn't agree with me."

Todd was disgusted, but two seconds later he was even more disgusted. He quickly opened his window. "For God's sake Minton, put your window down."

"Sorry boss," apologized Minton, as he opened his window. The smell began to quickly dissipate.

Minton now focused on the winding road ahead. "Wouldn't you say that the Pennsylvania countryside is the most beautiful at this time of year," he said.

Todd was still enjoying the relief of not having a do-over job hanging over him. "It is nice."

"I've actually been this way before, as a kid with my parents," said Minton. "If I remember right, we should soon be coming up to an historic bridge just around the next bend. My mother always loved to sketch bridges, but she has arthritis now and just can't do it anymore."

Todd was surprised that Minton was talking about bridges and his mother. He wasn't exactly the nostalgic type.

Suddenly, a tiny insect flew in through the window and began to zip around the front of the van. "A bee!" screamed Minton. He began shrieking and hitting out at it whenever it flew close to his head.

"Stop it!" shouted Todd. "It's just a bee. Calm down! Look where you're driving!" When the bee came his way, he tried to knock it out of his window, but only managed to chase it back towards Minton.

"Ahhhhh!" Minton screamed, as he wildly hit out in every direction.

"The wheel!" yelled Todd. "Turn the...."

* * *

"Please Jack, sit down," said Magnus, gesturing towards the table and chairs on his patio. "It's nice of you to join me for lunch."

Jack took a seat. "After the news conference and the interviews, I should think you might be tired of seeing me," he said.

Magnus smiled, pulled out a chair and sat down. "I never tire of seeing good friends."

A friendly plump woman in her thirties appeared, carrying a tray with a pitcher of lemonade and two already filled glasses. She placed the tray on the table, smiled at the two men then turned and walked away. "Thank you, Maria," said Magnus. He then took one of the glasses and placed it in front of Jack. "I suppose it's growing up in the south, but it just doesn't seem right to drink anything else on such a beautiful hot day. It's like a little piece of home in the middle of New York. Is this okay with you, or is there something you would rather have? Need something stronger?"

"No," answered Jack. "This will be just fine, thank you."

"So," said Magnus, in such a way that Jack knew this meeting would be more than just two friends getting together for lunch. "You know I never like to beat around the bush on things. I invited you here today because I want to talk to you about something important.

204

There's been some talk, Jack. There's been talk that Elijah is looking for something he really shouldn't be looking for."

Jack took a sip of lemonade. *It could use a little more sugar,* he thought. *Magnus must be trying to get in shape for all of the offers that must be coming his way.* "You don't mean that he's looking for *something,* Magnus. You mean he's looking for *someone.*"

"Well…yes," responded Magnus. "There are some people who are very concerned."

"I'm sure there are," said Jack.

"He's breaking the rules, Jack. You know that."

"Whose rules?" asked Jack.

Magnus looked at him in surprise. This was not the answer he was expecting. "They are the rules. They're our rules and we have always followed them. We must continue to follow them."

"Why?"

Magnus was again taken aback by Jack's reply. "Don't you realize that the rules have been in place for centuries? We can't just decide to break them whenever we please. That's what has preserved us all this time. It kept the Bloodline going. It saved lives. The rules must be obeyed. If you allow this to happen, God help us all."

Jack could see how deeply Magnus believed that following the rules was the only way, and it was beginning to raise old doubts in his mind once more. *Was he right that it had saved lives in the past? Could I have over-stepped my mark? Maybe all the wonderful things that have happened have now gone to my head? I'm not part of the Bloodline. How can I make such a huge decision—a decision that could prove to be devastating for a lot of people? And Stuart didn't tell me I should allow Elijah to go on this search. Stuart didn't say anything about searching for the woman. Perhaps I have it all wrong. Maybe it's still not too late to turn back.*

Glancing over at the patio garden, Jack noticed, among the carefully tended plants, a potted rose vine in the corner. It was snaking up a white triangular trellis. The vine was sparse and seemed to be struggling in the heat and smog of the city, but there was one off-shoot of the plant near the bottom where the leaves were rich green and a single golden rose had beautifully blossomed. A golden rose. That is what Stuart had called her. He called her the Golden Rose.

Jack suddenly knew what he had to do. "Frankly Magnus, I'm tired of the rules," he said. "Call me a rebel if you like, but I'm tired of all the lies and foolishness that almost got me killed. I'm tired of the same old ideas around what the Bloodline is and what it means. I want something new. Something pure. Something that can take us beyond anything we have ever accomplished before. These past few years I have felt as if I have been going in circles. Round and round, where nothing changed. No matter what I did, nothing really changed. When Elijah came along, that stopped. He made me feel like I was accomplishing so much. I'm not going to turn my back on him now. He says this is important, so I will believe him, and I will do everything I can to try and help him."

At first, Magnus did not know what to say. Was Jack becoming a little mad with power? No one had ever just flouted the rules like that. Perhaps it was the shock from what had happened at the TCMA. Post-traumatic syndrome can last a very long time.

"I know a lot of things have happened lately," Magnus said. "It's a very confusing time for all of us. And Elijah was—well he was a bit of a miracle in himself, but that still doesn't mean he can just break all the rules—rules that people have made sacrifices to uphold. He's out of line, Jack."

Jack laughed a little. "Oh Magnus, tell me exactly, where o' where is the line? Do any of us really know the answer to that question? The truth is people just make up the line as they go along— a line of convenience. Elijah may be the only one of us who is actually in line—the real line." Leaning over the table, he looked his friend straight in the eye. "Elijah is not just anyone. He knows things. He feels things. Things we may never know or feel. I've allowed him this freedom because I'm confident that he can somehow bring about those changes we have longed for. Think about it. All those songs we send around the world and even into outer space. All those songs pleading for our salvation. From the Book of Psalms to the latest hit single, we have been pleading for as long as our species has been in existence. It's time to take a risk. Let's break the rules. Let's be honest with ourselves and admit that we don't have any real answers. Let's give Elijah a chance to answer some of those questions. Give him a chance to change the world in the way we have always dreamed of. Wouldn't that be something wonderful? To finally taste, not just a tiny morsel, but a true all-out victory! I can't think of anything I want more. Can you?"

Magnus had definitely not been expecting this. Jack was not power-mad, but he was full of faith. Was faith even worse than madness?

"Can you not see?" said Jack. "We keep waiting and waiting, and for what? For Godot? After all these years of waiting, Elijah says that if he finds her, things will change. There'll be no more waiting for any of us. Wouldn't that be incredible? Finally, after so long, we will see it all happen. We will have goodness and love follow us all the days of our lives. The world will at last be saved. Is there any happier ending?"

Magnus was astonished by the extent of Jack's passion. Jack had always been known for his zest for life and for business, but this was different. It was intense—almost frighteningly so. This was a side to his old friend he had never really seen before. And the things that he had just said—things no one else had ever dared utter.

As Magnus sat there looking at Jack, it all began to become clear. If what he was saying were true, then all those years spent in clandestine meetings and making secret plans were not what any of them thought. It would mean that they didn't have the power to bring about the great changes. In some ways, they were nothing more than chattering children at play. What a humbling thought. And yet wasn't humility supposed to be one of their main credos? At least there was much talk given to it. Somewhere along the line, had they lost their humility, and along with it, their imagination? Why couldn't the entire world be changed by one man? It has happened many times throughout history. Could this really be what they had all been waiting for? In the end, the entire world would change not by the loud booms of guns and bombs, as they all believed, but by the single quiet choice of one man—Elijah.

"Jack," said Magnus. "Do what you have to do to help Elijah, and I'll try to quell the fears of the others."

"Thank you, my old friend," smiled Jack. "It's good to know that you can see it too."

Just then the patio door opened and Maria cheerfully wheeled the lunch cart out to the table. "Lunch is served," she sang. As she set a full plate in front of Jack, she beamed, "And just for you Mr. Jack, *food fit for the gods!*"

* * *

Elijah was at Mona's, leaning back on the sofa, his feet on the coffee table and the remote control in his hand. *Is this it for Thursday morning choices,* he wondered, *cooking, celebrity bull-shooting and emotional exhibitionism?* He switched over to one of the news networks hoping to find something slightly more substantial. A woman with too much makeup, piano key veneers and a plastic-hard face was delivering random bits and pieces of stories:

Early this morning, the second man, a passenger who was in the van that went off an historic Pennsylvania bridge last week, has died in hospital. The driver was killed instantly at the time of the accident. This is not the first time this famous bridge has seen death. In fact, many in the area consider it to be haunted, and have unofficially named it the Killer Bridge...

Just then, Mona walked in and sat down close beside Elijah. "I was on the phone to Jack," she said. "And I have some good news."

Elijah switched off the television. "What is it?" he eagerly asked.

"Yesterday Jack had a long discussion with Magnus Tabor and apparently, he's now on our side. He's willing to support us in our search for Rose."

"Great!" exclaimed Elijah. "He has some pull in this world, doesn't he? Maybe he'll be able to provide us with more information."

"Yes, some pull, but not enough that he might know anything about Rose. At least, this is what he told Jack." Mona could see that Elijah was disappointed. "Still," she said, "he may have access to someone who would know where to look. If we could recruit Magnus, we may be able to recruit others as well—maybe someone higher up who has the address."

"And what about our trip to Canada next week? Should we still go?" he asked.

"I don't see why not. We need to try everything." Mona rested her head against Elijah and he wrapped his arm around her. She then curled up tighter against his body.

"It's nice to have a day off," Elijah said, kissing her hair. "It's just like heaven to spend it with you."

"Mmmm," Mona breathed. She closed her eyes and wished everyday could be like this.

Elijah wrapped his other arm around her and began to quietly hum *Love Rising*. In his head, he sang the words. When he reached the line *Rise up my darling*, something strange happened. Suddenly, he felt as though he were being lifted right off the sofa. Shocked by the experience he immediately stopped humming and the sensation abruptly ended.

"Don't stop. I was singing along in my mind," said Mona.

"Something just happened," Elijah said. "As I was singing, I felt something strange happen to me."

"What do you mean?" Mona asked him.

"It was…it was different. I mean, I was different. I felt like I was taking off."

"Taking off?"

"Yes," said Elijah, trying hard to describe the experience. "I know it sounds weird but I felt like I was beginning to…well…beginning to fly."

Mona laughed. "Perhaps being a superstar is going to your head, if you now think you're a superhero."

"Maybe," laughed Elijah. "But you know what I can't help thinking?"

"What's that?"

"I can't help thinking that somehow Rose was responsible. Somehow, she heard me singing the song and caused me to feel that way."

Mona placed her hand on his leg. "Do you think she could be a fan?"

Elijah stopped and thought about Mona's question. Even though she had asked it in jest, it was no joke. Why had he never considered this before? "Why wouldn't she be?" he exclaimed. "After all, she comes to me in dreams. If I dream of her, could she dream of me? Wouldn't you be a fan of the man of your dreams?"

Mona thought about it for a moment and then smiled. "That makes perfect sense," she said. "Rose would have to be a fan. How could she not be?"

Elijah took his arms from around Mona and sat straight up. "If she's a fan," he said, "then maybe she's on our mailing list."

Mona sat up straight too. "Of course!" she exclaimed. "Why didn't we think of it before? We need to check the mailing list! I'll contact Ron in Marketing and see if we can find her name on the list."

"Oh Mona, could it really be that simple? Will we really find her there?" Elijah was a little nervous about getting his hopes up too high. He wanted to keep a level head.

"Why not?" replied Mona. "Why shouldn't it be that simple? If she's going to be a fan of anyone, it would be logical that she'd be a fan of yours. Let me go make a quick call. My phone's in the other room. I'll be just a moment."

Elijah sat alone on the sofa. What if the information is really there? How would this change him? Before, it was easy to keep an emotional distance. He could think and talk about Rose with some degree of detachment. She was real but not that real. She was still safely tucked away in his dreams. But now, the idea that he might be getting closer to seeing her face was both elating and frightening at the same time. Elijah could feel his heart beating faster.

Mona came back into the room with her phone in hand. "Okay, I spoke with Ron, and he's going to do a search to see if he can find her."

Elijah said nothing as he stared at the floor. Mona became concerned. "Are you alright?" she asked, sitting down next to him, and taking his hand.

"Yes," he replied. "Stupid as it sounds, I'm a little frightened. Here I am, wanting more than anything in the world to make my dreams come true, and now I'm frightened that it may finally happen."

Mona stroked his face. "I think it's normal. I'm a little frightened myself. This is big Elijah—huge! If we find this woman, we could be changing the entire course of the world. Who wouldn't feel scared?"

Elijah reached over and pulled her to him. "I'm so glad I have you, Mona. You mean everything to me."

Just then there was sound of the *Love Rising* ring tone. Someone was calling Mona's phone. She picked it up and looked at the call display. "It's Ron," she said.

* * *

Jack was wearing sweats, a ball cap, and dark glasses, as he enjoyed the beautiful morning in Central Park. He decided to disguise himself, not because he was afraid of another assassin, but because people just couldn't get enough of him since the incident at the TCMA. He didn't think it was possible, but he was now an even bigger celebrity than before. As soon as the first person recognized him, he knew he'd be swarmed, and this was a morning Jack really needed some quiet park time.

He leaned his arm on the back of the bench and watched as all the different people walked, jogged, and wheeled by. Jack always loved to watch people and try to imagine their lives. Billions of people on this planet—everyone unique with a complicated life--every one of them separate but connected. It was amazing! *What a piece of work is a man*, he couldn't help thinking.

Looking up at the clear blue sky, he watched as an airplane flew overhead. Once he had seriously considered getting his pilot's license, but his natural lack of prowess with large machines kept him from pursuing this dream. However, the idea of having the freedom to fly anywhere at any time had never lost its appeal.

His eye followed a bird that swooped down into a nearby tree. Once it landed, he could see it was a robin. Jack smiled. It reminded him of Stuart and about how much he still missed him. He never told even Mona the truth about what he had felt after the attempt on his life. When he was finally alone in his room that night, he couldn't help feeling a little disappointed that the killer had not been successful. If he had, perhaps he and Stuart would be together right now. Jack knew he shouldn't think like that, but there were times when it was difficult not to.

When will we be together again? he silently asked.

"Soon," said a voice in his ear.

Jack jumped and quickly looked to the right and then to the left, but there was no one there. He looked behind him—still no one. He stood up and looked behind the bench, but again, there was no one. He looked up in the tree and the little bird was gone.

That was not my imagination, thought Jack. *As I know that the images in the unicorn case and in the looking-glass were not my imagination. That was not my imagination. That was Stuart! What did he mean 'soon'? Oh Stuart, come back! Tell me more!"*

Just then, Jack felt his phone vibrate. He took it out of his pocket and answered.

"Hello," he said.

"Jack! Oh Jack! It's incredible! It's wonderful!"

"Mona, calm down. What is wonderful?"

"Oh Jack, we found her! We really found her!"

Jack couldn't believe it at first. Was Mona confused or was he mishearing? "You mean you found Rose?"

"Yes Jack! Oh yes! And you won't believe where. All this time she was on Elijah's mailing list. Can you believe it? Why didn't we think of that first?"

Jack sat back down on the bench. *They found her! Did you hear that, Stuart? They found her!* He could feel tears starting to well up in his eyes and was happy that he was wearing dark glasses. "Where are you?" he asked.

"We are at my place," said Mona.

"I'll be over as soon as I can," said Jack. "We need to make plans about how we should approach this." He then shot up from the bench and headed out of the park to flag down a cab.

* * *

Before Jack could step through the door, Mona threw her arms around him, almost knocking him down.

"We did it!" she shouted. "We did it, Jack!"

"Let me inside and we'll talk about it," he laughed.

"Oh, of course. I'm sorry. Come in." Mona released Jack and stepped aside to let him enter. After quickly closing the door, she then grabbed him by the arm and pulled him to the living room.

Jack saw Elijah who appeared to be in quiet contemplation. He looked up at Jack and in a calm voice said, "Hello."

"So, you have found her," Jack said, sitting down on the sofa. Mona sat down close beside him, still holding on to his arm.

"We did, Jack! We did!" exclaimed Mona.

"And you are sure that this time it is really her?"

"Everything fits Jack. Even her birth date. We know it's really her!"

Jack patted Mona's arm. To Elijah, he asked, "What do you believe we should do next?"

"I want to go alone," Elijah answered. "I think it's best."

"But Elijah," said Mona, "don't you think we should all go?" Ever since her failed trip to Canada, Mona had dreamed of this day. She wanted to be one of the first ones to meet Rose.

"I can't tell you why Mona because I don't know the answer. All I know is what I feel, and I feel I should go alone. For some reason, it's important."

"I think we should go with Elijah on this one," said Jack to Mona. "He had the dreams and she is, after all, his fan."

Mona sighed and looked at Elijah. He smiled at her and said, "Don't worry. If all goes well, you will be meeting her soon."

"We'll all be meeting her," added Jack.

Mona got up from the sofa and walked over to Elijah. She sat down on the arm of the chair and wrapped her arms around him. "I didn't mean to be pushy," she said. "I'm just so excited."

"I know," replied Elijah. "And without you and Jack, I know that none of this would have been possible. But for this journey, I just feel that I have to go alone. I'll be booking a flight to Canada tonight, and tomorrow, I intend to show up at her door."

"When do you think you'll be back?" asked Mona.

"You know I have a concert at Madison Square Gardens in three days, so I'll be back here with you tomorrow night. When I see her, I'm going to be giving her tickets for both the concert and for the plane to get here. In my dream, that's where we were, in a large concert hall. It seems to make sense to do it this way."

Jack sighed and closed his eyes. Were they really on the edge of something so big it would change the world? Had they finally reached the end and come to the beginning—the beginning of everything? All those years of struggling to know if he was on course—all those years of reminding himself that believing in Stuart was the right thing to do. Stuart, his *ever-fixed mark*. Was it finally going to all come together? He almost felt like crying.

"Jack are you okay," asked Mona.

"Yes," he said, feeling a single tear fall down his cheek. "In fact, I haven't felt this good in a very long time."

27

Elijah slowly walked up the stone path. He stopped and stared at the grape vine wreath hanging on the front door. Cloth flowers of many beautiful colors had been delicately placed throughout the ring. The wreath had a finished, but yet natural look—the look of something thoughtfully crafted by a caring hand.

He stared at the doorbell and thought about what might happen when he pushed it. What would she think to see the famous Elijah standing on her threshold? And what on earth would he say to her? Would she have any idea—any sort of instinct about why he was there? Would she react like just a regular fan? *I suppose there is only one way to find out*, he thought to himself, as he pushed the button.

It seemed to take a long time before he heard a click of the latch. When the door finally opened and he saw her face for the first time, there was a strange flash of light as if from a camera. It took him a moment to focus and see her welcoming smile.

"Elijah!" she beamed. "I knew you'd come."

* * *

Jack sat down at his weight machine. He was feeling determined to lose at least a couple of pounds this week, but he also needed to do something to take his mind off what might be happening with Elijah. He had not slept well for thinking about it.

He increased the tension. Today was the day he'd finally get into perfect shape—turn all that old man fat into youthful muscle. The other day he had seen men on television, older than him, still competing in body building competitions. It could be done. All he needed was the willpower.

Jack strained to push his arms out straight. He pulled and pulled but could not lift the weight. *I know I can do it*, he thought. *It's simply mind over matter*. He tried again until the pain was too much and he had to let go. *One more time*, he thought, determined to lift it

214

no matter how much it hurt. Jack strained once more. He could feel his heart pounding and his face turning beat red. Then suddenly, *crack*! An intense pain was burning through his lower back and Jack found that he couldn't move.

He sat for a few moments, hoping it was just a passing thing, but whenever he tried to move even the slightest, the pain was so intense that he felt like he was going to pass out. Finally, he had to admit that he needed help.

Jack looked over at his phone. *Thank God, I placed it within arm's length.* Slowly and carefully, he reached over and picked it up. As he did, every tiny movement in his shoulder sent a fiery knife into his back. Once he had the phone finally close enough to see the numbers, he hit the speed dial and then the speaker button. *Please answer! Whatever you do, don't send me to voicemail!*

"Hello," Mona said, much to his relief.

"Mona," Jack grunted in pain. "I need your help!"

"What happened? Are you alright?" He could hear the worry in her voice.

"I was exercising and I hurt my back."

"Oh Jack!" Mona was laughing now. "I told you to slow down. You're not as young as you think you are."

"Only yesterday I saw men older than me competing in body building. I'm not past it."

"Jack, those men are on steroids. You should know that."

Jack started to laugh silently at himself. *Of course they are. For someone in the business of illusion, how did I miss that?* "Well, this old fool needs some help now. I'm stuck on the weight machine. Can you come over?"

"Actually, I'm shopping just a couple of blocks away. I'll be there in ten minutes."

"Thanks. It's nice to have a friend you can always count on."

"Have you heard from Elijah?" asked Mona.

"Not yet."

"I didn't even want to go shopping, but I needed to do something to take my mind off of Elijah."

"I understand," said Jack. "That's precisely why I am now in so much pain. Please hurry."

* * *

Elijah was sitting on the sofa, quietly waiting. Rose came from the kitchen carrying a tray with two cups of tea and a plate of homemade cookies. She placed it down on the coffee table and then held out the plate of cookies. "Try one," she said. "They are called Honey Surprise."

Politely taking one of the small golden cookies, Elijah then took a bite. Its sweet sugary goodness melted in his mouth. "These are amazing!" he said, and then quickly finished it off.

Rose sat down close beside him. Their bodies were almost touching and it made Elijah feel both hot and cold at the same time. "Have some tea to wash it down," she said.

He picked up one of the teacups and drank back some of the warm refreshing brew.

"You don't know what this means to me," said Rose. "To open that door and see you finally standing there is just so wonderful!"

Elijah looked at Rose briefly. It was difficult to maintain eye contact with this woman for very long without feeling overwhelmed. He looked at the cup in his hand and said, "You seem to have been expecting me."

"Oh yes!" she exclaimed. "I always knew you'd come around, but some days I was afraid it wouldn't happen. Every day I listened to your music, hoping that…well I know it sounds strange…but hoping that you could hear me listening. And that you would come to find me. Now here you are."

"I have something for you," said Elijah, who then took out the tiny white plastic shoe from his pocket and held it out. "A friend of mine, Mona, wanted me to give this to you."

Rose took it in her hand and laughed. "How beautiful!" she exclaimed. "That's my doll's shoe! I still have her." She then got up and went over to a credenza. Opening the drawer, she took out something and then returned to the sofa. Elijah could see she had a small doll in her hand. The doll had dark skin and was dressed in a nurse's uniform. One of the white shoes was missing.

Placing the tiny shoe on the doll's foot, Rose then stroked the doll's red hair. "Do you know that her hair used to be black," she said. "But time somehow changed the color." She set the doll on the table and looked directly at Elijah. "Please tell your friend Mona, *thank you.* It was so kind of her to do this for me."

Elijah smiled and blushed but wasn't sure why. He felt like a child sitting next to her. "I dreamed of you," he said. "In the dream, you changed." *Why would I say that? I'm babbling now. What must she think?*

"That's wonderful," she answered, much to Elijah's surprise. "I am changing in many ways."

For a moment, there was only silence between them as Elijah thought about what to say next. The words and ideas were all scrambled in his mind. He then suddenly blurted out, "There were some who didn't want me to come here—to see you. They said I would ruin things. They said it was against the rules."

"So, there are others who know of me. How long have they known?"

"Many years," answered Elijah.

"Oh, I see. So, what made you break the rules?"

"Dreams," he answered.

"Oh dreams!" sighed Rose. "Dreams are what have always broken the unjust rules in this world. Have another cookie."

Elijah accepted the cookie and took a large bite.

"I'm a great fan of yours," Rose smiled. "Your song *Love Rising* is my favorite."

"You inspired it," said Elijah. "The dreams of you."

"That makes me so happy to hear you say that!" Rose picked up her cup and took a small sip of tea. "I'd love to hear you sing it live."

Elijah reached into his pocket and took out the tickets. "The day after tomorrow, I'm playing at Madison Square Gardens," he said, handing over the tickets.

Rose took them in her hand and then looked through them. "There is even a plane ticket here. How thoughtful!"

"Can you be there?" Elijah asked.

"I wouldn't miss it for the world."

"In the dream, you are there. You hear the music and you change."

"That would be nice," she replied. "Like I said, I have already been changing for a while—in many ways. Shall I tell you a secret, Elijah?"

Elijah just nodded his head like a small child.

"I don't get sick anymore," she smiled. "I used to. Like everyone else, I'd get colds and the flu, but not for a few years now. I'm changing."

Powerful emotions suddenly welled up in Elijah, and for a moment, he thought he was going to burst out weeping. "I also have this," he said, handing an envelope over to Rose.

She opened it and quickly looked over the papers inside. "Oh Elijah!" she exclaimed. "It's my family history. How beautiful that you brought this to me. Thank you so very much!"

"Did you know that you are a descendant of Jesus?" he asked.

Rose then surprised him again when she answered, "Anyone who has the spark of love in their soul is a descendant of Jesus. Those are His true progenies in this world. Those are His true children. Blood turns to dust, but the spark of love is eternal like our Lord."

Elijah could feel the tears in his eyes. He didn't know what to say. Glancing over at her, he noticed the faint crescent shaped scar on her forehead. He then quickly looked away before she would see him looking.

"It's been a very long road for me, Elijah. It's not been easy living in this world. I tried so hard to fit in, but it never really worked. Finally, I had to admit that it just wasn't my world at all. I saw my world once. It was when I was only seventeen. Just a girl really. I was sitting on the ground sunbathing, the way I liked to do, when it just happened. I was suddenly in my world—the real world."

Elijah finished off the cookie. He felt just like a child being told a bedtime story. "What was the real world like?" he asked.

Rose softly laughed. "It was indescribable! It was perfect in every way! Oh, the feeling, Elijah! The feeling of being reunited with the one and only true Love. I saw everything through the eyes of Love. The grass, the insects, the trees, the road and even the telephone poles—all through the eyes of Love. And the most amazing part is that this real world—this true world is here and now. We are blind and just can't see it. I don't want to be blind anymore, Elijah. I need to return. I need to return to my one and only Home, and I believe that you have come to help me find my way."

Elijah was feeling overcome with emotion. He wasn't sure what to say next. He knew there were plenty of questions in his mind, but at the same time he couldn't think of even one.

"You had better get back to New York," said Rose. "You have a show to prepare for, and I think I should go out and find myself a new dress. I've never been to New York before. They say it's the city that never sleeps, so I should have something nice to wear if I'm going to be wearing the same thing for a very long time."

* * *

Jack was stretched out on his favorite chaise lounge. He was supposed to stay in bed, but he insisted on moving to the great room. Staying in bed would make him feel like too much of an invalid, and it was bad enough that he needed Mona's help to do the simplest of tasks. He refused to be just another feeble old man.

Mona came in with a tray of fresh fruits and sparkling water. She set it down on the table beside him. "I know you will not like this advice," she said, "but try to take it easy."

"But I'll miss the concert," said Jack. Elijah had already phoned them with the news that Rose would be there.

"It's going to be televised live. You won't miss a thing." Mona held the glass of water up to Jack's lips.

"I am quite capable of drinking from a glass by myself," he said.

Mona laughed. "Sorry. Whenever I start caring, I suppose I get carried away."

Jack took the glass in his hand. "It's alright. I truly appreciate all you are doing for me."

Mona leaned over and kissed his forehead. "What are friends for?"

Just then the sound of *Für Elise* echoed throughout the house. Someone was at the door.

"Elijah!" shouted Mona. She jumped up and ran out of the room to let him in.

Jack reached over to the bowl of blue berries and popped a few in his mouth. He waited patiently for Mona to return. She seemed to be taking an awful long time. Finally, Mona showed up in the doorway with Elijah in tow. "He's back," she said.

"Hello Elijah, please come in and sit down," said Jack, gesturing towards the settee opposite him.

"How are you feeling?" asked Elijah in concern.

"I have been better," replied Jack. "But I'm afraid I'm likely going to miss the concert tomorrow."

"The good news is that it will be televised," said Elijah.

"That's what I told him," said Mona, sitting down beside Elijah. "Jack you must concentrate on getting better."

Jack looked closely at Elijah. He was looking different somehow. It reminded him of the way Stuart had looked after returning from America. "How did it go?" he asked.

Elijah sighed. "It went well, Jack—very well."

"Was she surprised to see you?" Mona asked.

Elijah reached over and grabbed Mona's hand. "Strange enough, no. She had been expecting me. She was…she was not like other people."

"So, what did she say?" Jack asked eagerly.

Elijah lifted up a small brown bag he had carried in his hand. "She sent you cookies," he proclaimed.

"Cookies?" Mona was not sure what to make of that.

"Yes," said Elijah, opening the bag and offering a cookie to Mona. Mona took one and looked at it. Elijah then reached across and held out the bag to Jack. Jack also took a cookie.

As they began to eat their cookies, Elijah said, "She's amazing and she's going to change everything. Just like we hoped."

Jack and Mona could taste the sweet cookies melt in their mouths, and felt chills run through their bodies with what Elijah had just said.

Elijah set the bag of cookies down on the table. "I need to go prepare for the show," he said getting up. "Jack don't worry. Don't worry about not being there, it's out of your hands anyway. You just need to focus on getting better." He then turned to Mona, "For now, you will have to stay here to look after Jack. But will I see you at the concert?"

"Of course," interjected Jack. "I'll be fine on my own for a few hours. Mona will be there when the time comes."

Mona stood up beside Elijah. "I wouldn't miss it for the world," she said.

Elijah ran his hand down her face. "It wouldn't be the same without you." He then began to walk towards the door.

"I'll see you out," said Mona, following after him.

Jack sat alone and looked at the paper bag on the table. He painfully reached over, grabbed it up and then placed it in his lap. Reaching in and taking out a cookie, he then lifted it in salute to the painting that was Stuart's gift. "This is to you, Stuart. Our dreams will soon be realized. We will have all that we have been waiting so long for. Finally, we will break through to the other side."

28

Elijah was nervously pacing backstage. When he felt Mona's hand on his shoulder, it instantly relaxed him. He turned and asked, "Is she here?"

"According to the computer records, someone with her ticket is in the building. She'll be on the floor in the VIP section. Would you like me to go and see if I can spot her?"

"No," replied Elijah, taking her in his arms. "There's not much time and I want you to stay with me until I go on."

Mona ran her hand through his hair. "It's going to be alright. Don't worry about anything."

"The funny thing is I'm not sure if I'm worried. There are just so many emotions going through me at once. It's as if I can feel the vibration of every molecule in my body right now. Strange as it may sound, it feels like I'm starting to turn into pure energy."

Mona looked up into his eyes. How did this man become more beautiful every time she saw him? "I'll stay with you, if it helps."

"It does," he answered and kissed her mouth.

* * *

Jack shifted a little on the chaise lounge. Before leaving, Mona made sure that the mini-fridge on the table beside the chaise was full of food and drinks, and that the remote was close at hand. The television was already on and the pre-show was well underway. Jack listened to the over-dressed entertainment reporters as they chattered away about Elijah.

Reporter 1: *What an amazing comeback this has been for the man! To go from stardom, to hitting rock bottom, and then back up to the number one singer in the entire world—what a story!*

Reporter 2: *Yes, it is an amazing story. Speaking of amazing, who are you wearing?*

Reporter 3: *Isn't it amazing! This dress is by Leaping Lemon Lizard designs. And did you see my shoes? They are just amazing!*

Jack hit the mute button. Despite the mini-fridge being so close by, it was still painful as he reached over and pulled open the door. Mona had filled it with mostly fresh fruits and cut vegetables. He stared at this healthy cache in disappointment. Nothing looked remotely tempting, and he wished he had another one of Rose's cookies.

He shut the door of the fridge and then looked back at the television. The entertainment reporters were finally gone, and now he could see what was happening inside Madison Square Gardens. The crowd looked stoked and ready to go.

* * *

"Three minutes Elijah," said the stage director.

Elijah held Mona tighter. "You know that you can't take me out there with you. All your lady fans will be broken-hearted," Mona said, not really wanting him to let go.

"I just need a few more moments of your love to help get me out on that stage," he replied. "This is going to be the biggest thing I have ever done."

They stayed in this embrace until the stage director said, "One minute Elijah."

Elijah could hear the music begin to play and could even feel the intense anticipation of the crowd. This would be a show like no other. He kissed Mona once more and then headed up the steps towards the stage.

* * *

As the camera scanned the waiting crowd, Jack munched on a carrot stick and searched for any sign of someone who could be Rose. It was difficult to discern individuals in that huge throng of people. *She has to be there. I know she's there.*

The camera swung back to the stage and suddenly everything in the stadium changed. The loud buzz of the waiting crowd had now instantly risen to a thunderous boom, as Elijah walked out.

Jack smiled and sighed. He couldn't help but remember when Elijah had first arrived at his office. How unassuming he looked—and now here he was—the biggest singer in the entire world—the King of Hearts—and he looked every bit the part.

Elijah walked straight up to the microphone and began to sing *Love Rising*. Usually, he would sing this song last, but tonight the last would be first.

* * *

Mona quickly moved to the side of the stage, where she would be unseen, but able to see everything. As Elijah began to sing, she closed her eyes to listen. Despite all of the times she had heard him sing *Love Rising* so beautifully; she had never heard him hit those notes that perfectly before. The sounds filling the theatre were unbelievable.

Opening her eyes, Mona saw a strange look of amazement on Elijah's face. It was then that she realized someone else was on stage with him. There was a woman standing in front of him a few yards away. Mona's first thought was that a fan had somehow gotten by security and climbed onto the stage, but she knew this was not possible. There was only one woman who would have been allowed to breach security. It was Rose!

Suddenly, Mona could feel it all through her body. She could sense it in those around her. She could hear it in the now absolute silence of the crowd. And then there was the light! There seemed to be a strange light coming down from the ceiling and straight to Rose. But it wasn't a stage light. It was more natural. It didn't just shine on her. It absorbed her. It emanated from her and reached out to touch the crowd. It was filling the empty space. It was drawing people in— drawing them near—filling them up.

As Elijah continued to sing like an angel, the woman slowly walked towards him. He then dropped down to his knees and sang like the world depended on it.

* * *

224

Jack leaned forward slightly in the chaise. "It's Rose! Oh, dear God! It's Rose!" he exclaimed.

Elijah, on his knees, seemed almost overcome with emotion. Yet, he never wavered from the song. The camera panned the crowd. Tears were streaming down every one of their faces. Not one person was unmoved. Not one person was untouched.

The camera turned back to Rose who was looking so incredibly beautiful—shining in such an unimaginable way. She continued to only move silently towards Elijah. But everything was being said in that silence—in that presence. What call could there be for words? Rose was the Word.

Jack moved to the end of the chaise and placed his feet on the floor. "Oh God, it's true! It's really true!" he exclaimed, leaning into the television to see it all closer. Elijah, still on his knees, continued singing while Rose now stood directly in front of him. She gracefully reached out and gently touched him on the crown of his head. Tears were flowing freely down Elijah's face, and although he still sang each note with perfection, his voice was trembling with emotion.

As Jack watched the screen in amazement, he suddenly, out of the corner of his eye, caught something moving in the darkness of the hallway. Turning his head quickly towards the movement, he saw that someone was there! He was not alone! *How was this possible? Mona had turned on the security system before leaving and it was fool-proof. Could it be another would-be assassin?* Unafraid, he jumped up from the chaise ready to face any intruder.

He watched as the shadowy figure moved slowly into the light. Now Jack was very confused. The unlikely assassin was an unassuming man of about his own age.

"Hello Jack," the man said.

Jack closed his eyes. *No, it can't be! It must be the painkillers! This can't be real!* He opened his eyes again, but he was still there. "Stuart!" he gasped, as he grabbed the top of the mini fridge to steady himself.

Stuart moved closer until they were face to face. He smiled lovingly and a small tear fell from the corner of his left eye.

Jack was struggling with all the thoughts that were racing through his mind. *Is this a dream? How can this be? I know I'm not asleep. None of this makes any sense.* "Stuart, you are old," Jack blurted out in his confusion. Immediately, he realized what a foolish thing this was to say.

Stuart just laughed. "So now that you are rich and famous, I am not young enough for you anymore?"

Jack was too much in shock to see the funny side of things. "Oh no!" he exclaimed, suddenly afraid that he had insulted Stuart. "No! It's just that when I saw you last..." He then reached out and touched Stuart's arm. *He's here! He's really here!* "H...How?" asked Jack, just barely able to get out the one-word question.

"There are more things in heaven and earth than are dreamt of in your philosophy," replied Stuart, laughingly. "I know that you still appreciate a little Shakespeare."

As Jack felt the tears rolling down his face, he no longer cared how. What did it matter how? It was Stuart! Stuart was right in front of him! Jack grabbed Stuart and held him tightly. "Please don't disappear on me!" he begged. "I can't live if you go away again. I need you!"

"I won't leave, Jack," replied Stuart, embracing him back. "I won't ever leave you again."

"Am I dead?" asked Jack, suddenly considering this possibility. "If I turn around now, will I see my body slumped in that chaise?"

"Turn and see for yourself."

Without letting go of Stuart, Jack turned his head and looked back. The chaise was empty. "Stuart! Oh Stuart!" he cried.

Stuart gently touched Jack's face. "How is your back?" he asked with a smile.

It was then that Jack realized that he had felt no pain when he jumped up from the chaise. Now, he was standing...standing straight and there was still no pain! He looked at Stuart in disbelief and answered, "It is better...I don't know how, but my back is all better."

Stuart kept smiling. "That's good news—very good news." He then looked up at the wall and the painting he had given Jack all those years ago. "I see you have kept the painting I gave to you. Will you look at it now, my love?" he asked.

Jack looked up at the painting. The whiteness of the unicorn appeared more brilliant than it had ever looked before. "Do you remember what you said to me the last night we were together?" Stuart asked.

"I said a lot of things," replied Jack, who was still having trouble believing it all was really happening. "I said so many things, I can't remember them all."

Stuart laughed again. "You said, 'Look Stuart. Do you see what she is? She is a mare.' Well now look at the telly, Jack. Do you not see her? Do you not see our unicorn?"

Still holding tightly to Stuart, Jack turned his head to look at the television. Elijah had finished singing and was now slumped on the stage in apparent exhaustion. The woman was standing in front of the microphone and speaking to the enthralled crowd. Jack couldn't really focus on what she was saying, but he knew it was changing things. He knew that whatever she was telling them, it meant that nothing in this world would ever be the same again.

"Do not worry about how I have returned to you, Jack," said Stuart. "Only know that I have, and that I am not ever leaving you again. We now have work that must be done—work that we must do together. It was in our stars from the beginning. That is why we were first brought together and also why we were separated. Now, we are reunited because the time has come. Our beautiful unicorn has finally broken her chains, and a Divine power has been unleashed in this world. She has set herself free! She will set us all free! Oh Jack, do you realize what is happening? Humankind is saved! We are all saved! Our Queen, our Unicorn, our Golden Rose has come! She has come to do what no one else has been able to do before her. She has come, at last, to slay the beast!"

Love Rising

Written by: Elijah
Produced by: Mona Solman
Einhorn Records

Just when
I thought you'd never show
The wind told me so
You were on your way,
Spring of living water flows.

Just when
I was giving up
The lightning struck
And the whole world shook with laughter.
At a pomegranate cut.

Just when
I said
All love lay trampled dead
I saw it rising.
Kiss me with your scarlet thread.

(Chorus)
Oh baby I see you
Oh baby I need you
Oh baby rise up
Come save me
Come save me
Come save me
Love Rising.

Tell me it is really you
Please no more cruel lies
I've waited over two thousand lifetimes

To be a seal upon the heart of Love Rising.

Rise up my darling.
Rise up
Open your lips behind the veil.

I see your face
I hear your voice
I feel your grace
I have no choice
But to surrender
To Love Rising.

(Chorus)

Wrap me
In your ribbons of gold
Silks and satins
To heal the soul.
Wrap me like a gift
A gift to be opened
On your birthday.

(4x Chorus)